ONCE UPON AN AUTUMN

Various Authors
Foreword by H. L. Macfarlane
Edited by H. L. Macfarlane and Adie Hart

Table of Contents

For everyone who really needs a good book and a hot drink

PLEASE NOTE: The formatting in Once Upon an Autumn follows Macfarlane Lantern Publishing's house style. However, in order to preserve the voice of each contributor in the anthology, the version of English the individual authors chose to write in has not been changed. As such some discrepancies in spelling, punctuation and language between stories should be expected.

Now westlin winds and slaught'ring guns
Bring Autumn's pleasant weather;
The moorcock springs on whirring wings
Amang the blooming heather:
Now waving grain, wide o'r the plain,
Delights the weary farmer;
And the moon shines bright, as I rove by night,
To muse upon my charmer.

Composed in August (Robert Burns; 1783)

FOREWORD

H. L. Macfarlane

Autumn, or Fall, heralds the death of all things. But that is not a bad thing. Nothing can grow without death. *We* cannot grow without death – the death of our loved ones, the death of who we used to be, the death of ideas abandoned for new ones.

Perhaps this is why autumn is so synonymous with celebration instead of sadness. We celebrate the harvest so that it might get us through to spring alive and well, yes, but we honour the dead first and foremost. Samhain, All Hallow's Eve, All Saint's Day, Day of the Dead, and countless more. All in the name of those we've loved and lost, and to remind us that though we are mortal, if we are remembered we never truly die.

It is in this way that autumn, dear reader, is the spark that ignites so many stories. Werewolves and witches and wickedness. Sunsets and songs and soulmates.

Promises made in life doomed to be broken in death...or the other way around.

This anthology, as with its predecessors, contains a little bit of everything. What better way to celebrate our cycle of folk & fairy tales than to repeat and build on what came before it?

It has been an honour working on *Once Upon an Autumn.* I hope that you, dear reader, love each and every story as much as everyone involved loved bringing them to life.

THE NETWORK

Katherine Shaw

Lungs burning, heart hammering in her chest, Abigail pressed her back against the wooden fence, her already aching feet grateful for the moment of respite. Straining her ears, she listened out for more gunshots, but could hear nothing above her own heavy breathing.

She looked down at her hands, where she clutched a small sack of root vegetables with cracked and dirty fingers. Only sixteen, and she already had the hands of an old woman.

A howl rang out behind her, and Abigail's heart leapt into her throat. That *shithead* farmer had set the dogs on her! And for what? Stealing a handful of food he wouldn't even miss just so she could survive the rest of the week?

It wasn't fair.

A second howl erupted, closer this time. There was no more time to waste – she had to get out of there, and fast.

Abigail took a deep breath and sprinted forward, her tight leg muscles already protesting at the forced movement. She took random turns down farm tracks and country lanes, the encroaching dusk making it harder and harder to discern which direction she was running in. Barks and growls followed every step of the way, sending panic rising up Abigail's body until tears were streaming down her face. Farmer Kotter had the biggest farm in the village, which made it ripe for stealing from, but his hounds were renowned for their savagery, great hulking beasts whose primary function was to frighten off intruders. And if that didn't work, they tore them apart.

Finally, farmland gave way to woodland, dry fallen leaves crunching under Abigail's feet as she raced behind the nearest tree – a thick-trunked oak she could use for cover while she caught her breath. She slumped behind it, bent over with her hands on her knees, gulping for air. Each breath stung like razor wire was being dragged down her throat, and her thin legs trembled under her weight. Abigail hadn't eaten a scrap of food in days; her body was in no state for this level of physical activity.

After several minutes of laboured breathing and some uncomfortable retching, Abigail stood up straight and dared to peer out from behind the oak tree. Night was closing in earlier now that autumn was here, and despite most of the branches being half-bare, it was impossible to see further into the woods than the next couple of rows of trees. She wouldn't know if the dogs had caught up to her until they were already on her. The thought almost made her retch again.

Abigail worked to smooth her ragged breathing and listened. Leaves rustled across the ground in the breeze that was picking up now night was falling, and somewhere in the trees a pair of blackbirds sang to each other. But underneath that, if she really concentrated, Abigail could hear something else, something that turned her blood to ice. The unmistakable snuffling of a sniffer dog on the hunt.

The hounds had found her scent, and they were close.

Adrenaline flooded Abigail's body and she bolted, all sense leaving her as she hurled herself deeper into the woods. Twigs, leaves and underbrush crunched beneath her feet, the flurry of sound almost immediately answered by the baying of two ferocious canines hot on her trail.

In her haste, she considered dropping the sack of vegetables, but what would be the point? It wouldn't sate the dogs' thirst for blood, and she wouldn't survive much longer without the nourishment. Either way, she was dead if her luck didn't change very soon.

Abigail zigzagged between tree trunks and leapt over fallen branches, terror the only thing fuelling her dilapidated body. She threw herself between two huge rowan trees with low-hanging branches, wincing as bunches of plump scarlet berries caught in her unkempt curly hair and dragged at her scalp. She lurched forwards, but skidded to a halt as a familiar but dreadful sight came into view.

A fairy ring.

A perfect circle of ghostly white mushrooms sprinkled with red-brown spots, daring Abigail to step inside and suffer the consequences.

Superstition wasn't a strong enough word for how the people of Abigail's village felt about such things – it was a healthy respect for a very real danger. All her life she had been warned not to reveal her true name to strange folk, to always refuse food or drink she hadn't seen being prepared herself, and to never, *ever* enter a fairy ring.

Today, however, she didn't have much of a choice.

Low growls sounded from behind her, turning her insides to water. She turned slowly and locked eyes with a hulking bullmastiff, its snarling lips pulled back to bare large, sharp teeth.

The dog looked to weigh as much as Abigail – likely even more – and she had no doubt that it could easily overpower her emaciated frame and tear her limb from limb.

It crouched, preparing to lunge, and Abigail's decision was made for her.

She stepped back, and as soon as both feet hit the ground,

everything changed.

***

Blackness, in every direction. And a damp, earthy odour that seemed to come from all around.

And... was she moving?

It was difficult to tell without a visible focal point, but Abigail felt like she was being pulled forwards, transported against her will at tremendous speed. Having grown up poor, she had never so much as ridden a horse, and her body reacted strangely to the quick movement. Her stomach roiled and she grew light-headed. She tried to take a deep breath, but nothing happened. No matter how hard she tried, she couldn't draw any air into her lungs. Panic stirred in her chest, and yet a niggle of curiosity tugged at the back of her mind.

If she couldn't breathe, how was she still conscious?

Unless...

Abigail pinched her arm, and felt the sharp sting of pain. So, she wasn't dreaming and hadn't passed out. This – whatever *this* was – was really happening.

Wait, where was the sack of vegetables? Though she could see nothing, both hands felt empty. Had she dropped it, after everything she had gone through to get those damn things? The prospect was galling.

Before she had time to dwell on her situation further, Abigail was propelled into a new one entirely.

The movement stopped, and she stumbled forward, landing hard on her knees. Only... it *wasn't* hard. Abigail placed her palms on the ground around her, and it felt like nothing she had experienced before. Softer than dirt paths, stone steps and wooden floors, but firmer than wet mud or dry sand. She sat back and crossed her legs, and ran her fingers along the unfamiliar ground. It was dark, and strangely fibrous, as if it was made of thousands of separate strands.

Abigail raised her head, eyes widening at the alien surroundings.

Though she was shrouded in darkness, Abigail could make out that she was in the entrance to some sort of cavern. There were no openings to the outside world, but a faint green glow illuminated the space just enough to make out some of its features. Before Abigail stretched a vast, empty floor made out of this odd, fibrous material, the strands crossing over and under each other almost like the roots of some great plant. The edges of the space were shrouded in shadow, but as Abigail craned her neck upwards, she saw huge webs and fronds of the unusual fibres, connecting wall to ceiling and criss-crossing above her in fantastic hanging arrays. Green light rippled through them at seemingly random intervals, making Abigail think of mice scurrying through pipes.

She rose and turned, expecting to see some sort of tunnel or pathway that had brought her to this bizarre place, but there was just another wall of dark fibres. She walked up to it, stepping carefully as she got used to the spongy texture beneath her feet. Unlike the floor, the fibrous surface was not flawlessly interwoven. Instead, there was a circular area at waist-height made up of hundreds of smaller circles. Close up, they looked almost like cut flower stems. Unable to stifle her curiosity, Abigail brushed her fingers over them, recoiling at the unexpected silkiness. It was a sensation that on a soft pillow or a fine gown would be pleasing, but in this dark, surreal environment was deeply unsettling.

Turning back to face the cavern, Abigail's gaze swept over the area once again, searching for anything resembling an exit. As grateful as she was for being spared the wrath of Farmer Kotter's vengeful hound, this place did not feel like somewhere she wanted to linger in for very long.

The hound.

Abigail spun around again, panic threatening to return. She held her breath and listened for any sign that she was being followed. Nothing. Perhaps the dogs had also been trained to keep out of fairy rings, and – unlike Abigail – they had heeded the warnings.

She didn't belong there – didn't know if she could even survive there for very long – and needed to find a way out. The darkness was thickest at the far end of the chamber, so that seemed to Abigail to be the most sensible source of an escape. She straightened her back, took a deep breath, and strode forwards, into the unknown.

***

The gloom enveloped Abigail as she crept to the end of the mysterious cavern. Small flashes of light erupted in the darkness all around her, but didn't penetrate the shadows enough to illuminate the path forward.

She walked, feet sinking into the springy ground, her steps unpredictable and awkward. Moisture hung in the air, clinging to her hair and settling on her skin. Whether she was walking down a passage or another open space, Abigail couldn't tell, and the uncertainty twisted her stomach.

A warm breeze brushed Abigail's face, and she stilled. The air seemed to slither across her cheek like a gentle caress, raising the hairs on the back of her neck.

"Wh-who's there?" she said into the gloom, cringing at the quiver in her voice. She turned on the spot, staring into the shadows; the lights continued to flicker, green and white flashes seeming to travel up and down whatever walls held Abigail in this place. "Is anyone—?"

A noise emanated from the blackness, a croaking moan that made Abigail's blood run cold.

"Aaaaaaaaaaaahhhh…"

She froze. The sound seemed to come from everywhere at once, the vibrations running under Abigail's feet and trembling through the air around her. It set her heart pounding, but she couldn't move, rooted to the floor with fear.

"Eeeeeehhhhhh..."

A second, higher-pitched groan broke the spell, and she bolted.

Abigail sprinted, blindly plunging into the darkness ahead. Fear drove her onwards, fuelling her aching feet until she could barely lift them anymore. A raised fibre protruding from the ground snagged her flimsy shoe, sending Abigail tumbling forward so she landed hard on her bony elbows.

"Ow!" The shriek tumbled out of her mouth before she could stop it, echoing around her surroundings until it seemed as if the walls were screaming back at her. If someone – or some*thing* – was looking for Abigail, they certainly knew where she was now.

Easing back onto her knees, Abigail rubbed her throbbing elbows and looked around. The shadows were a little thinner here, revealing more of the luminescent webbed material growing from wall to ceiling. And there was something else Abigail noticed as her gaze swept over the ground around her – something that she did not expect.

A river.

A slow-moving channel of water ran alongside the edge of the passageway to Abigail's left. She crept towards it, eyes darting around for any sign of movement. In truth, she wasn't sure what she was looking for – this place was like nothing she had ever imagined, and Abigail couldn't fathom what creatures or people might dwell in the shadows – but there was comfort in vigilance.

Abigail peered over the edge of what, up-close, appeared to be a narrow stream. The water was crystal clear, reflecting Abigail's face perfectly in the luminescent glow around her. It was a while since she had seen herself, and her stomach dropped when she saw how gaunt and scruffy she looked. This coming winter would mark three years since Abigail had lost both her parents, and the bright-eyed, mischievous girl she used to be was long gone, replaced by a skeletal waif she barely recognised.

Blinking away the hot tears threatening to burst free, Abigail tried to focus on the water. It looked cleaner than any river or stream she had seen around the farmland she called home. In fact, it was bizarrely clean, devoid of any plant or animal life whatsoever, the riverbed made up of more of the strange material that this entire place was constructed from. Abigail licked her dry lips as she gazed into the water, only now realising how thirsty she was. How long had it been since she had a good drink? Farmer Kotter had moved his water butts closer to the farmhouse since he caught her drinking from them, so it had been shallow streams and dirty puddles for the last couple of months, and it was never enough.

Unable to deny her thirst any longer, Abigail plunged her hand into the stream and scooped up some of the sparkling water. The cool liquid had barely touched her lips when another creaking shriek sounded out behind her.

"Aaaaaaaaaaahhhh! Eeeeeeeh!"

Abigail spun around, heart racing. The passage appeared to be empty: the same glowing tendrils criss-crossing the walls and ceilings, the same sprawling, fibrous ground.

Something grabbed Abigail from behind, and a shock of cold struck her as she fell backwards into the flowing water, knocking the breath out of her lungs. The second her full body was submerged, the current grew stronger, and Abigail was washed downstream.

Water flooded her eyes, ears and nostrils as she fought against the flow, kicking and scrabbling until her face finally burst through the surface and she could breathe again. Abigail lay on her back, exhausted but alive – for now, at least.

Drained of all energy from her fight against the current, Abigail let the stream carry her. She floated on her back, straining just to keep her eyes open, and watched the glowing lights on the ceiling dart across her vision.

Tiredness seeped into Abigail's bones, wrapping her in a cocoon of numbness. The adrenaline from her narrow escape and her tumble into this strange, new place was long gone. The sound of rushing water warped and shifted in her ears, morphing into something akin to a melody. Discordant notes penetrated Abigail's consciousness, lulling her into a reluctant drowsiness. Her eyelids grew heavier, and she blinked rapidly, urging herself to stay alert.

She couldn't fall asleep, not here.

The lights danced on the ceiling, swimming in and out of view until they coalesced. Monstrous luminescent faces formed before Abigail's eyes, staring down at her with gaping maws. They seemed to be wailing something at her, but their cries were lost in the song of the current. Abigail tried to decipher their words, but the numbness was spreading. Her head was full of cotton, her eyelids made of lead. She couldn't hold on any longer, and as the faces screamed their protestations, Abigail slipped into oblivion.

***

Drip, drip, drip.

A cold splash struck Abigail's forehead. She wrinkled her face and blinked her eyes open. The ceiling was above her again, the lights now benignly glowing with no apparent shapes or messages, but what really struck Abigail was the hardness beneath her body.

She sat upright and ran her hands over the ground. Sure enough, she was on dry land. She grabbed at her dress, and was astounded to find it equally free of moisture. Except for the hem, which was still damp... or was it?

Abigail leaned forward, squinting to see in the gloom. The edge of her dress – which had been wet a moment ago – was already almost dry, as if the moisture was being sucked out of the fabric. She wriggled her toes, feeling the familiar discomfort of soggy shoes and socks. Since losing her parents, Abigail had had to make her clothes last as long as possible before scavenging new ones, and these old, cracked boots had long-since lost their waterproofing. Summer was over, and as autumn once again rolled in, she had grown used to perpetually damp feet. But as Abigail rocked her feet back and forth on the ground, she felt a new – and very welcome – sensation.

Dry toes!

Then dry soles, and then dry heels. It was as if the moisture was being siphoned from Abigail's body directly into the ground. Within moments, it was as if she had never touched a drop of the stream's fast-flowing water. She rose to her feet and, in the glow of the moving lights, could just make out the shrinking patch of wet ground where her body had been. Although she was glad to be dry again, knowing some unknown entity had sucked every drop of moisture out of her clothes, from her skin, her hair... It sent a shiver down Abigail's spine.

She raised her head, dismay rocking her as she took in an another dark cavern, almost identical to the one she had started in. What sort of hideous maze was this place? Dread prickled the back of her neck. What if she was trapped? Doomed to wander this dark, dank labyrinth until she succumbed to either starvation or madness – whichever came first? The thought was almost too much for Abigail to bear.

No. Abigail had been a smart kid before everything went wrong, and since then she'd learned to survive on her own. If she could keep herself alive despite the wind, rain, and savage farm dogs, she could figure out how to escape this fairy trap.

Taking a deep breath, Abigail reassessed her situation. She had stepped into that fairy ring and... then what? She'd been transported to another world? Captured by the fae? Sent to a nightmare realm? Each option seemed equally implausible, but an impossible place required an impossible explanation.

She tried to think back to the warnings the elders of the

village had shared about fairy rings. Old men and women would tell dark tales of children not watching their step and being forever changed by the magic of the ring, but now she thought about it, the details of such changes were always vague. They instilled fear through sheer conviction; their bulging eyes and bared teeth ensured each generation grew up with a healthy respect for these dangerous features of the forest.

But how real were those dangers?

Emboldened by this new rational line of thinking, Abigail strode through the chamber with purpose. She would learn more about this alien place, and she would find a way out – or die trying.

***

Abigail's tentative fingertips slid slowly across the soft surface, sensing something that she hadn't noticed before.

Hairs.

Thousands – no, *millions* – of tiny hairs covered the entire surface of the chamber wall. Abigail brushed her hand over a swathe of the strange follicles, and jumped as a vibration thrummed away from her touch. It rippled away from her, back through the chamber, the eerie glow of the tendrils brightening along its path until it disappeared around a corner.

Abigail had a feeling she had just sent a message she couldn't take back.

Standing in the opening between caverns, half-cloaked in shadow but all too aware of how vulnerable she was, Abigail waited. The primal part of her brain screamed at her to run, to find some dark corner to hide in and avoid being found by whatever had just been alerted to her location. But Abigail stood firm. She had tried running away and it had got her nowhere. She would face whatever came for her, and she would use it to get home.

A far-off shriek echoed towards Abigail, turning her stomach upside down and sending her pulse racing once more, but still she stood. Something like warm breath tickled the back of her neck, but she didn't move.

"Aaaaaaaaaaahhhh…"

That voice again. It sent a wave of ice down Abigail's spine, and she fought the urge to run away. Instead, she listened.

"Aaaaaaaaaaahhhh… Eeeeeeh!"

It was getting closer, but it was also getting clearer.

"Aaaaaaaaaaahhhh… beeeeeh!"

When she really listened, Abigail realised it wasn't just a nonsensical screech she was hearing, it was a word.

"Aaaaaaa-beeeeee!"

"Aaaabeeeee!"

Her chest tightened as recognition hit.

Abby.

They knew her, and they were calling out to her.

Abigail's legs trembled and her throat tightened, but she didn't move. The voices drew closer, the nickname she hadn't heard for years echoing all around.

"Aaabbbyyyyy… Aaaabbbyyyy!"

"What?' She shouted into the gloom, nervous energy thrumming through her entire body. "What do you want with me?" Tears brimmed her eyes, the fear and the exhaustion and the frustration spilling over. "Just tell me!"

Silence.

The sudden absence of sound made Abigail's ears ache. She could hear her own blinks, her pulse throbbing in her neck, but nothing else. She swallowed, the noise impossibly loud in the silence.

She wanted to move, to explore the cavern and see what had

changed, but couldn't bring herself to make a sound. The stillness was so perfect, so absolute, Abigail couldn't break it.

Then something broke it for her.

Great tendrils burst away from the floor and walls, curling away from the surfaces and arcing towards Abigail. They rose up like cobras, ready to strike, and Abigail's resolve finally broke.

She turned and ran, sprinting blindly into the next chamber. It was stupid to think she was brave enough to stand up for herself against who knows what. Abigail ran - it was how she had always survived until now, and it was how she would survive whatever nightmare she had stumbled into.

The shadows and glowing lights blurred together through Abigail's tears, but she hurtled forwards regardless; self-preservation was steering her body now.

Something grabbed Abigail's ankle and she fell, landing hard on her elbows. The springy ground absorbed some of the shock, but pain still ricocheted up each arm. She twisted onto her side to see one of the fibres wrapped around her leg.

"Aaaabbbyyyy..."

Panic seized Abigail as the tendril tightened and began to drag her backwards. She scrambled onto her front, desperate hands grasping for a handhold, but there was nothing. Her nails – brittle from months of malnutrition – snapped and splintered as she dug her fingers into the ground. Fleshy material tore away from the fibrous surface, earthy and almost sweet-smelling. Abigail wasn't gaining any purchase. With each failed attempt she was dragged further towards the voices, towards potential doom.

"Let go of me!" Abigail wailed, thrashing and kicking with all her might. She knew it wouldn't work. She knew her reserves were already depleted and she was squandering what little energy she had left, but wherever she was going, she would not go without a fight. "Let go!"

"Aaaabbbyyyy... pleeeeaaaaase..."

She froze. Please? Was this strange monstrous entity really saying *please* to her?

"Please, what?" she asked slowly, in disbelief that she was conversing with whatever this thing was.

"Coooooome. Pleeeeaaase."

What other choice did she have? Abigail allowed her body to go limp, the fight finally draining out of her. Closing her eyes, she let herself be dragged off towards whatever lay in store.

***

Whispers. Hushed, and hurried, just out of earshot.

Abigail stirred, and scrunched up her face. Somewhere along her long journey across the ground she must have fallen asleep, somehow. She knew she was tired, but to drift off while being carted off to some unknown danger seemed wrong. She rolled her neck, stopping when she realised her head was no longer against the ground.

She was upright.

Abigail blinked her eyes open. Sensation flooded her body as she became aware of her surroundings. This chamber was different. Where before there had been a vast stretch of relative nothingness, now there was a riot of colour. Reds, oranges, yellows and browns blossomed along the walls, floor, and even the ceiling. Huge swathes of colour streaked each surface, made of up clusters of strange shapes: discs, spears, frills, domes, bells... Abigail blinked again, forcing her vision into full focus. She knew those shapes.

They were mushrooms. Hundreds, if not thousands, of them.

Abigail's mouth hung open. If there were this many mushrooms to be found in the woods around the village, she would never have to resort to raiding Farmer Kotter's field again. She was no expert, but Abigail counted at least four varieties she knew from experience were edible. As if on cue, a rumble erupted in her stomach.

The whispers stopped, the silence reminding Abigail that they had been there at all. She had been so fixated on the magnificent fungi that she had blocked out everything else. Her gaze swept the chamber, but she could not pinpoint the source of the whispering. Veins of bioluminescent flora snaked around the mushrooms, lighting the space enough to see them in all their glory, but shadows still gathered around the edges, and could potentially conceal beings of nefarious intent.

What caught Abigail's eye the most was in the centre of the chamber. A large table-like structure stood ahead of her, formed of twisting fibres of brown, red and orange, and edged with draping fronds of white. On the surface lay a plethora of edible fungi: brown fieldcaps, white wood mushrooms, vibrant orange peel fungi, grey spotted amanita, crimson ruby boletes, frilly chanterelles, and even a few autumn truffles. Abigail's eyes bulged as she took in the smorgasbord before her, saliva filling her mouth.

She moved to walk towards the table, but couldn't. She looked down, horror creeping through her body. Thick tendrils wrapped around her from the waist down, holding her in place. Abigail pushed forward, but the binding held fast.

"Damn it!" she hissed, twisting and struggling, to no avail. Did her captors mean to torture her? To place nourishment just beyond her reach until she starved? It was cruelty beyond measure. Hot tears welled in her eyes, anger and frustration and desperation building up inside her until she couldn't hold it inside.

"Why are you doing this to me?" she screamed, her shrill, anguished cry echoing all around. She didn't care if they could hear her anymore. She didn't care if they found her. "What do you want from me?"

Abigail dropped her head and felt the splash of tears against her cheeks. The whispers came to life again, this time hurried and almost panicked.

"Just do whatever you're going to do to me," she muttered, not bothering to raise her head. "I don't care anymore."

Abigail's body sagged, and she almost fell forwards as the tendrils holding her in place began to unwind from around her. She jerked upright, astounded, as her bindings fell away and dropped to the ground by her feet. She was free. Her eyes shot to the table, where a bounty of delicious mushrooms awaited.

Abigail took a step forward. The whispers rose in volume, almost excited-sounding. Abigail listened hard, straining to pinpoint their source. The acoustics of the chamber made it difficult, but the loudest whispers appeared to be emanating from Abigail's left. Her gaze swept over the multi-coloured fungal foliage, but amongst the myriad of colours, shapes and patterns, it was impossible to pick out anything remotely human.

Abigail's stomach growled, and her attention returned to the table. So many mushrooms could sustain her for days if she was careful, and the thought of having a full stomach for the first time in months was almost overwhelming.

She walked to the table, the whispers never fading. Up close, the earthy scent was intoxicating. Abigail raised her arm and tentatively reached for a small field cap,

The whispers stopped.

It was as if they had taken a sharp intake of breath. They were waiting for Abigail to move. Waiting for her to eat.

She drew her hand back, unease curdling in her gut. "What did you do to it?" she shouted into the room. "Is it poisoned? Cursed?" Abigail turned around, still unable to locate the hidden spectators. "Is this a test, or some sort of twisted game? Tell me what you want!"

"Eat." It was barely more than a whisper, coming from somewhere to Abigail's left. "Please."

"Why?" Abigail challenged back, eyes continuing to search the wall of the chamber. "What does it matter to you?"

"You are starving." It was a woman's voice. Soft and pleading, but with an otherworldly quality that gave Abigail goosebumps. "Please, Abby."

"Don't call me Abby!" Angry hot tears pricked the back of her eyes. "No one has called me that since... since..."

She couldn't say the words. She had never said them aloud, couldn't bring herself to verbalise the most painful experience of her life. She swallowed down a sob as their faces swam across her vision. Her parents. They were the only ones who had ever called her Abby. It was their private nickname; at school and in front of respectable society, she was *Abigail*, but at home, she was still Abby. Their little girl.

"Abby..."

That voice again. Underneath the ethereal whisper, it was somehow familiar. Abigail felt drawn to it, but she didn't move. It was a trick, it must be.

"Don't..." She stifled a sob. "Don't call me that."

"My Abby."

Abigail froze. That voice... She shook her head. No, it couldn't be.

In spite of herself, she approached the cavern wall, eyes searching. "Where are you?" She murmured, her voice on the verge of breaking. "If you're here, show me."

The wall shifted, veins of colourful fungi drawing together until a slender figure appeared. It creaked and groaned as it pulled away from the surface, fine fibres keeping it attached to the remaining fungi, as if they were all one great network of organisms. A myriad of mushrooms of every shape and size covered its body and face. It was beautiful, and terrifying.

"Abby..." The figure spoke with tenderness, lowering to its

knees and opening its arms wide.

Abigail hesitated. This could easily be a trap. A way to lure her into their fungal network and turn her into one of them.

"It's me," the figure said softly. It lowered its head for a moment, and when it lifted it again, Abigail's heart leapt into her throat.

The fungi had shifted again, rearranging into features that were painfully recognisable. Soft brown eyes, a sharp, slender nose, and a small, delicate mouth.

I couldn't be. This was a dream, or a nightmare.

"M-mum?"

Her voice was shaking. Her whole body was shaking.

The fungal figure nodded. "Yes." It drew its arms to its chest. "Oh, Abby, it's been so long."

It could be a dream, or a hallucination, or a trap, but Abigail didn't care. She ran into her mother's arms, sinking into her embrace. The sweet, earthy fungal smell hit her again, but there was another scent lurking underneath. Chrysanthemum and rose. Her mother's scent.

Abigail drew back, tears flowing freely down her cheeks. "It... it really *is* you."

Her mother nodded. She cupped Abigail's cheek and ran a soft hand through her hair, just like she used to. The last two years melted away – the cold nights, the hunger pangs, the constant fear – and she was a little girl again, safe in her mother's arms.

"I've... I've missed you so much." Abigail's breath caught in her throat as she fought back a sob. "It's been so hard."

Her mother pulled her in again, squeezing her tight. "I've missed you too, my sweet, darling girl."

"Does this mean you're alive?" Hope swelled in Abigail's chest. It was dangerous, but she couldn't help it.

Something like a sigh rippled through her mother's fungal body. She pulled back, gentle hands resting on Abigail's shoulders. "I'm afraid not, sweetheart. Not in the way you would hope for, at least. After we... after we left you, we were returned to the earth. For most people, that's where it ends, but we were lucky." She waved an arm towards the rest of the cavern. "The magic of the network found us, and took us in, made us part of it. So our spirits, and our memories, live on at least."

A swirl of emotions warred in Abigail's chest. Spirits, magic, networks... it was incredible and heartbreaking and wondrous and tragic all at the same time. Something her mother had said tugged at her, pulling Abigail out of her spiral.

"Us?" She asked, a small twinge of excitement stirring. "Is Dad here too?"

Her mother rose to her feet. "Of course! He didn't want to overwhelm you. I'll call for him."

She turned and faced the wall she had broken away from, but didn't make a sound. Abigail watched as a wave of luminescent blue light thrummed through her mother's body, pulsing down the fibres connecting her to the network. Moments later, several clusters of brown and white mushrooms grouped together and coalesced into a human-like form. It broke away with a groan, and lumbered over to Abigail and her mother.

"Jonathan," her mother murmured, rushing up to the figure and taking its mushroom-covered hands in hers. "She's here. She's really here!"

The fungal form of Abigail's father looked at her, his face shifting until deep-set eyes, a Roman nose and the strong chin she remembered so well became visible. When he spoke, his voice was deep and rumbling.

"My little girl."

Abigail didn't hesitate. She ran to him, a giggle escaping her mouth as he swept her up into the air and spun her around.

"Daddy!"

She hadn't said that in a long time. She hadn't felt so free, and safe, and happy in a long time, either.

"Glad you finally found us," rumbled her father, placing Abigail carefully back on her feet. "We were calling for a while."

Abigail stared up at her parents. "That was you? Screaming at me?"

Her mother slapped her father's shoulder. "I told you that would scare her!" She turned to Abigail again, and placed an arm around her shoulder. "I'm sorry, darling. We are still quite new to the network, so we did what we could to call out to you, but only had the strength to speak to you properly once we brought you here, to our chamber. This magic is powerful, but strange, and still new to us. Compared to the other entities here, we're like toddlers still learning how to walk."

"And you..." Abigail pointed towards the fungal table, still laden with a plethora of delicious treats, "did this?"

Her mother stood straighter. "Oh, yes!" She dragged Abigail to the table, Jonathan following quietly behind them. He had always been the quiet one. "We noticed you had gotten awfully thin, and wanted to help. Here." She gestured at the table, waving a hand over the colourful array of edible fungi. "Take as many as you would like."

Abigail picked up a chanterelle, already salivating at the thought of a good meal, but something her mother had said stopped her.

"Take?" She looked up at her parents, a bad feeling replacing the hunger in her stomach. "I can't stay with you?"

The silent look that passed between her parents was painful. They wanted her to leave. She had just found them again – after years of struggle and loneliness – and they were going to send her away already?"

Her mother spoke first. "Abby..."

"You don't want me here." Fresh tears brimmed in Abigail's eyes and her cheeks flushed hot. "After all this time... you don't want me."

Her father reached for her, but she stepped away. Sobs bubbled up her throat, shaking her chest in great heaves.

"You don't... you don't..."

Abigail turned away, the disappointment crushing.

"Abby..." Her mother's gentle voice pulled at her, but Abigail didn't move. "Of *course* we want you."

Abigail spun around. "Then why can't I stay?" She was shouting, but she didn't care. "Why do I have to go?"

Her mother kneeled so they were face to face, and the scent of rose and chrysanthemum washed over Abigail again, breaking her heart. "If we could be together forever – the three of us – it would bring us more joy than you could ever imagine."

"But?"

"But," she continued, another ethereal sigh rippling through her fungal form. "You can't survive here, not indefinitely. The air here isn't for humans. You may feel fine now, but there are spores everywhere. They get in your eyes each time you blink, on your tongue each time you speak, in your lungs each time you breathe..."

"Your body can only take in so many," her father continued, shaking his head. "It would slowly kill you."

"I couldn't take it." Even with its ethereal ghostly quality, Abigail could hear the sadness in her mother's voice. "You need to live, to survive."

Abigail knew the grief of watching those she loved fade away in front of her eyes. She couldn't put her parents through that. "It's just..." she began, scrubbing the tears from her eyes with the back of her hand. "I *just* found you, and it's been so hard. I can't say goodbye again. I can't."

"Oh, Abby." Her mother hugged her tight, pressing her cheek against Abigail's. "You can see us again, any time you need us."

Abigail's eyes widened and she pulled back, staring incredulously into her mother's colourful face. "What? Really?"

A low chuckle rumbled from her father. "You didn't think this would be it, did you?"

Abigail gaped. "What do you mean?"

"Now you know how to find us," her mother continued, the fungi on her face shifting into a smile, 'you can return. Not straight away, of course – you need to let the spores clear your system – but after a week, or so. Step into the fairy ring, and you'll enter the network. And then we'll find you again."

Abigail stared, her head spinning. Then she threw herself at her parents, wrapping an arm around each of them. Warmth spread through her body as they pulled her close, a family again.

"I love you so much," Abigail whispered.

"We love you too," her parents said in unison, holding her tight.

Abigail closed her eyes. For the first time in a long while, she was content.

***

Dry leaves crunched underfoot. Autumn was almost over, and almost every branch overhead was bare. The air carried the chill of impending winter, but Abigail hardly felt it. Excitement buzzed in her chest as she practically skipped through the trees, her heart racing.

Almost there.

A grin spread across her face as the familiar circle of mushrooms came into view, and Abigail had to resist the urge to sprint straight into the fairy ring. Instead, she stood on its edge, preparing herself.

She had made the journey into the network five or six times already, but was yet to get used to the strange sensation of travelling through the mycelia. It helped to calm herself beforehand and take a few deep breaths.

She checked she had everything she needed for what was probably the third time, to settle her nerves. A small sack for carrying mushrooms – her parents insisted that she not only eat her fill during every visit, but that she also take some back to ensure she would never go hungry – a bracelet of dried horse chestnuts she had made for her mother, and a particularly beautiful pheasant feather she would give to her father. They had no use for such items in their current form, but they seemed delighted with each thing she brought them, and so Abigail always tried to find a gift before each visit.

They had saved her, after all.

There was no more stealing, no more starving, no more running away for what might be the last time.

She was safe, and she was happy.

Taking one more deep breath, Abigail stepped forward, and into the network.

She was going home.

Katherine Shaw is a multi-genre writer and self-confessed nerd from Yorkshire in the United Kingdom, spending most of her time dreaming up new characters or playing D&D. She has a passion for telling stories of injustice and battles against oppression, often with a focus on female protagonists. She has published her debut novel Gloria, a contemporary domestic thriller, and has work appearing in multiple anthology collections.

You can find out more at her website www.katherineshawwrites.com

GOD IS A HETEROPALINDROME

S. Markem

For Scooter.
I miss you, buddy.

Bill the gnome removed his little red gnomish hat and wiped the sweat from his brow and the top of his balding head.

He jumped from the wagon, patted the pony that pulled it, and then called out for the stable boy.

Moments later, a young boy, who is not important enough to have a name in this story, appeared and saluted Bill.

"Welcome home, Master Bill," he said. "We wasn't expecting you back so soon."

"It's good to be home," he replied. "I would have stayed with my cousins longer, but it's nearly 'anthology' season again and Autumn is the season of misfortune. I suspect the old fool will need my assistance. How is Blagre, anyway?"

(Author's note: The only background you need to know is that Blagre was a medieval wizard. He lived on the fairy-infested island of Lyonesse and was possessed by the idea that he was a

character in a novel.

It's a ridiculous premise, I agree. But then again, you are reading a book full of leprechauns, centaurs, fairies and ghosts, so the plausibility bar is already set pretty low.)

The stable-boy-with-no-name shuffled his feet and stared at the ground. "Tell the truth, Master Bill, I've not seen him for a while. He went away."

"Went away?"

"Uh-huh. He went for a walk – or that's what he's said he was going to do."

"When exactly?"

"Er – bout a week ago. M'be a bit more. Said he was hiking up to the summer house."

" The summer house? In October? Good grief. Did anyone go with him?"

"No sir, t'was just the dog an' him."

Bill wagged a finger at the stable boy (who was only about fifteen but easily twice the height of Bill). "Do you know how much trouble that old wizard can get himself into? Why did you not send a servant up to the house? Good grief, good grief. No wonder the author hasn't bothered giving you a name, you fool."

"I'm sorry, Master Bill, but I didn't know what was best and all. You know how funny he gets if he's disturbed when he's doing his wizard-y things."

"Get me a fresh pony for this wagon, boy. And some food – and beer. I better go and see what's what."

***

A couple of hours later...

When Bill arrived at the summer house, everything seemed quiet – eerily so. The house, a small cottage with extensive gardens, was usually busy with servants, goblins, and faerie folk whenever Blagre was in residence. But no one was to be heard or seen on this particular day.

Bill searched the cottage – no Blagre.

He checked the bedrooms – no Blagre.

He checked the wine cellar – no Blagre.

Finally, he wandered out to the rose garden. "Ahoy, Blagre, are you there?"

Nothing.

He walked through the rose garden to where there was an ornamental fish pond. And there, sitting quietly, was Blagre.

Fortunately for this author, Blagre was a trope – big hat, long beard, that sort of thing. Saves a bit of unnecessary blurb on my part.

Oh, I nearly forgot. Wizards are not, in fact, wholly human. It's a complicated business that involves demons and women of questionable morals. But we won't go into that in a short story. It is somewhat relevant for later, though. Just an FYI, as they say.

Anyway...

"Hey there, Blagre. What gives?"

The wizard remained silent, somewhat oblivious to Bill's arrival.

The little gnome drew near and nudged Blagre on the shoulder. "Did you not hear me calling?" he said.

"Hey now, what's that you say?" replied the wizard. "Oh, Bill... Bill, my lad, I am glad to see you; I truly am. Something very puzzling has happened. I suspect witchcraft."

"Witchcraft?"

"Yes, yes. Look over there," he said, pointing to the other side of the pond. "It's Merlin. He has not moved for two days. He is motionless. Some strange magic has overcome him."

Blagre pointed to his dog, a shabby-looking reddish brown dog who appeared to be sleeping peacefully on his side in a patch of long grass.

Bill went over to the dog, knelt, prodded him, and then returned to where Blagre sat.

"Well?" said the wizard. "What do you think?"

Bill took a deep breath and shook his head slightly. "My dear wizard, surely you can see that Merlin is dead."

The wizard jumped to his feet. "Dead? Don't be ridiculous."

"I'm afraid he is. How could you not tell? How long have you been sitting here exactly?"

"A couple of days, I think. I have been trying to figure out what enchantment can have overcome him. He can't be dead. He wasn't doing anything. He just went over there and lay down."

"I can assure you he is, old chap. Dead, and quite a severe case of it. Could you not tell that for yourself?"

"How would I know? No one I know has ever died before."

Bill scrunched up his face. "What about Sir Betonix? He died trying to headbutt a stone golem. Or Revelato the Righteous? He was killed by a falling ogre, as unlucky and as improbable as it sounds. Or what about your friend Galdius, who got his head... "

"Yes, yes, but that is different. They were all architects of their own misfortune. The perils of adventure. But Merlin wasn't doing anything."

"Everything dies eventually, Blagre – everything mortal anyway – though faerie folk are an exception."

"And wizards."

"Yes, and wizards. But Merlin was neither. Moreover, how old was he?"

"I'm not sure. Barely twenty-one, I should say."

"Well, that is surely a long life for a dog. He was fortunate."

"Fortunate? How is being dead fortunate?"

Bill reached up and tried to put a reassuring hand on Blagre's shoulder, but the wizard was too tall, so he just tugged his robe instead.

"It's a sad thing, but it is time to grieve. Where would you like me to bury him? If you feel like crying, I can leave you alone for a while."

The wizard, red with anger and his brow narrowed most alarmingly, thrust his face toward Bill's and shouted, "Dead? Buried? Cry? Are you mad? That dog is my best friend. I *love* that animal. This state of affairs is unacceptable."

"I can see you are upset, but we should... "

"Upset? Upset! I am not upset; I am *incandescent.* Return to my manse, fetch horses and provisions for a long journey. We are going to put this matter right. And put Merlin in the cold room for now; he'll be fine there until we return."

"Put it right? You can't put death 'right'. Unless you are suggesting necromancy?"

"Don't be absurd, Bill. I do not propose to raise a zombie dog. No, we will take this matter up with the fellow responsible. Now, on your way. Enough chat. Do as I command."

***

Later that day...

Bill sat on his pony next to Blagre, mounted on a white stallion.

"Where to then, Blagre?"

"We seek an audience with the one being who can help us. The one person who can make this wrong right and give me back my best friend. We are going to see God."

"Which one?"

"Don't be facetious, Bill. You know perfectly well who I mean. The real one. Cherubs, angels, impressive beard... that one."

"Very well, I will humour you. But is it wise to seek out God? I am told he takes unkindly to such things and has quite a temper. It might mean banishment, purgatory, hell... Scotland, even."

"Do not worry, Bill, that's mostly Old Testament superstition. He's actually quite charming. And besides, *I* am not mortal. He does not hold sway over my fate."

"But, what about me?"

Blagre laughed, "You are faerie folk; he doesn't believe you exist. It would cause some sort of theological problem. You'll be quite safe."

Bill found himself almost taking the wizard seriously. "So, are you telling me you know where to find God? He who is everywhere and nowhere; He who men spend their lives seeking; Him, the great mystery; He who many quest for and... "

"I do. Trevena, on the Tintagel coastline."

"Cornwall?"

"That's right. He has a nice little cottage there; you'll like it. Come, Bill, let us go forward. It is a week's journey from here, but He will put many challenges in our way."

***

More than one week later...

Bill sat on a large rock and wiped the dragon's blood from his boots. It was an inclement day, and an icy breeze swept along the coastline, where he and Blagre rested.

The weather is entirely irrelevant, but as this was the island of Britain, it seemed odd not to mention it. It also provides a somewhat tenuous link to the theme of this anthology; it is that kind of literary magic that keeps this author gainfully employed.

"I really can't believe it," said Bill. "I have never packed so much adventure into a few weeks. Dragons, sea monsters, temptations galore and peril at every step. It's taken us nearly forty days and nights to get here."

"You don't get to see God without enduring hardship, Bill. Let us hope this is not a short story because our journey was a bona-fide epic. It'd be a shame for our readers to have missed it. But we are here now; follow me."

The two adventurers made their way to the small village overlooking the North Atlantic coastline. Waves crashed, seagulls swooped, and the smell of freshly baked pasties – Cornish stuff – filled the air.

They came to a small cottage, a humble affair that seemed no different from any other nearby dwelling.

Blagre knocked politely on the door and waited, hands behind his back.

"Is this it?" said Bill.

"Ssshh. Let me do talking."

Presently, the door was answered by a tall man with short dark hair and a countenance so beautiful that if he'd had pointy ears, you might have mistaken him for an elf.

"Ahh, Gabriel," said Blagre. "How nice to see you again. How goes it?"

"Blagre. Second most famous of all the wizards. I am well. How goes it with you?"

"Not as well as I might like. But then, you already know why I am here, I imagine?"

"Yes, I do. Won't you come in? Leave your boots at the door; I've just finished cleaning the floor, and you know how much He likes a tidy house."

Inside, Bill took a sharp breath. For one thing, the inside was much bigger than the outside. The floor was polished marble; magnificent pillars held up a ceiling that must have been a hundred feet high, and gold and silver etchings decorated all the walls. Brilliant sunlight streamed in from unseen windows, and cherubs sat around cherubbing *(Dearest Editor, please do not correct - I made that word up. I have no idea what cherubs do, nor if there is an actual word for it. But whatever it might be, that's what they were doing.)*

"So," said Blagre, clearing his throat, "you know why I'm here, and we've done the obligatory forty-day-trial stuff. When can I see Him?"

"I am sorry for your loss, Blagre. Truly, I am. And I am moved by what you have endured to get here. But He will not see you. You knew this, surely?"

"Yes, yes. I know the usual rules. But it's *me*. I am sure He can make an exception. Is He here?"

"He is everywhere."

"Gak. Spare me that nonsense. Just go and give Him a nudge, will you? We don't mind waiting."

"He will not see you, Blagre. Although He knows your pain. He understands."

Blagre grew visibly cross, which always made him seem a foot or so taller. It's something wizards can do, so I'm told.

"Enough of this. I am not in pain; I am angry, and you are only making it worse. I warn you, I do not take kindly to being ignored."

Gabriel smiled a gentle, all-knowing smile - the sort of thing that might make you want to punch him in the face - and said, "I cannot help you. He *will not* see you. I am sorry your journey has been wasted."

The wizard's expression grew even darker; a shadow seemed to fall around him, and he gazed intently into the archangel's eyes.

"We will see who has wasted what, Gabriel. Come, Bill, we have work to do."

*****

Two days later...

"This narrative is all over the place, Blagre. Where are we headed now?" said Bill.

The wizard got down from his horse and pointed to where a stream ran down and out of sight.

"Down there," he said. There is a cove and a village within that cove: Anvon. It lies under the cover of an ancient rocky outcrop. A place of safety and shelter. The locals call it 'Big Hat', which isn't very imaginative, but that's the Cornish for you.

"I also know that He is rather fond of the place, good fishing or some such thing."

"And how does this help us?"

"Well, if Muhammed wants the mountain to come to him, as the saying goes... "

"I think you may be misquoting."

The wizard and the gnome walked alongside the stream, following it as it wound down toward the rocky cove.

If you've ever been to Cornwall, you'll probably know there are many little fishing villages like this, and they all look pretty identical – tourists love 'em. If you haven't been, take my word for it.

But this little place was unique because a massive rocky outcrop on the easterly side provided a roof over the dozen or so cottages.

A small harbour completed the picture with a few fishing boats and a smattering of Cornish folk going about their idyllic, pasty-fuelled existences.

"It looks *lovely*," said Bill.

"Oh, it is," replied the wizard, "and that rocky outcrop is a most unique and charming feature, wouldn't you agree?"

"I would."

Then the wizard smiled. His eyes glinted, and he rubbed his hands together. "Viewed from *another* perspective, however, one might conclude that it is somewhat precarious. I mean, suppose that rocky ledge collapsed?"

Bill nodded, "I suppose so. But that's highly unlikely. It's not as if Cornwall suffers from earthquakes."

"Indeed."

The wizard looked up at the sky. "One last warning," he shouted. "*You* took my dog from me, and I want him back. It is such *a small* thing to ask; why are you leaving me no choice?"

"What are you going to do?" said Bill, suddenly alarmed.

"I intend to bring that rock down on their heads. If He takes something I love from me, I will do the same to Him!"

"But you can't."

"Just watch me."

"No, no," said Bill, "I mean that you are *unable*. You do not have *that* kind of power."

Blagre chuckled and placed a hand on his friend's shoulder.

"A wizard derives his power from many sources – the various energies that surround us all – fire, earth, wind and water. But there is one source of power far, *far*, greater than any other."

"And that is?"

"*Indignation.*"

Blagre stood atop a large rock (that I placed there earlier for dramatic purposes) and rolled up his sleeves. His pupils grew more expansive, so much so that his eyes became pure black. He waved his arms above his head, a hypnotic motion. The ground began to tremble, and a mist formed around him. It seemed to Bill that the sky suddenly became overcast, and clouds appeared to gather together. It was very cinematic: technicolour, super-wide aspect ratio... but that never works quite as well in literary form.

More ground trembling, more arm waving, and now Blagre began chanting in a voice much deeper than his own – the words were indecipherable.

Bill saw the rocky outcrop above the village begin to shake. Several villagers also noticed and ran for their cottages.

And then...

A blinding flash followed by a burst of pure sunlight so bright it took Bill by surprise, and he stumbled backwards.

The initial burst over, and the bright light became warm and calming. Tranquillity settled around them, and Bill saw that Blagre had fallen to the floor. It felt as if time stood still – as if one were in the faerie kingdom where all things persist forever.

But the 'Big Hat' remained intact, and the village was unharmed.

"Blagre, are you all right? Your magic did not work, or at least it would appear not."

"Very well, Blagre, you have made your point," came a calm, soothing voice.

Bill squinted and saw a small figure approaching them. A short man, or perhaps even a gnome, his head was mostly bald, with long white hair flowing around the edges. He wore a red robe, and around his neck hung a topaz amulet.

Behind him stood Gabriel.

The diminutive figure smiled and then pointed a finger toward Blagre. A beam of light shot out from the tip, and when it fell on Blagre, the wizard came around and got to his feet.

"Ah ha," said the wizard. "You see, Bill, it *did,* in fact, work. Bill, meet God. God, this is Bill."

"Who?" said God, looking around, somewhat bemused.

"You see, Bill?" said Blagre. "They are in total denial," and the wizard chuckled. "So, you came. Good. You have seen reason and will bring my dog back to me."

God smiled, shuffled over to the rock Blagre had been standing on, and sat down.

"I felt I had to come. For one thing, I saw grief clouded your judgement and that you may be determined to execute your plan. That would have been unfortunate. I am fond of this village. The local tavern makes the most delicious pickled cockles. But that aside, I felt I owed you an explanation."

"Are you bringing my dog back or not?" Blagre's voice wavered slightly.

"Alas, I am not. Such things cannot be done."

"But, I am fairly sure that book of yours sets a precedent."

God frowned, "If you mean the Bible, then an exception is not a rule. But let us not get into semantic arguments about resurrection. Death is part of life. *That* is the rule. And I should know because *I* made the rules. I made all things, and I made them this way."

"Ha, you didn't make me though," said Blagre.

Gabriel stepped forward, "The Lord God made all things, Blagre. This is his creation and... "

God coughed, "Ahem. Actually, that's not strictly true, Gabe. There are three things in creation I am not responsible for. Three things that are not divine. Porridge (yuk), literary criticism, and wizards. These things were not part of my grand plan."

Gabriel was taken aback, shocked even.

God laughed, "Don't worry, Gabe. I was joking about the porridge."

"And faerie folk," said Blagre.

"Don't be silly," replied God. "There's no such thing as fairies."

God slid down from the rock and took Blagre's hand. "I do pity you, though, a child who is not a child of my own. You occupy a special place in creation; thus, it is no fault of yours that you fail to understand its intricacies. "

"Intricacy? Sounds like blatherskite to me."

"Death must follow life, and I cannot interfere. It's all about free will, which is highly complicated to explain. So, you'll have to take my word for it on that score. And as that is the word of God, it's pretty reliable.

"And so, for this reason, I have come to you today. I take your hand, and I share your pain. But you must understand, Blagre, that all things with a beginning must have an end."

God rubbed his chin and walked around in a little circle. Then he continued, "As you are fond of stories, imagine, if you will, finding an old book. It is a big book, and it is filled with a beautiful story full of drama, love, sadness and joy. It's got some juicy action sequences, too. It's a wonderful story, and you are mesmerised by it. And then, you discover it is missing the final chapter. Perhaps the author failed to finish it, or the pages had been torn out.

"Imagine now how that would be. A story with no end. An incomplete tale."

As Bill listened, he noticed that Blagre's countenance began to change. His strength seemed to be leaving him, and his expression changed from defiance to resignation.

The wizard looked down at God, who returned his gaze.

"But... but please," said Blagre, "I just want my dog back... please... I raised him from a puppy, and... and... " his voice trailed away as he saw God gently shaking his head.

Few things are more pitiful or uncomfortable than watching a grown man - a powerful man and a proud man - reduced to tears.

I will not dwell on it save to say that if the expression is 'to cry a river', then Blagre may have cried an ocean.

When he finally composed himself and the initial pain subsided, he looked back at God and said, "But what about the happy ending? There's supposed to be a happy ending, isn't there? I have been in so many stories, and it has never failed to be thus."

God squeezed the wizard's hand and said, "Life is not a fairy tale, Blagre."

***

The End (almost)

Bill and Blagre stood in the rose garden of Blagre's summer house. Bill carried a little ceramic pot.

"Here?" said the gnome.

"Yes, I think so, Bill. It's as good a spot as any, and he loved it here. I doubt it matters to him now, but it brings me some comfort."

Bill opened the little pot and tipped the ashes amongst the roses. Blagre wiped a tear from his eye and looked up at the sky.

"This is not how I imagined any story of mine would end. In fact, I am somewhat annoyed with our author. No more anthologies for us, Bill."

Bill gasped, "No more stories? But what will become of us?"

Blagre smiled and clicked his fingers.

"I said no more *anthologies*, Bill. From now on, it's epic novels for us! Life is too short for anything less."

S. Markem is an accidental writer of fiction. You cannot find him anywhere.

To Wield the Blade of Autumn Sunlight

Laila Amado

The moment the blasted peony exploded in her face, Katharina decided that she'd had enough. Pale pink petals were still tumbling to the floor, when, with a whirl of the heavy silk train of her floor-length skirt, she exited the lab, slamming the door shut.

Katharina had graduated from the Runebell Academy of Enchantment Arts six months ago and could have gone out into the world as a newly minted Green mage, but she was hesitant to do so. The Academy's hospitality clause allowed her to stay for another year, and, while she told everyone who would listen that she was too attached to the ancient halls and libraries to leave, if she were entirely honest with herself, the reason for her stalling was that she was afraid. Afraid that she wasn't good enough.

Green mages were the masters of plant magic, of growth and nourishment. They were hired to salvage the forests damaged by war or fire. They cultivated crops resistant to parasites and disease, saving thousands from hunger. They were hired by the royal courts to create magnificent gardens that showcased the beauty of magic. As for Katharina, she could not even make the plain peony change the color of its petals from pink to blue. The stupid flower kept exploding in her face.

Katharina had passed all of her theoretical exams without trouble but the practicals made her cry. Driven to despair, she'd cornered her mentor, Professor Adonarum, in the lecture hall, and demanded to know if her magical talent had been identified incorrectly during her admission trials. She was certain there was a mistake. It would have certainly made her family happy, if this was so: Katharina's family had a long history of strong magical affinity, having regularly produced wielders of fire and powerful necromancers, ocean whisperers and blood healers. They were less than thrilled with one of their offspring being assigned to "garden variety" magic.

"There was no mistake." Her mentor had shaken his head. "Your magical affinity is to all things green. You just need to find your vibe, your personal connection to the power you hold." He'd smiled a beatific smile, and the vines tangled in his white beard had blossomed with delicate little flowers.

Katharina tried to follow his advice. She really did. She cast more spells. Experimented with vegetables and flowers. Pumpkins failed to grow beyond regular size. Flowers exploded in her face. But six months had passed and her magic wasn't getting any better. She was in desperate need of a break, and she was taking it now.

Katharina tossed the key to the lab into her Department's letterbox and left the Academy building.

* * *

Outside, the city street was a river of movement – bicycles, tricycles, and steam-powered carts raced along its length. Katharina raised her hand. A carriage drawn by two mechanical horses stopped by her side, and she climbed inside.

"Where to?" asked the driver.

Katharina paused. She hadn't really considered where she was going.

"Take me to the Central Railway station," she said. The driver nodded and the carriage moved from the curb, joining the flow of traffic.

From her handbag, Katharina extracted a folded paper pigeon. She scribbled a few words across its wings and let the messenger fly from the window of the carriage. Cleverly enchanted by the Air mages, paper pigeons delivered letters and small parcels across the city and beyond. Katharina had half a dozen of them folded away in her purse's compartment. The messenger fluttered off in the direction of the Academy's residence building, where her own apartment was located in one of the turrets.

By the time the carriage reached the railway station, Katharina's traveling bag, delivered from the residence, was waiting for her at the ticket booth. Katharina bought a one-way ticket to the seaside town of Colthor, famous for its long, sandy beaches and cozy hotels. In Katharina's opinion, seaside towns off-season were severely underrated. Autumn thinned the crowds and tempered the sun. The mere thought of quiet walks along the beach, eating oysters in half-empty diners, and falling asleep to the sound of rolling waves made Katharina happy. What, if not a seaside vacation, could help her find that internal vibe of magic that Professor Adonarum believed she possessed?

Ticket in hand, Katharina boarded the train. Four seats in her compartment for six were already occupied. She ended up sitting in the middle, wedged between a matronly lady equipped with a pair of knitting needles and a sleeping monk of the Three Divinations. Settled in her seat, Katharina took out a book and prepared to enjoy herself. Ever since she was a child, she'd enjoyed traveling by train.

Not more than a minute after the departure, some sort of commotion began outside. The door slid open and a tall, lanky gentleman in a gray traveling suit, fell rather than stepped into the compartment. In his hands, he was trying to hold a leather valise, a box, a stack of books tied by a cord, and a long cylinder that looked like something containing a portable telescope. The gentleman in question made a brave attempt to heave all of these items into an empty space on the luggage rack right above Katharina, but the train swayed, taking a bend; the gentleman lost his balance and the valise tumbled down, followed by the tube and the box. He made a chivalrous attempt to prevent these objects from landing on Katharina's head but, in the process, almost fell on top of her himself, which she did not enjoy. After a bout of profuse apologies and harried movements to fit all of his items onto the rack, the gentleman landed in the remaining seat across from Katharina and lapsed into embarrassed silence.

Katharina re-opened her book. Now that the commotion was over, she was hoping to enjoy the journey. The train sped along its route. Rain droplets streaked the windows, washing away the grime of the city. Things were almost perfect, but then the gentleman of the many tumbling bags cleared his throat and spoke for the first time in three hours.

"Are you really a Green mage?" he asked, blue eyes behind round spectacles, full of unbridled enthusiasm.

After a moment of confusion, Katharina realized that what gave her away was the book she was reading – The Green Path of Enchantment. "Yes, I am," she had to admit.

"Wow," said the bespectacled gentleman, and Katharina realized that he was very young, hardly older than her. It was just the boring gray suit that made him appear older. "I've never had a chance to talk to a Green mage before. What's your position on the application of photospectrum spells in the cultivation of non-indigenous species?"

This was the last conversation Katharina wanted to have, and she opened her mouth to say so, but, apparently, the bespectacled gentleman belonged to that excitable breed of people that were unable to stop talking once they had begun.

Eyes gleaming behind the round spectacles, he carried on. "I've always found the natural world fascinating. Insects, for the most part, but also plants, fossils, and celestial events. I'm an amateur naturalist, you see." He gestured vaguely towards the bags on the rack, which Katharina was now certain, contained a telescope. "Unfortunately, I do not have any magical talent of my own. Such a disappointment. What do you think of the post-enchantment hybrids found in the Eastern River valley?"

Katharina opened her mouth again, this time fully prepared to tell the gentleman off for his lack of conversational manners and also to let him know that having magic might, in fact, be a bigger source of disappointment than not having any. She took a deep breath to deliver her points, but at this moment the train lurched forward, shook, and came to a screeching halt. Bags and boxes tumbled from the racks; somewhere a woman screamed; Katharina was thrown from her seat and landed right on top of the bespectacled gentleman with a shocked "umph". Up close, his eyes were a shade of turquoise rather than simple blue.

"Oh my rainwater gods, are you all right?" he asked, eyes full of genuine concern. He helped her to her feet, holding her hand until she was safely back in the seat, then dove under the table to retrieve her book, and placed it, with utmost care, in her lap. Katharina found this strangely pleasing. She wasn't able to explore this thought any further, because at this moment the door to the compartment slid open to reveal a very distressed conductor.

"Esteemed passengers," he said. "We're sorry to inform you but it appears that, due to heavy rains in the area, a mud slide came down on the tracks. The train cannot move until they clear the obstruction and repair the damage."

"What does this mean, exactly?" asked the monk, who up until now had appeared to be sleeping.

"They're bringing carriages to take you to the nearest village." The conductor checked the scribbles in his notepad. "The village of High Hollows. You'll be staying there a night or two until they fix the tracks. All expenses paid by the carrier, of course."

"Sounds lovely," said the rotund lady in green and resumed her knitting.

Katharina's view on this development was much less benevolent. Seaside, and peace, and clarity were being ripped from her by an oversized lump of dirt. The unfairness of it made her eyes well up with angry tears. Yanking her traveling bag off the rack, she left the compartment and stomped towards the exit, where a queue of passengers was already forming in wait for the arrival of carriages from the village.

* * *

The ride to the village did nothing to improve Katharina's mood. The choice of open-top carriages in the autumn weather of the Rakefall highlands was, at best, thoughtless. The rain continued in a steady drizzle throughout the journey, soaking her dress and jacket. By the time the caravan reached the village of High Hollows, Katharina looked and felt like a drowned rat.

They were brought to an inn that sat at one end of High Hollows' main square, which currently resembled a labyrinth of half-assembled market stalls, beer barrels, and piles of orange pumpkins. The preparations for Harvest Day celebrations were in full swing. This was not how Katharina meant to spend her break.

She dragged her traveling bag upstairs to the room assigned to her by the harried proprietor of the inn. Katharina could safely bet that the poor inn had never seen this number of guests at the same time.

In her room, Katharina unpacked her bag and changed into a dry dress. She was almost done with trying to fix her soaked hair when the sound of a soft chime made her pause.

On a silver tray sitting on the table by the bed, a golden apple began to roll. Round and round it went, chiming with the sound of crystal bells: the sound of her mother calling. Katharina contemplated ignoring the call. Then she sighed. Knowing her mother, not taking the call would eventually cost her more. She touched her finger to the rolling apple, and the surface of the plate first turned to liquid silver and then cleared, showing Katharina's mother. Baroness von Holz sat, straight-backed, in her favorite chair; behind her, a small fire levitated within the confines of an hourglass.

"Whatever happened to your hair?" said the Baroness by way of greeting.

"And good day to you, Mother." Frustrated as she was, Katharina was unable to control her sarcasm. By the way her mother's lips tightened momentarily, she knew that the Baroness had noticed her tone and was not pleased.

"I'm hoping that you won't be this snappish when you come to visit next weekend. Your brother has won a commission to renew the enchantment of the Wyndemier waterways..."

Katharina's heart sank. She had entirely forgotten about the invitation to spend the weekend at her parents' estate.

Mother was still talking about Katharina's brother's latest achievement and could go on like that for quite some time, as Katharina's brother, unlike her, was gifted with some serious magic and could do no wrong. Of all the days, today Katharina was not prepared to listen. It was time to use a trick learned at the boarding school she'd attended as a child.

She rapped her knuckles on the side of the plate, making the apple jiggle. The image of her mother began going blurry at the edges. Her voice started to break up, making the clipped accent of her voice sound almost comic.

"Mother, the connection in this village is very poor, I'm afraid," Katharina squeaked, trying to sound distressed. "You're breaking up." She made a frustrated face and plucked the apple off the plate. The connection died.

Katharina was fairly certain that her mother wasn't trying to grate on her nerves on purpose. She was genuinely unable to hide her disappointment that her only daughter had no valuable magical talent. The magic of plants and growing things did not entice the Baroness, and her daughter's inability to make the best of the poor hand she has been dealt and add some achievement - at least of decorative value - to the family's impressive tableaux was a bitter pill she was unable to swallow. Katharina, if she was being honest, shared the feeling of disappointment, but today was a long and tiring day and she couldn't stomach talking to her mother any longer. She left the apple lying at the side of the plate, preventing any further calls, and left the room. If she was stuck in this village, the least she could do was treat herself to a nice dinner.

* * *

The dinner was surprisingly good. The stew was rich with flavor, grilled mushrooms - sumptuous. She was almost done with an excellent pumpkin pie when the owner of the inn approached her with an apologetic smile.

"Magistra von Holz," she said, addressing her by the proper title given to fully qualified mages. "I'm sorry for interrupting your dinner, but I'm afraid the mayor wants to talk with you."

Taken off guard, Katharina could not prevent her eyebrows from climbing up. She had no idea what the mayor of the village could possibly want with her. Still, her upbringing had taught her some manners and years at the Academy had polished them to perfection. Katharina offered the owner of the inn her most polite smile. "I'd certainly be honored to have a conversation with the mayor," she said.

The owner of the inn, Ms. Dorotea Abercraft, as she introduced herself, led her to a small sitting room. The walls were decorated with a lovely peacock tail wallpaper, and an enchanted flame burned in the fireplace.

The mayor was a short man with a graying mustache. He leaped from his chair to greet Katharina, enveloping her hand in both of his. "We're so, so happy that an esteemed Green mage like yourself is paying a visit to our humble village. We almost lost hope, but I told Ms. Abercraft here just yesterday that miracles happen. That the rainwater gods will not let us fail the Harvest festival in such an abysmal manner. And here you are. We're saved!"

Katharina had no idea what was going on. She was also pretty certain that she wasn't an esteemed anything. Over the mayor's shoulder she caught a glimpse of Ms. Abercraft rolling her eyes, which, as funny as it was, didn't help Katharina much. She was worried that whatever help this village needed, she would fail at it miserably, and fail not in the safe confines of the academy but out in the open, for everyone to see and judge. Still, she couldn't just say no.

* * *

The mayor led Katharina out of the inn. All around them, preparations for the impending Harvest Day celebrations were in full swing. The air smelled of early autumn – warm earth, cider, and the first breath of cold. They took one turn, then another, and the streets changed to flat, rolling hills. The village was, indeed, small. Right in front of them stood a tall gate. Katharina traced the lines of bronze flowers and leaves decorating its surface with her fingertips, wondering at the intricate metalwork. Beneath her fingers, the gate hummed with magic. It was very old – you didn't see enchantments like this one anymore.

"Welcome to the famous orchard of High Hollows," said the mayor, pushing the gate open. "We have been producing our premium apples for almost a hundred years."

Katharina was not sure if the orchard was indeed famous, as she had never heard about it before, but she was sure that not only the gate but the orchard itself was enchanted, as no apple tree could survive and bear fruit for so many years without a little help. She wondered what mage had laid the spellwork on this orchard, and why.

The mayor kept talking. In fact, he had never stopped talking since they left the inn, and Katharina was seriously impressed by his stamina. She was also relieved that she didn't have to uphold her end of the conversation, as it carried on without any active participation on her part.

"Our orchard grows apples not seen anywhere else in the region. Sauce, cider, jams. We produce all of those, and sell throughout the Rakefall highlands and beyond. You must have noticed the apple on the crest of our village."

Katharina had not, but felt that sharing this with the mayor wouldn't help anything. They were still standing in front of the gate, the mayor's hand locked on the handle in a white-knuckled grip. Beyond the gate, Katharina could see nothing but the thicket of evergreen brambles. The mayor was hesitant to lead her into the orchard, for some reason.

The only thing Katharina wanted was to return to the inn and have another portion of their glorious pumpkin pie. She needed to get this over with before it was finished by other guests. "Mr. Mayor," she said. "What happened to your orchard?"

The mayor looked sheepish. "It's my fault," he said. "Two months ago, a hedge witch traveling through the village told me she had a potion that would double the yield of the orchard in time for the Harvest festival. I jumped at the chance. This year we're expecting the Duke of Ambly and his wife, two representatives of the merchant guilds from the West, and the famous dessert maker, Flavoris. Can you imagine what this could mean for our village? To make a long story short, we added the potion to the water feeding the trees, and everything was going well, in the beginning. The trees sprang more apples than we have ever seen. But then something went wrong, and now the Harvest Day is looming. If this can't be fixed, the village will be ruined."

Katharina wanted to point out that that was what happened when the services of unlicensed practitioners of magic were solicited out of greed and vanity, but the Mayor looked so crestfallen that she kept her mouth shut. In a way, Katharina felt relieved. To fix a mistake made by an amateur dabbler did not require complicated magic, and her chances of failure were minimal. She put on her most magnanimous smile and asked the mayor to show her the affected trees.

The mayor sighed. They stepped inside the gate of the orchard and Katharina's sense of smell was assaulted by a strong, disgusting odor. The fact that she hadn't smelt it standing just outside the gates confirmed that there was a magical barrier around the orchard, and it was stronger than she'd assumed. Her apprehension growing, she followed the mayor.

Apple trees towered over the sanded paths and flower beds, planted in what looked like a series of concentric circles. Katharina counted a total of twenty-one trees. Three times seven; the triple replication of the strongest magic number. Amid the trees' green leaves shone the bright red orbs of apples. But the mayor was right. Something was wrong. The closer Katharina came to the trees, the stronger the smell became. Like something rotting, sweet and putrid at the same time.

The apples dripped with viscous liquid, and, where the droplets fell, the grass was discolored, as if the green was being eaten away by a corrosive substance. Katharina did not want any of this to drop on her, so she was hesitant to approach. But thankfully, no tree is a separate entity: beneath the ground, they are connected with each other by the multilayered network of roots spreading far and wide. Katharina could get a sense of the nature of the damage by consulting this network. She lowered herself to the ground and pressed the tips of her fingers into the soft layer of earth.

She let her magic spill into the ground. Eyes closed, she saw with her inner vision how its pale green light connected with the underground structure of roots and mycelium strings. It looked strange, the knots too big, the cords spread out too evenly for a natural system. She'd already known that the orchard was affected by magic, but she had never seen something like that before. Why would anyone want to dictate the shape of the underground systems? It made no sense, but she had no time to deal with that right now. There was a more pressing issue at hand. Here and there, healthy roots were smudged with patches of slimy black. Katharina was not entirely sure what that was. Some form of fungal infestation? A parasitic species introduced by the traveling charlatan's potion? She was certain, however, that it needed to be eradicated if the apples were to be saved. The obvious way to do it was to use her magic to burn it off.

She concentrated, pulled together the strands of power, and directed its flow at one of the ugly black clumps. To her surprise, instead of yielding, the black smudge unfurled like a coiled snake and snapped back at her.

Katharina yelped, yanking her hand out of the ground. The tips of her fingers stung. While she had learned not to expect stellar success from her magic, no agricultural fungus or parasite had attacked her before. Just how much power did this infestation possess to resist a fully trained, if not particularly competent, mage like that?

"I will need some supplies," she said to the mayor. "A dozen copper rods, at least ten inches each, and a roll of hemp rope."

The mayor nodded, head bobbing with enthusiasm Katharina herself did not feel. "We'll get you anything you need to save the orchard!" he exclaimed, before asking the question that, obviously, bothered him the most. "You will be able to save those apples, right?"

Katharina did not answer. She turned and walked back in the direction of the village. The day that hadn't begun well was becoming worse with every hour. In the Academy, eradicating fungal growths and removing infestations had been one of the few things she did well. Classmates joked that destruction came easier to her than creation. This was not untrue.

Here, however, her confidence in that one ability that she never questioned was beginning to waver. Something was happening in the ground beneath that orchard, and she did not fully understand what was going on, but there was no way she could step away from the task or fail at it without losing face in front of this whole village, fellow passengers from the train, the Duke and Duchess, and the whole crowd attending the Harvest Day celebrations.

In short, if she failed, her reputation would be ruined, she would never find employment, and she would have to go back home to her parents' estate and face her mother's gloating for the rest of her life. She had to make this work.

* * *

The mayor was evidently invested in saving the orchard, because by the time Katharina changed into a dress more suitable for "garden variety" magic and collected the few instruments she'd brought with her, he was already standing by the door of the inn with a bag full of copper rods and a coil of hemp rope.

"Thank you very much." Katharina hauled the bag on her shoulder. "These will do."

"Would you like me to accompany you, Magistra von Holz?" asked the mayor, without moving from his spot by the door of the inn.

"This would be unnecessary," she said.

The relief on the mayor's face was quite amusing.

The magic surrounding the orchard tingled when she crossed the boundary. Oddly, it felt like a greeting. Yet, the smell of decay was now even stronger. It filled Katharina's nostrils, clung to her skin in a way that made her want to scrub herself clean.

Katharina took the first rod out of the bag and stuck it in the ground. She did the same with the next rod, and the one after it. When she'd been here with the mayor, extending her magic to clean off the black rot from the intertwining roots had seemed like a logical step. But it hadn't worked; the likely reason for this was that the infestation was too big. Katharina needed more power. That was where the copper rods and the hemp rope came into the picture. She would create an enchanted circle surrounding the orchard, with copper as a conduit and hemp as a reservoir for her Green magic, and when she poured her power into the circle, the power of her cleansing spell would be amplified.

She was almost halfway across the perimeter of the orchard when she made a step backwards to get a look at the circle she was setting up from a different angle. The rope of hemp was quite hard to see. So she took one more step, and another, and, all of a sudden, her back connected with something solid. Katharina yelped and jumped. Whatever she'd run into also yelped. She turned around, copper rod at the ready, and found herself face to face with the bespectacled gentleman from the train.

"Dear lords of rainwater barrels, what are you doing here?" she half-screamed at him.

He made a small apologetic bow and said, "I'm so sorry for startling you, Magistra von Holz. I didn't mean to run into you like that, but I was backing up to get a better look at the nest of honey wasps in the tree top and didn't see you there."

"No. What are you doing in this orchard?"

"Ah," he said as if just now realizing the meaning of her question. "I'm a naturalist, you see. And I've heard that some quite unusual variations of Western long-leg insects can be found in this orchard. Also, have you noticed what's going on with the apples?"

Katharina made an effort not to roll her eyes at him. "Yes, I have."

"I took a sample of that liquid dripping from them."

"You did what?" Katharina couldn't believe her ears. Did this guy have no sense of self-preservation whatsoever?

The bespectacled gentleman fumbled with the lock on the small leather case he carried and extracted two glass plates pressed together. Inside, Katharina could see a small blob of cloudy liquid. Holding the plates up to the light, he said, "You cannot see it well, but there are eyes in this liquid. A myriad of small eyeballs. At least that's what it looks like."

Katharina squinted at the liquid. Something, eyes or not, was moving between two pieces of glass. Momentarily, she felt nauseous. She turned to face the bespectacled gentleman. "Do you realize that what you did could be dangerous?" she inquired.

He had the decency to blush. "No, I didn't think of that."

Katharina sighed. "Please go to the inn, stay away from the orchard, and do not touch that glass with bare hands. I will tell you when it's safe to come back and study your insects."

The bespectacled gentleman hurried away, looking sufficiently harassed. His ability to create chaos in the immediate vicinity of Katharina was annoying, but she had to admit that he had a lovely smile and, if she was totally honest with herself, a really attractive backside. And this was definitely not the right time to think these kinds of thoughts. Katharina shook her head and got back to work.

One after another, all the copper rods went into the ground of the orchard. The circle was ready. Katharina closed her eyes. She concentrated on releasing the slow current of cleansing magic into the rope of hemp joining the rods, felt it stretch in a taut line, humming, as its force amplified. Katharina concentrated, channeling the accumulated power into the spots of blackness marring the roots of the orchard. By her estimation, she'd need anywhere between six and a dozen bursts of amplified power to clean the entirety of this infection. At least, that's what she'd written in her theoretical paper on the subject.

She was already imagining the mayor congratulating her up on the stage and the duke offering her stellar recommendations for a Green mage position at the royal court when the black smudges she was targeting, instead of fading out of existence, sucked in the magic Katharina threw at them. They became bloated, blackness leaking from them across the unaffected roots, and then exploded outwards in a fountain of upturned earth, ichor, and wriggling worms. The wave of ricocheting power hit Katharina in the chest, throwing her to the ground, breathless.

This was not supposed to happen. This never happened, if the textbooks at the Academy were to be believed. She rose to her knees, bewildered. All around her the orchard was going berserk. Slimy tubes erupted from the ground, unfurling to become parodies of trees and grass in a bizarre perversion of everything that Green magic represented.

This was a catastrophe of proportions Katharina had never experienced before, far beyond exploding peonies and puny pumpkins. She remained frozen in place, staring at the horror unfolding in front of her, when the copper rod closest to her began to tremble in the ground. An invisible force yanked it out of the ground and launched it at Katharina. She was barely able to dodge it.

At least the shock of the attack brought her out of her stupor. She got to her feet just in time to see another rod hurtling towards her. Then another. From the ground beneath her feet erupted long purple vines. They reared up, aiming to snare Katharina in their coils and hold her in place for the next copper rod to skewer her like a bug. Her only chance of saving herself was to run.

* * *

Katharina raced away from the orchard, tears streaming down her face. She had no idea what she'd done to cause such a catastrophic fall out. All she knew that she had to get away from this town immediately, not to face the humiliation that was awaiting her. It was time to admit she was a failure and should not be allowed anywhere near apple trees and other growing things.

The streets of the village were mercifully empty, its residents tucked in bed for the coming night. At the inn, Katharina hauled her traveling bag out of the closet and onto the bed. She threw in her shirts, her dresses, and her shoes, dumped the silver plate with its darned apple on top. Perhaps it was this bizarre image that made her stop.

In place of overwhelming humiliation, anger began to sizzle in her chest. What in the actual rainwater hells? Katharina von Holz, a fully qualified Magistra of Green magic, was not going to be defeated by some overgrown fungus. She was going to go back and finish the job. She had no idea how to do it, but she wasn't backing off. She stomped down the stairs and stepped outside.

The night was now a black blanket studded with silver stars.

"So, you've decided against running," said a somber voice behind her.

Katharina jumped and turned around. Ms. Dorotea Abercraft was sitting on a bench by the door of her inn.

"No, I'm not going to run," Katharina sighed. "And I'm going to do what I can to fix the damage that I caused." The wave of anger was receding, and her usual doubts were raising their ugly little heads.

Ms. Abercraft shook her head. "Child, whatever makes you think that you *caused* whatever is going on down there?" She gestured in the direction of the orchard. "Let me tell you something. This garden was planted many years ago by my great-grandmother Wilhelmina Abercraft."

Katharina gasped. "*The* Wilhelmina Abercraft, one of the twelve founding mages of the Runebell Academy?"

Ms. Abercraft smiled. "Yes, that was her. For better or worse, none of us inherited her gift, but we've stayed around to keep an eye on that orchard. Wilhelmina buried something there, you see. Something she could not kill, but only cage in the roots of those apple trees."

"That's why the roots looked so odd, so unusually systematic in their structure," gasped Katharina. "And that black rot... is not really a rot. Something in the potion of that hedge witch interfered with Wilhelmina's enchantment, and the evil buried underneath the orchard is now breaking free."

"I told the mayor and the council that I didn't like the idea of adding that potion to the water," sighed Ms. Abercraft. "But they were too enthused to listen. Now, unfortunately, you'll be the one to deal with the problem they have caused."

Katharina was caught off guard. "Me? But what can I do? This is so far beyond my ability."

Ms. Abercraft shrugged. "You're the only mage in the vicinity. We have no one to help us but you. Besides, I think you underestimate yourself."

"But you don't understand," Katharina said, feeling again on the verge of tears. "I'm really not good at magic. Never was. I cannot grow or heal plants. A peony exploded in my face right before I came here. I'm a complete failure."

This was the first time Katharina had said these things out loud. And, surprisingly enough, the earth did not open to swallow her up.

Ms. Abercroft looked up at her with a soft smile. "I might not have magical ability of my own," she said. "But this I know: there are different ways for Green magic to manifest. And Wilhelmina herself was also no good with growing things. Her talent lay elsewhere. I've got something for you."

Just then, Katarina noticed that Ms. Abercraft was holding a flat black wooden box on her knees. She moved to open its lid. Inside, on a bed of green silk, lay a wickedly curved sickle blade shining rose gold. An inscription in the letters of the first alphabet ran along its edge. Katharina could almost hear the sharp consonants of the spell powering its magic.

"This was Wilhelmina's blade. I cannot wield it, as I have no magic, but you can put it to good use," said Ms. Abercraft.

For Katharina, everything clicked into place. She remembered the full-length portraits of the three founding mages of the Green magic school within the Academy: Anselm Elsprit with a bag of seeds; Tova Jurun with a smoking mortar; Wilhelmina Abercraft with a sickle blade. The Seeder. The Healer. The Reaper. These were the three faces of Green Magic, three types of power. The talent to create life, the talent to nurture it to health and shape it to your will, and the talent to cull malevolent growth.

That was the calling of the Reapers. They had been among the warrior mages that had fought in the Spellcaster wars so many centuries ago. They'd hunted monsters that had found their way into the ancient cities of the Western planes. Exorcised corruption from the spells that had gone bad. Reapers were rare, though. So rare, in fact, that the Academy hadn't encountered one for many decades. Katharina was not untalented in Green magic, as she'd thought, she just held an ability that remained unrecognized due to its rarity. And Professor Adonarum had been right in a way; she did need to find her vibe with the magic she possessed. And that vibe was right in front of her, pulsing in the glowing metal of the sickle blade. She reached out to touch its wicked curve and felt it resonate with joy and recognition.

"Thank you," she said to Ms. Abercraft with deep gratitude. She took the sickle blade out of its case and ran back towards the orchard to face down the monstrosity crawling up from beneath the apple tree roots. There was no one else who could stop it.

* * *

It was bad. The orchard behind the gates was a writhing wall of darkness. The outer boundary still held, but the air above the gates trembled with the strain of containing the malice inside. It would not hold much longer. Once it fell, the darkness inside the orchard would spill out, rolling over the flat incline of the hill and towards the sleeping village below. Katharina took a deep breath, tightened her grip on the handle of the sickle, and pushed the gate open.

What had been, just a few hours ago, a looked-after garden was now a wild thicket of unnatural growth. Vines covered in thick, protruding bumps twined around the stalks and branches of things that wanted to be trees but weren't. Katharina was loath to call them "trees", for they were nothing but a travesty of the real thing. The air in the corrupted orchard was thick with the foul smell of rotting fruit.

Katharina moved forward, as silently as she could, tiptoeing along a path still visible in the nightmarish landscape. She didn't know what waited for her ahead, but felt that it would be unwise to attract attention.

She was almost halfway to the trees of the orchard, when to her left, somewhere in the depth of the thicket, she heard a noise, the desperate sound of someone or something trapped and struggling to break free. Then, a voice, hoarse and thick with effort, managed a half-strangled "Help!"

That was definitely not an animal. Katharina raised her sickle blade and let it fall forward, cutting through the branches barring her way to the poor soul trapped in the twisted garden. There was no one else to help them out. So much for keeping quiet.

The garden screamed. Bumps on the vines all around Katharina opened to reveal blood-shot eyes. She remembered the glass plates with cloudy drops trapped inside. So, that was what had been in the liquid dripping from the apples. One mystery solved.

Since all opportunity for stealth and subtlety was lost, Katharina hacked at the leaves, stems, and vines with full abandon. The blade sang in her hands, enchanted metal shining pale gold like a sliver of sunlight in early autumn. Wherever it touched the toxic green, the severed growths fell to the ground like so much ash.

Straight ahead, wrapped in a tight cocoon of vines, dangled a human figure. It took Katharina another few minutes to set the poor soul free, using the tip of the sickle blade as a hook to cut through the loops. When the last of the vines gave away, the unfortunate tumbled to the ground in a rather undignified manner. It was, quite evidently, the bespectacled gentleman.

Katharina stared at him, bewildered. "I thought I told you to leave the orchard. How are you still here?"

He sat on the ground, still struggling to catch his breath. "I was just about to leave when I saw a perfect specimen of a long-stick insect," he sighed. "I had to stay and document its behavior. I was just about finished with describing its habitat when everything exploded around me. I was knocked out, I think, and then when I came to my senses, these vines were everywhere and I was trapped. I thought I was going to die." He wiped the glass of his spectacles and got to his feet. "Thank you for saving my life." He attempted a rather old-fashioned ceremonial bow, which turned out a bit wobbly as he was still unsteady on his feet, then glanced at the shining sickle blade in Katharina's hand and his mouth opened in a silent "O". "You're going to fight this thing, right?"

"Yes, that's the plan," she answered. What else she could have said?

"I want to help!" said the very disheveled – but no longer wheezing – gentleman. He looked very earnest.

Katharina should have lied about her plans. "You really want to help?" she asked.

"Yes!" He looked much steadier on his feet and, again, enthusiastic. She was beginning to think that enthusiasm was his fundamental characteristic, one that even being trapped by nightmare, dark magic plant-like things could not shake. She had to make sure it didn't get him killed.

"If you really want to help, run to the village, wake up the mayor and ask him to prepare the village for evacuation."

He looked at her, his turquoise blue eyes suddenly somber. "You don't know if you can overcome this thing, do you?"

"No, I don't."

He nodded, looking pensive. "I wish you all the power and luck to prevail." He made another bow, this one steadier. "I will warn the village." He turned and ran towards the gate.

Katharina hoped that he would make it to the village in time and that the mayor would heed the warning. Otherwise, things could turn really bad.

Katharina had no more time to waste. Now that the horror Wilhelmina Abercraft had locked under the orchard had managed to crawl up to the surface, she needed to defeat it before it gathered its strength. Hacking through the pungent growth, she made a beeline to the center of the orchard. Her hand wielding the sickle was beginning to tire when, finally, the vines parted and she tumbled out into a clearing.

She made just one step and stopped in her tracks. In the middle of the clearing, on a large stone sat a girl no older than ten. Her shoulders shook, as if she was crying. This was no place for a child. Katharina had to get her out of here.

"Hey," she cried out. "Don't be afraid. I'm coming to save you."

The girl raised her head. She had eyes so big and transparent they looked like two pale opals. Katharina hurried towards her. She had no idea how a young girl like this could wander into this orchard alone in this time of the night. The thought stopped Katharina in her tracks.

The girl frowned. "What gave me away?" she said, and her voice sounded flat and abrasive, like blunt metal dragged across stone. Its contrast to the tiny frame of a child made the hair on Katharina's head stand on end.

She tightened her grip on the sickle.

The girl screamed. Vines, branches, and leaves flew at

Katharina, as if the entirety of this putrid garden was being flung at her. She cut them down, dodging and turning. The blade in her hand was burning bright.

"You can't defeat me," hissed what was pretending to be the girl. "I'm the god of things that rot in the eternal darkness, things the rainwater doesn't touch. Those better than you couldn't defeat me, and you won't."

Another vine flew into Katharina's face. The blade of the sickle was becoming heavier in her hands by the minute. Katharina could not keep up this battle much longer, and the enemy knew it.

The girl snickered and stepped forward, her fingers stretching towards Katharina, becoming impossibly long. Katharina noticed a thin thread, akin to a pulsing intestine, snaking behind the girl in the grass. As a Green mage, she recognized a tendril when she saw one, an off-shoot connecting the likeness of a girl to all of the terrible growths overcoming this orchard. They were but one system.

"No, I cannot kill you, but I can return you to your trap," Katharina said and swung the blade up, bringing it down on the snaking, slimy tendril in the grass. It burst, spraying everything around it with a rain of dark red, foul-smelling droplets.

The girl opened her mouth to scream but no sound came. Her form shriveled and dried until she was no more than a withered creature struggling to crawl away. All around, the dark parodies of plants fell to the ground, turning to ash.

Katharina drew in a deep breath and focused on the current of her magic. She directed its light green flow at the cowering form in front of her and pushed, driving the escaped evil down into the upturned soil of the orchard. Her Green magic connected with the memory of Wilhelmina's spell still held in the network of healthy apple tree roots. Joined together, these powers pushed the creature down, down into the depth of the orchard's soil where it would remain trapped.

When the spell was done and the ground closed over the banished darkness, grass spilling over the spot, following the command of Katharina's gestures, she took a deep breath. The air was filled with promise. For the first time in her life, Katharina felt in control of her power, proud to be who she was.

* * *

The golden apple rolled along the rim of the silver plate. Mother was calling Katharina every day since the news of her daughter rescuing the royal prince and imprisoning the ancient evil had got out into the world beyond the village of High Hollows. Katharina thought that this newly found maternal love was mildly amusing.

Outside, the leaves of maple trees blazed orange and crimson. The rain had ceased. In the square, people gathered around cider barrels, laughed at the old jokes and sang gaudy songs. The Harvest festival was in full swing.

A carriage carrying the royal crests rolled to a stop in front of the inn. The door opened and a tall gentleman stepped out. He looked very different dressed as the heir to the throne, but Katharina would recognize his disheveled curls and round spectacles anywhere. She was beginning to like him more than she was willing to admit.

Great things were waiting for Katharina at the capital. The Queen had offered her a position at the court as the first Reaper in generations, someone needed to investigate who had brought the poisoning potion to the orchard and why, and the prince's eyes were a shade of turquoise blue she was unable to resist. Katharina took the plate and apple off the side table and unceremoniously dumped them in the suitcase. Mother would have to wait.

Laila Amado is a vagabond storyteller who writes in her second language and has recently exchanged her fourth country of residence for the fifth. Her stories have been published or are forthcoming in Best Small Fictions 2022, Daily Science Fiction, Cotton Xenomorph, Three Lobed Burning Eye, and other publications. She is on Instagram at Laila Amado and on Bluesky at amadolaila.bsky.social

Pay the Troll

Josie Jaffrey

The troll sat underneath her bridge, picking her teeth with a bone.

It was an old bone, as gnarled and yellow as the molars she was cleaning with it, well-honed for extracting pieces of bug carapace and wing. But the troll had no particular attachment to the toothpick; she only continued to use it because it had been some time since she'd eaten anything substantial enough to provide a replacement. That was about to change.

Clip clop. Clip clop.

At first, she thought she must be hearing things.

Although her bridge was in the best possible location - in the middle of the forest, halfway between the two biggest towns in the region, caught between mountains and gulleys, and the only viable crossing over the raging Carver River for miles - no one had come this way in years. Decades, maybe. It was hard to keep track when the days blurred together as her brain withered with each missed meal. The troll didn't know much of the world beyond the forest, but she knew something must have changed in one town or the other, or in the space in between, for her diet to have become so abruptly curtailed. She felt the hunger more keenly now, with the fallen leaves thick in the river, knowing that it wouldn't be long before another lean winter descended.

She could have upped sticks, perhaps, but it's not in the nature of trolls to abandon places in which they have become entrenched. Their homes get wrapped around their bones and threaded into their hearts, until they begin to grow into their dens: their hands gnarling like tree roots, their hair flowing like water, their skin scaling into the pale stonework of the bridges that shelter them. For this troll, leaving her lair would have been like ripping out her insides and leaving them behind. So instead, she had resigned herself to a bare diet of bugs and worms until such time as her body was rendered so dry and spare that it became part of the bridge itself.

But then—

Clip clop. Clip clop.

She put the bone aside, hobbled through the river shallows and peered tentatively out towards the leaf-littered forest path. The troll rubbed her eyes in disbelief.

There was a cow, and the cow had a herder. And they were heading her way. For her bridge.

She ducked back under cover and waited for the telltale sound of hooves on stone.

Trip trap. Trip trap.

She smoothed down her river-wet hair, flicked a maggot from her shoulder, and cleared her throat.

"Who's that trip-trapping over my bridge?" she thundered, her voice reverberating so deeply that the water at her feet shook.

The hoofbeats paused.

"Oh. Er..." And then nothing.

"I said," she said, stepping out to peer up at the newcomers, "who's that trip-trapping over my bridge?"

"Just me," the man said. Barely even a man, really. He had only the very first whisper of beard on his face and his limbs still gangled with the uneasy weight of adolescence. "And Daisy, of course. My cow."

"Then I shall eat you now and save her for dinner," the troll roared, reaching up with one impossibly long arm to snatch at the ankles of the morsels above.

"No, please," said the young man as he tried to dance out of her reach. "You don't want to eat us. Look at us. We're all skin and bone, gristle and nail. We'll get stuck in your teeth. But there are others coming down the path behind us who are much more appetising. You don't want to scare them off with our screams, do you? Just wait a little and you'll have a much richer feast."

The troll was about to argue that since no one had come this way for years, he could hardly expect her to give up this rare meal for the mere chance of another, but then she heard the footsteps in the distance. He was right: there were more coming. And, now that she looked properly at him and his cow, she could see that he was right about that, too. There was nothing to them. Frankly, there was more meat on the grubs she dug up from the riverbank.

"Very well," she said. "But you go quickly now, and don't speak a word of our meeting to anyone."

The young man and his cow hurried off, and soon enough the troll's favourite sound was ringing through the air once more.

Trip trap. Trip trap.

"Who's that trip-trapping over my bridge?" she thundered, her voice reverberating so deeply that mortar dust rained down from the stonework above her head.

"Oh, no," a voice squeaked.

The footsteps came to an abrupt stop, then started to race away.

Ah, the troll thought with a wave of pleasant nostalgia. *A runner.*

Her long arms reached up and snatched, holding her quarry in place.

"I said," she said, stepping out to peer up at her captives, "who's that trip-trapping over my bridge?"

"Just a poor shepherdess," said the young woman, so full of nerves that her voice shook, "and her last remaining sheep."

"Then I shall eat you now and save your sheep for dinner," the troll roared.

"No, please!" the woman screamed. "Can't you see that we'd make a meagre meal? We are thin and hungry, and wasting away. Please, have mercy."

The troll assessed the young woman and her sheep, and saw that she spoke the truth. Beneath her clothes and the sheep's fleece, there was so little flesh as to make the chewing of it more trouble than it was worth. And besides, the troll could already hear more footsteps along the forest path, and could only imagine that they were carrying tastier fare her way.

"Very well," she said to the young woman. "But you go quickly now, and don't speak a word of our meeting to anyone."

The woman hurried off, and soon enough the troll's bridge was trespassed upon once more.

"Who's that trip-trapping over my bridge?" she thundered, her voice reverberating so deeply that the ants living in the riverbanks bubbled up out of their nests.

"Oh dear," a familiar voice said. "You're still here, then, are you?"

The troll stepped out and peered up at her visitor.

"*You,*" the troll said, pouring every acidic pang of hunger into the word. "You *dare* to come back to *my* bridge?"

"Yes, I do," the old woman said. "Me and my goat, here."

For it was this woman – older now, but still with the same malicious glint in her eye – who had curtailed the troll's last repast by pushing her into the river and sending her swirling away downstream. By the time the troll had finally made her way back to her home, waterlogged and broken in places, the woman had been long gone, along with the rest of the travellers on the forest path. It couldn't be a coincidence that she had returned on the same day as the rest of them, but the troll didn't stop to think about that. Instead, she let her hunger carry her into a rage.

"Then I shall eat you now and save your goat for dinner," the troll roared. "I'm not so green as I was back then, and I'll be dining on your flesh before you have a chance to drown me again."

"Will you, really?" the old woman said, then she raised the hem of her skirt to display a shin so gnarled and fleshless that it could have been carved from wood. "I'd like to see you find an ounce of meat on these old bones."

"Bloody hell!" the troll groaned, throwing her hands up in defeat. "You're even scrawnier than the other two! Am I never to find a decent meal?"

"Not in these parts, not these days."

"Why not?"

The old woman pinned the troll with a level look. She had hazel eyes that hadn't dimmed with age. They danced with colour in the afternoon sunshine that dappled through the tree canopy, giving them a magical quality that left the troll feeling as through the old woman could see right through her.

"You really don't know," the old woman said when she had finished her assessment of the troll. "You're supposed to be part of this place. Can't you feel the change in the trees, in the earth around you? Don't you sense what's being done to the river that flows underneath your bridge?"

Now that the old woman mentioned it, there had been some changes recently. Ever since people had stopped using the troll's bridge, in fact. The Carver, which had once been a veritable torrent, was now just an ordinary river. Water that used to flow clear and clean was now murky and filled with odd bits of detritus that the troll didn't recognise. And, perhaps most egregiously of all, the fish that had been in plentiful supply were now a rare supplement to the troll's meagre diet.

"Tell me," the troll said.

"Go upstream and see for yourself," the old woman replied.

The troll hesitated. To leave her bridge, particularly when so much else was already compromised, felt like a terrible idea. When she had so little left, how could she leave her last constant in the world unguarded?

"I could," the troll said. "Or I could just eat you, even if you are a little stringy."

"I'll make you a deal," the old woman offered. "If you don't eat me, then I'll take you with me right now and lead you to the source of the problem."

"Then what am I supposed to eat?"

"I might have an idea about that. I think we can both agree that no one around here is going to make you a decent meal at the moment. Correct?"

"Correct," the troll admitted grudgingly.

"But if you give us a little time and, during that time, permit us to cross your bridge to the pastureland on the other side of the forest, then we and our animals will be able to fatten ourselves up before winter and become much more appetising. You just have to wait a little, and then you can have my goat."

"Only your goat?"

"The town will see that you're well fed. If they don't, then you can eat me too. Do we have a bargain?"

The troll thought for a while. She was hungry, it was true, but she was not yet starving, and her long life had taught her the value of delaying gratification.

"Very well, I shall wait," she agreed. "But only until you're nicely fat. And if my appetite is not satisfied then I shall eat you all, one by one, starting with you and your goat."

"Can't say fairer than that," the old woman said. "Come, then. Follow me."

* * *

"Do you see it?" the old woman asked as they emerged from the trees.

"I see something," the troll replied.

They'd followed the river upstream across the entire width of the forest, the old woman and her goat on the path that ran alongside the river, and the troll with one foot in the water at all times. It reassured her that she was still connected with her bridge through its flow.

Now they were standing just at the edge of the brush in the dusk, looking across the fields to where some monstrous fabrication crouched menacingly over the water, choking the river.

"What is it?" the troll asked.

"It's a bridge."

"No, it's not."

"It's a new kind of bridge," the old woman insisted. "The water passes underneath and turns those wheels, and then the squire uses the turning to power the lamps on the balusters. See?"

The troll gently shook her slick-haired head, sending water droplets this way and that. There were lights on top of the bridge, but she didn't understand what they had to do with the wheels, or what any of it had to do with the bridge.

"It's awful," the troll said.

"I agree. Didn't use to, though, I'm ashamed to say. When the squire first built the thing, I have to admit, I was just as impressed as the others. I thought, *Now we can all get to the pasture without having to cross the troll bridge*, which – back then when all our livestock was getting et, you'll remember – felt like a godsend. It felt like pure charity, and we loved the squire for it. But then he said the mortar needed work, so we'd all need to pay a toll to use the bridge by way of contributing to the upkeep, and that seemed fair enough at the time because it was only a few pennies a year and the bridge saved us more than that in the cost of feeding you, if you don't mind me saying so. But then the squire said the bridge had to be lit, and he had this bright idea about the wheels, and suddenly we're paying more than a month's wages to cross the river and people are starving just to graze their animals, and at a certain point... Well, we'd rather you than the toll."

Which explained a lot. Except the wheels, which seemed to be some kind of inexplicable and magical abomination.

"Well," the troll said, "I don't like it."

"I didn't think you would. What are you going to do about it?"

"Do?" The troll hadn't been planning on doing anything at all. Perhaps she might have shaken her head again before trudging back downriver, but that would have been it. In the old days, when she was the only power in these parts, she would have pulled the whole damned structure down, but she was not what she once was and she had no energy for such exertions in her diminished state.

"Well, what use are you, then?" the old woman asked dismissively, before turning to lead her goat back towards the town. "Some troll you turned out to be," she muttered under her breath as she walked away.

The troll was not so stupid that she was unaware that the old woman was trying to manipulate her, but neither was she so devoid of ego that she didn't feel the sting. She was not just any old troll, she was *the* troll of this forest. She'd fought off hundreds of other would-be bridge-dwellers in order to claim her current abode, widely accepted as one of the most desirable and picturesque bridges in the country. It was *hers*, and the flow of the Carver belonged to her as well.

She marshalled her strength, gathering support from the water that ran through her toes, the breeze that rushed through her hair, the solid earth beneath her. She had earned her home, and she would protect it until her dying breath.

"I should have done this sooner," the troll said, then she dove into the water with all the grace of a kingfisher, swam against the current towards the offending construction, and pulled the centre of the bridge out of the earth by its pilings.

Bricks tumbled into the water. The lamps went out, and someone screamed. When the rumbling of masonry stopped, the river was free once more.

A little way along the path, the old woman grinned.

* * *

There were a lot more people crossing the troll's bridge the next day, but she'd made a bargain, and she stuck to it. She didn't snatch. When she heard the trip-trapping, she kept her grasping hands to herself and sat quietly with her feet dangling in the flow of the river – stronger now, she noticed – wondering with pleasant anticipation how long it would be until the townsfolk were fat enough for her to eat, and what they would taste like when she finally did.

At the end of the day, shortly before dusk, the old woman came by again.

"They're rebuilding it," she said.

"Not for long," the troll replied.

She went upstream again that night and found men patching the old masonry back together with wattle and daub. It didn't take more than a minute or two to deconstruct what they had rebuilt.

The next evening, the old woman came again with the same message, and again the troll made her pilgrimage against the current to the place where the river was being strangled with machinery. This time, men were trying to bridge the gap with wooden beams. Again, she pulled them apart and threw them into the water.

But the next evening, it was the same again.

"The squire will never stop," the old woman said. "With the tolls he's collected from us over the years, he has the wherewithal to rebuild the bridge a hundred times over."

"Then I have simply to destroy a hundred bridges, so he can extract no tolls to pay for more," the troll replied.

The old woman sighed with exasperation, bid the troll do what she would, and shook her head as she walked away.

Although the troll pretended once again that the old woman's reaction had not found its mark, in truth it pinched. All the way upstream that night, she wondered whether her plan was proving more futile with every repetition. Each time she broke down the bridge, the squire merely rebuilt it stronger, and indeed as she approached the site of the cursed machinery she could see that this time it was being reconstructed in brick and stone, just as strong as the original.

Something more drastic would have to be done.

Then she saw a smartly-dressed figure walking along the emerging skeleton of the new bridge, looking down at the water with a suspicious eye, and she knew exactly what she must do.

While she put things in motion, she pulled the bridge down one last time, just for fun.

* * *

The troll sat under her bridge, washing her hair in the increasingly-clear water.

Trip trap. Trip trap.

"Oi, there!" a man yelled from the bridge above. Without waiting for a response, he began to rap his cane on the stone. "The old woman told me you'd be lurking under here, waiting for me, so out you come, right now, or I'll have my men drag you out!"

"Who's that trip-trapping over my bridge?" the troll roared, relishing the growing strength in her voice that made the grass shake and the stone sing and the man above her stumble – just a little – in his stance.

"I am the squire of these parts and I own this forest," the man yelled, a little more shrilly this time, "and you will stop destroying my bridge or be slaughtered like the monster you are. Your days terrorising the townsfolk are over. Come out, you coward, and face your doom!"

The troll did as he asked, but slowly, unfolding herself carefully, limb by limb, so by the time she rose to her full, towering height, the squire could appreciate the magnitude of his error.

For the troll hadn't spent her day in idleness. Instead of sitting under her bridge counting the bricks as she might otherwise have done to pass the time, she had spent every minute of the day – ever since speaking to the old woman this morning – preparing herself to meet the squire this evening. She had spoken to the bees and the ants and the worms; she had spoken to the birds and the rats and the fish; she had spoken to the trees and the water and the earth. They had all lent what they could spare to augment her in body and strength, whether by adding to her physical form or by loaning their power to her, just for a few hours.

Now, with all of the strength of the forest behind her, she had become a creature as tall as the trees, as wide as the river, and as uncontainable as the earth.

"The old woman tells me that you collect a toll for every traveller who crosses your bridge," the troll said in a voice that shook the few remaining leaves from the trees.

"Yes," the squire replied in a voice that also shook, but in a different way.

"Well, if you and your men want to cross my bridge, you must also pay a toll."

"Oh?" the squire sneered, pulling a purse full of gold from his belt. He was trying to save face in front of his men – twenty or so of them, standing back on the path – but there was such a tremor in his hands that the coins were tinkling merrily against each other. "What do you want for it?' he asked. 'A penny? A crown? A sovereign, perhaps?"

"Oh, no," the troll assured him. "Not nearly so much as that." She thought, *a squire will do,* laughed a little to herself, then she said out loud: "Do you know what the difference is between troll bridges and toll bridges?"

The squire tapped his cane, as though he were impatient, but the troll could see that he was now so unsteady in his fear that his feet were slipping on the wet leaves that carpeted the bridge. He said, "I don't have time for your stupid, antiquated riddles."

"Then I'll tell you," the troll replied. "With a toll bridge, you pay the toll and then you are allowed to cross. But with a troll bridge, you pay the toll and then... Well. That's it, actually. There is no *then.*"

* * *

When winter came, it found the troll sitting under her bridge, picking her teeth with a bright, new bone. She had grown fat on the tributes the townsfolk now brought to her: cows and sheep and goats and, just occasionally, a nice plump squire.

Josie Jaffrey is a fantasy and historical fiction author who writes about lost worlds, dystopian societies and paranormal monsters (vampires are her favourite). She has ten novels published so far, along with lots of short stories. Most of those are set in the Silverse, an apocalyptic world filled with vampires and zombies. She's currently working on vampire murder mysteries (the Seekers series) and a YA series about the lost civilisations of the Mediterranean (the Deluge series). Researching the latter is the first time she's used her Classics degree since university.

Josie lives in Oxford with her husband and two cats (Sparky and Gussie), who graciously permit human cohabitation in return for regular feeding and cuddles. The resulting cat fluff makes it difficult for Josie to wear black, which is largely why she gave up being a goth. Although the cats are definitely worth it, she still misses her old wardrobe.

Heartless

Elanna Bellows

I didn't recognize the sky the first time I saw it between the spread fingers of my mother's hand trying to shield me from the sun. Even now, with my face tipped up toward the rain that patters and pools on the leaves around me, the sky is a stranger to me.

But my heart has known differently.

Some people will tell you that hearts are safer kept in your chest, but that's no more true than caged birds are happy. Which is not to say that my heart is happy now, lying there in its own ashes, bare and struggling to find a pattern to its beating, to recognize itself with the new streak of red that cuts down its center. But it was happy once, if only for a little while. For the briefest of moments, my heart knew what it felt like when hope was smooth and sweet like honey, before it remembered that every taste of honey comes with a thousand barbed stings.

I pull the veil of black lace from my face and wrap my poor, infant heart in the woven patterns of flowers - the same flowers that had been set around the bowl now filled with ashes in which my broken heart flailed. Hyacinth and lilies and gladiolas. But the ceremony is over now. Everyone has seen my heart die, puffing out its final breath in a smoky sob before bursting into flames and consuming itself. Everyone saw, and everyone left.

I am alone.

Swaddled in its new lacy armor, my heart coos and settles into silence. I place it back among the soggy ashes where it will sleep until the red, no longer seeping, feathers over with the rest: feels less like a wound and more like a scar.

Above me, a maple leaf falls, swirling on the currents of air and spiraling toward the forest floor where it will rejoin its brethren and find its final rest. But I pluck it from the breeze, stealing its future for this moment, for myself, and run my fingers along its pocked veins and the smooth surfaces between them. It's red, the same red as the new stripe on my sore heart, with a splotch of yellow near the stem no bigger than the print of my thumb. It's still hearty, just having changed its color, not yet dry from the separation from its tree. There are no scars on its face.

There is no skin on mine that isn't running rivulets. I think I have stopped crying, because my lungs feel tired but steady. They remembered how to breathe when my heart burst into flames and my tears ran out. There's nothing left now but the rain.

My heart whimpers from where it sleeps in the ashes, and I know why because I have dreamed those dreams before. I dreamed them last night, and the night before, and the night before... I don't want to dream them again.

There's a way out, an old wives' tale that no one believes anymore, and most have forgotten. If it's true, then I know what I need to break free:

Something living, something dead, something stolen, something red.

I look back at the leaf. It couldn't be so easy.

My heart will find me when it wakes in fresh, full feathers and searches for the empty chest that waits to be filled. It will grow back stronger, more colorful, and equally brave. It will leap into the sky again, seeking happiness. Seeking the kinds of dreams it doesn't remember how to dream right now – dreams of light, and hope, and what it is like to be whole, to breathe deep without pain.

There are two roads, and I don't know which is worse.

A sick feeling curls in my gut when the wind picks up and the leaf trembles. It pulls against my fingers as I hold it too long, but I can't let go. With the leaf pinched between two fingers, I unlock my chest and put the leaf inside.

When I look back at my heart, all bound in lace, I feel nothing. When it whimpers in the ashes, I see flashes of the dreams it is stuck living, but they cannot hurt me anymore. I am powerful like this. I am light as the air that carried the leaf to my fingers.

It only takes me three minutes to trace the wind and the trail of leaves back to the maple tree. Red as flame and swaying in the storm, I would think myself Moses if each branch weren't weeping rainwater into puddles on the ground. Seven minutes more, and my heart is sleeping in the grave I have dug using my hands and a fallen branch. I fill it in and cast my eyes about for a rock to mark the spot. Nine minutes pass before I find one. It's gray and keen-edged, roughly the size of my fist, all sharp angles that aren't quite a trapezoid, aren't quite any shape at all.

I pull the ring from my pocket and place it in the dirt between the stone and my heart. It was a gift from someone who said they loved me – who couldn't, even though they wanted to. But I believed them.

I won't make the same mistake again.

I will tell you how it happened, so that you understand why I abandoned my heart.

It began as it ended, last year when the simmering summer heat shifted, and the wind became gentle and warm, or even cool, instead of searing like the hot, wet breath of a beast. I was sitting beneath my favorite maple tree as the birds sang morning into a brightening sky. The sun, as it rose, cut across the branches and patterned the ground all strewn with shed leaves. Two weeks prior, when I had come to sit after the previous time I'd left my whimpering heart asleep in its ashes, bleeding yellow, the tree had looked like a green match half lit, still in the process of shifting from the warmth of summer to the cool and flame of autumn. But that day it waved russet and crimson as the color faded and branches reached bare arms toward the wind. It had nearly shed its skin in preparation for the winter, as it does every year, so the snow would sit gently on its shoulders and not weigh it down too much.

I wished I could be so lucky. I dreaded the day my heart would find me, having eaten all the pain that had torn it apart, to weigh me down again. Brushing my fingers across the edges of the dried leaves around me, I wished I had found the courage to abandon my heart, even then. I had enjoyed those weeks of heartlessness – the lightness in my chest, the absence of feelings. I did not love, but neither did I hurt. It feels wrong to say, because I know I am not supposed to value emptiness, but this easy calm is worth the sacrifice.

I wish I'd made it sooner, before Timothy found me there, and brought my new heart back to me.

"Excuse me," he said, his tawny hair fluttering in the breeze and his blue eyes uncertain, shy. He extended his arms. "Is this yours?" My heart preened in his hands, ruffling its new streak of yellow feathers in excitement.

And I knew it was dangerous. "Unfortunately," I said, for I could say nothing else.

"It's beautiful," he said, with a shrug. "So many colors. I've never seen one so complex."

I stared at him, wondering if he realized what he'd just implied, and raised an eyebrow. "Keep it then. I've no more use for it. All it does is burn." I have always been too free with my heart.

"Oh," he laughed, the kind of laugh that squirms out of lungs that have lost their rhythm for a breath. "No, I couldn't possibly." He placed my heart on the ground and watched it hop around among the leaves. "I just wanted to be sure it was safe, and found its way home," he added, and smiled at me.

"Thank you," I said, and I think I meant it, but I also didn't. My heart has never been safe. It is safer in the ground, and I am safer heartless.

Safer, but a little less alive.

"You're welcome to sit, if you'd like to join me," I said. "I was just thinking about trees."

He sat a few feet away from me, cross-legged, and picked up a leaf to play with. "You were thinking about trees? I'm Timothy, by the way." He held out a hand.

"Corinne." I shook his hand and smiled. "Pleasure to meet you."

"Likewise. So, trees?"

I nodded. "They know when to let go of their burdens, how to protect themselves from the changes around them. They transform themselves every year. It's easy. Seamless."

Timothy frowned and his hands, which had been running aimlessly over the edges and face of the leaf he'd plucked from the pile, stilled. He looked at the leaf and traced the veins with a slow finger. "It certainly looks seamless, but how do you know that it's easy?"

I looked up at the branches and the leaves that still clung to their seat in the sky. "I suppose I don't. But they do it every year. How could they survive with that much pain?"

"How could you?" Timothy said quietly, his eyes finding my heart which had stopped searching in the leaves and come to curl up beside his ankle. Foolish, and fast asleep.

I didn't say anything.

He reached down and stroked my sleeping heart with the soft knuckle of his index finger and I shivered. It was dangerous, that. Even then I knew it, but I wanted nothing else. I was too brave for my own good. I met Timothy's eyes, still as gentle and even more unfathomable than his touch, and swam in them until he looked away. I told myself I didn't let it break me, but it did.

"Not all transformations are painful," Timothy said with his serious voice, the one that doesn't get lost in its own breath. I was learning to read these tones already, and I imagined the colors and stripes on his heart. I wondered what color it was, how long Timothy would keep it from me, if the answer was *always*. The thought stung. I should have held it anyway, but I couldn't, didn't want to, so I asked a different question instead.

"Tell me a story of a transformation that didn't hurt?"

The smile on Timothy's face that day could have lit up a stormy night. "This one," he said in his light tenor, the gentle voice that glided on the wind like my heart when it knew what happiness was. "An hour ago, I was a person who didn't know you, and now I am a person with a friend named Corinne. That is a transformation, and it didn't hurt."

I looked at my heart still asleep by Timothy's ankle, and I smiled, but it was sad. He was right, and also wrong, and I knew it from the start. It didn't hurt, talking with him while he pet my new heart.

But it would.

❦

On the eve of All Hallows, I clung to his arm as we walked up the stone steps to Locronan Manor. It's not quite a house, and not quite a castle either, and some say it holds twelve secrets, but every year on All Hallows Eve it fills with the satin slippers and voluminous skirts we bring to dance with the Lordyngs.

My silly heart rode on Timothy's shoulder, and I tried to call it back, but it wouldn't leave him. It's dangerous, I know, I've always known, to let myself get attached, but I have never known how to keep my heart from flying.

Except to bury it.

"It's fine," Timothy said in a cheery voice. "I am happy to hold your heart." I knew better than to trust that it would last. Everyone tires of my heart eventually.

Even me.

When we stepped off to the balcony to let our lungs and legs rest a moment from the dancing, Timothy handed my heart back to me and went to fetch some cider and mulled wine. Some days he was shy, but he was a butterfly that night, flitting around the room and talking to everyone. And, of course, everyone loved him. He was the belle of the ball.

I remember hoping the Lordyngs weren't jealous.

When Timothy returned, he was luminous. "Sorry," he said as he handed me a goblet of spiced cider, "everyone wanted to talk to me. I feel so popular."

I peered at him through the steam rising from my mug. "Everybody loves you."

He laughed. "It's nice to be loved." He sipped his mulled wine and glanced at me. "It's because I'm so pretty, isn't it?"

My fingers found his free hand and grasped it. "You are pretty, but I don't think that's why."

Suddenly all his bravado was gone and he was as vulnerable as a turtle hatchling on its mad dash toward the sea. "Why else?"

I ran my thumb across the skin at the back of his hand. "You have a good heart."

"You've never seen it."

Raising one shoulder in a shrug, I sipped my cider. The warm, tart sweetness filled me with hope. "I can infer."

"Would you like to see it?" His voice dripped uncertainty.

I shouldn't have let him, but: "I would like nothing more."

"I don't know if it's a good idea."

So I kept patient eyes on his and waited for him to explain.

"It's too ugly, too heavy. If I show you, you won't like me anymore."

To prove a point, I let go of his hand so I could open my chest and pull out my own heart, setting it on his wrist where it cooed contentedly. "Your heart can't be any heavier or uglier than mine."

He laughed, incredulous. "Are you kidding?"

"It feels heavy to me. I am glad you help me carry it sometimes."

He stared at me for a long moment before he made a decision. His motions were sure even as his hands trembled when he unlocked his chest and pulled out his heart. He didn't let it fly, but he offered it to me.

I remember his fingers stifling those frail wings. How could I not see that his trust in me was never the problem? The problem was that he did not trust himself.

I put down my cider so I could cradle his heart with both hands, and it huddled there with rumpled feathers. In the moonlight I could see the shades of color on its wings: midnight and cerulean and teal and mint green, like the uncertain sea before the change of the seasons. "Beautiful," I whispered to it, and smoothed its feathers. If only it were capable of believing me. It settled a little, but when I looked at Timothy he was pale with terror, so I offered his heart. He took it with relief and tucked it back in his chest, careful to lock it up tight.

"Thank you for sharing," I said, and picked up my mug of cider.

"You're sure it's not too heavy?" His eyes were searching, and he would never trust my answer, but I said it anyway.

"No, it's not heavy at all. I would love to hold it anytime you wish to share it with me."

He smiled, brighter than the moon, closer than the stars in the sky. I wanted to make him smile again and again, bathe in that joy forever.

"You make me feel warm," he said in his quiet voice, the one he used when he meant it but was feeling shy. It felt like a secret he'd shared with me only, and my heart leapt into the air, soaring circles around us.

Even then I knew it was only a matter of time before I would burn in the warmth of that smile.

In the weeks after I buried my heart, I walk through town like a hollowed-out shell rattling against the sand and letting the tide take it. People smile at me as I pass by, sending sympathy with their eyes, and I turn up the corner of my lips to let them know I appreciate it. It is a nice gesture, but I don't need it anymore.

On this All Hallows Eve, I approach the great doors with the mask of happiness on my face, the ruffles of my gown rustling around my ankles. It is nothing like last year, when my foolish heart rode on Timothy's shoulder. This year I have no heart to lose.

So I stand on the parapet and watch the Lordyngs dance. They swirl around the floor of the ballroom in patterns, and my eyes glaze over. I see them, and yet I don't. I can't bring myself to care, nor do I have the heart to join them. The mulled cider in my goblet is sweet and spiced, but it brings me no joy, though its heat seeps through the crystal. My fingers are warm, but my thoughts are cold.

It is no different when the ball ends. When my friends ask me how I am doing, I tell them I am fine, and it is not a lie, but I am not sure it is the truth either. We speak, and it is easy. I do not let them hold my sorrow, for I have none to share, and when they ask for compassion, I give them the words, but I cannot find the heart to care. They reach out for me, and I retreat like a turtle to the safety of my shell. I work, I eat, I wash my hair. I care for myself as Timothy never could.

He was a heart trapped with the wish of flying everywhere, and afraid to let it out of its cage. I remember his fingers stifling those frail wings every time he said, "I will marry you someday, Corinne, but I cannot commit to a date."

A year passed this way, and every time I believed him less as dust gathered on the lace of my dress, and his heart still languored behind bars in his chest.

In October, he handed my heart back to me. "I can't keep hurting you like this," he said. "I'm sorry my heart is so heavy."

So I took the dress I had meant for the exchange of hearts and dyed it black, wore it the day my choked heart went up in flames.

Those flames can't touch me anymore.

I return to the red maple tree in February to see if the sugar flows. When I pierce the bark with my spigot, the sap drips, thick and amber and sweet, and I thank the tree for all that it has given me – for all I have stolen. With its bare branches, it carries the snow with ease, just as I with my flat, red, dead-living heart that I stole from the wind have no cares for the pain I once felt, or the pain I would have felt if I hadn't cut it out of my life like a dead limb from a faltering tree. Below me, my true heart sleeps in the ground, bound in the veil of wedding-funeral flowers. I do not miss it.

Careful, dear heart. You're losing yourself again.

I spin around to face the voice that had no sound but somehow came from behind me. There, in the snow, a cat sits, tail twitching. He perches on the bulge of what must be a rock, though his white paws don't seem to actually be touching anything, and I see no prints behind him. With his fur black even to the tufts of his ears, and the wide white stripe down his nose and chest, and the pinstripe waistcoat, and the hat – not to mention the bowtie – he's dressed finer than any Lordyng in the high castle.

I raise an eyebrow. "Losing myself? Who are you to say?"

Your fairy godmother.

"Really."

No. His tail lashes and he glares at me. *My name is Nish.*

"I've never seen a Dandy before," I say.

You never did such a stupid thing before, Corinne, he replies, trilling my name.

I cross my arms, unphased. No longer have I any heart to wound.

He swivels an ear sideways, annoyed. *You're running out of time,* he all but growls, *and you don't even know it.*

"You're a grumpy one," I chuckle. "I never knew Dandies could be grumpy."

With a slow blink, Nish lifts his white chin and softens his gaze. *Does it amuse you?*

"Sure."

Do you fear me? He bares his teeth.

I shrug.

Does it fill you with joy, and wonder, and awe?

I shrug again.

So, Corinne, tell me: what does?

"Nothing."

Nish stalks over and winds around my legs, rubbing against my ankles and shins, and for a moment I almost feel—

But I am heartless now. I feel nothing but calm, and it is peaceful.

Do you remember what it felt like to be loved?

I shake my head, for I do not trust myself to speak, and I am not sure Timothy ever truly loved me.

Reaching up, Nish places his paws on my knee and widens his blue eyes. I bundle him into my arms where he purrs and touches his cold, pink nose to mine. He is not as heavy as I expected, despite his size, and he folds into my arms. *You have buried your pain, and hope with it.*

I nod.

Dig it up, he says as he lays his head on my shoulder and his deep purr resonates in the cavity of my chest. Even I know that the purr of a Dandy is healing magic, and I didn't ask for this, but I close my eyes and accept the gift. With my heart dead and buried in the ground, I should be stoic as a gravestone, but with Nish in my arms I remember what it feels like to be filled with the rhythm and vibrancy of life. I can go on like stone no longer.

"Okay," I whisper, and now there is no going back, for one cannot forsake a promise to a Dandy.

I will return once you have revived your heart, he says, *and teach you to love without losing yourself.*

"You're going?" The leaf in my chest flutters as if it were a real heart, as if it were still alive and feeling and will break when Nish leaves.

I always break when they leave.

I will return once you have revived your heart, Nish repeats, and his voice isn't real, isn't sound, but it *feels* patient, and soft, like a blanket to muffle my panic. *This part you must do alone.*

"I don't want to hurt," I say, though a tear already runs down my cheek, frosting me like a windowpane.

You must let yourself feel it or it will never go away. It is no insignificant wound you have to heal, but you are resilient enough to face it.

I want to believe him, but I don't know if I do.

Stand tall, dear heart, and if it breaks you, build yourself again.

And with that, Nish is gone. No puff of smoke, no flashy exit. Just gone, leaving only the scent of sandalwood to show that he'd been there at all.

I go for supplies, and the sun is low in the sky by the time I return, a shovel in hand and flint in my pocket. I do not know how much time it takes me to clear the snow, to find the place where I buried my heart. I only know that my toes ache with cold and my fingers are numb by the time I pry the flat stone from the frozen ground. The ring is there, but I couldn't get it out if I tried – the mud has molded around it, swallowed it, and hardened.

So I build my fire around it. A cabin, for heat, like the house Timothy promised, but never built for me. It almost hurts, but not yet. My heart still sleeps, numb, in its grave. I hesitate to strike my flint, because I don't know what will happen after that first spark. I've never heard of anyone exhuming their heart, and there is no Lordyng to preside over this ceremony, so I whisper the reburning incantation to the wind and hope the sun hears me.

In red and yellow, flame and ash

Restore thy spirit and heal the past

What happens is an unremarkable fire. I sit in the snow and warm my hands by it, let its heat seep into my weary body and keep me alive. And as my half-frozen limbs thaw, so does the ground. I feel it deep in my soul, somewhere both connected to and separate from my body. Matching my breaths to the crackle of the flame, I close my eyes and let the silent tears flow like the sap from the maple dripping, dripping into the bucket.

It is slow, this bleeding, while I wait for my heart to quicken.

When the fire has consumed itself, I scrape the pile of simmering ash and shimmering coals to the side and dig, careful to cut a wide berth. I would not recover if I sliced my own heart.

It is grueling work, for the ground is only partially thawed, and by the time I have uncovered my heart, I am slick with sweat under my layers of clothing, even having shed my coat. Brushing the last dirt away, I cradle my heart in my gloved hands and pull it from the earth.

It is stone cold, and motionless. The red wound still seeps through the black lace of its swaddling, but my heart is pale. I have let it bleed for too long, failed to close the wound. There is no folklore to lean on now, to tell me how to recover the feeling in this most vital organ that I made the mistake of abandoning. I can only try to undo what I have done.

I unlock my chest and open the door for the first time since I buried my heart. The leaf is unchanged, unscarred, a perfect face. I place it in the grave and cover it over, giving it back to the cycle from which I stole it. In time, it will fade and crumble into dirt. Only then will it bring new life, feeding the tree that brought it forth so a new leaf can be born.

My heart does not stir, but it feels more like a heart and less like a stone in my hand.

On the fresh grave of the hearty leaf, I build a crib of warm coals for my heart, build a house around it, fill it with kindling, and brace myself. I recite the ritual words of funerals and weddings, the binding and exchange and rebinding of hearts. My hand trembles around the flint, and I think that I might as well strike it on my thumb as on the steel, for we are equally rigid, equally brittle.

Ash to ash and dust to dust

Wing to wing and trust to trust

Sky to sky and song to song

Renew my heart and make it strong

When the spark ignites, my heart wails, and I turn away that my tears may not snuff the flames. I do not know how long the fire burns – I curl up in the snow and sob while my heart blazes hot beside me. It is all of the feelings I have avoided for the past four months. I feel them one at a time: the anguish, the guilt, the shame, the regret, the betrayal, the anger, the fear. And I feel them all at once: the longing, the uncertainty, the love, the hope and hopelessness of losing something dear.

There are icicles on my eyelashes and pockmarks in the snow, and I want nothing more than to sleep, but I did not suffer this and revive my heart only to succumb to the slow death of hypothermia. I melt my lashes with what's left of warmth in my fingers and open my eyes. My heart stands before me, pink and raw and bald, but alive. The wound has scabbed over, though not yet healed, and I have no tears left to shed. It is time to move now, to go home to a warm hearth, a warm bed, a warm dream, but I do not think I have it in me to rise. All I can do is open my chest so my heart can hop inside.

At least we will die together.

But then Nish is there, just as he promised, and his sandpaper tongue is scraping at the ice on my cheeks.

Get up, he says, and I obey.

Come, he says, and I follow him, leaving the shovel behind.

I wake wrapped in blankets with Nish beside me. For the next week he does not leave my side. He curls up on my chest and purrs when I cry. He watches out the window while I cook in the kitchen. He demands nothing from me except that I care for myself.

My heart sleeps closed in my chest. Though no longer heartless, I am now as skittish and guarded as Timothy.

It terrifies me.

Your fear, Nish tells me one night as I sew by the hearth, *is both rational and irrational. It is rational in that there is a reason for it. It is irrational in that it consumes you in excess.*

"I would rather not be afraid," I say, missing my fearless youth when I jumped into love boldly.

No, for then you would not have learned what you have learned. Ignorance and naivete are what led you here. It would not do to regress.

I do not know that I have learned anything from all this pain, but Nish is usually right, so I do not argue with him.

Every day he teaches me something new, and every day the scab on my heart softens until the day it flakes away.

The first time I open my chest and let my heart out to dance with the wind, it rushes into the sky with an eagerness I had forgotten how to fathom, and for a moment I understand what Timothy must have felt, for I am terrified of losing it again. But the breeze is sweet and clean, and it smooths the feathers on my heart, and I know that it will always come back to me.

As a child, Elanna Bellows pretended to be a horse, wrote stories on the back of napkins to fend off boredom, and had the audacity as a third grader to try to teach her much younger brother multiplication. Now she teaches for real at a public school in Massachusetts, writes in notebooks instead of on napkins, and pretends to be an adult. You can find her on Instagram at Elanna Bellows Writes.

A Tale Not About Frog Princes

Ella Holmes

We endeavour to write and plant this tale betwixt the castle's golden ash and scarlet oak, with the hope that even when we are gone, the story will live on. *(If you are reading this in a book, then it would seem our autumn wish to the forest was not only heard, but answered.)*

* * *

From her arched window high in the tower, Stepmother Wicker, Queen of Wreathwood, happened to spot the young princess stealing into the shadowed courtyard. The Queen had come to the kingdom only two moons ago, having met, warmed to and wed the King but two moons before that, and she spent most of her time burying her nose in mysterious leatherbound books or doing needlepoint with the older women of the palace.

The sun sank slowly below the horizon, spearing gold down to the cobblestones as the princess waited for the frog she'd come to expect would meet her when dusk fell. Wicker arched a fine brow, dark as pitch. The princess, sixteen years young and naïve yet, did not think to look to the tower window as she tried to keep her secret – the frog was a creature the cook might drop into his pot for supper, and there was also the small issue that if anyone found out he could talk, the King would surely begin his war campaign into the woods. Wicker knew more than anyone that the forest's mysteries and proclivity for stealing people away were more than imaginary.

The little green frog kept to the darkest shadows and deepest creases between cobbles as he approached the princess, hopping like he was not quite accustomed to his legs, kicking them out like a royal horse displeased with their farrier.

Frog princes were often shy and hesitant creatures, though once the promise of a kiss had been secured, there was nothing shy about them. Wicker watched as her step-daughter picked the cursed creature up, a weed of envy coiling in her belly. One could go their whole life never encountering a frog prince, and certainly Wicker had never been so lucky as to encounter one when she was young – unlike her sisters, who had kissed them and promptly married without complaint – but on this fine Autumn afternoon with red myrtle leaves blowing in the wind, Wicker imagined herself holding him, slick-skinned, in her hands – hands which ached deep in the joints, and whose fingers were crooked. People had claimed to have accepted food from those 'unnatural' hands, and sickened quickly afterward. There was no proof, of course, but those who are fearful are frightfully good at imagining terrible truths.

"The brave hero," Wicker murmurs to herself, thinking about her many stories, "injured and bleeding, battles his way through slavering dragons and bloodthirsty trees to achieve his prize. Suffering is a noble act."

Princess Grace whispered to the green frog and he whispered back, secret words Wicker couldn't hear, but which seemed to cause the princess to shift on her feet. Talking frogs were uncanny, so the princess's hesitation was not surprising. The men of the kingdom, the knights of the realm and even the King himself, often whispered amongst themselves about how they could catch the creatures of the magical wood, how they would lay belly-down in the undergrowth and wait with arrow drawn and aimed or dagger sharpened and naked, everything hungry for blood. It was more likely, Wicker thought, that the men would be bitten or spooked or dragged into a crack between this world and the otherworld, where they would have to fight their way back – and when the bards sang of it, the tale would be such that their fatigue was shaken off for bravery, their pain a mere obstacle to be surpassed, for there can be no heroic success until their bodies wailed for them to stop, give up, that lesser men would quit.

Wicker turned away from the window and returned to her needlepoint ladies: Ru, and Robin. Whether she watched or not, things would go as they always did.

* * *

Except, it happened that the princess was not interested in princes, nor men of any size, shape, or colour. It is not unusual, as some of us know, but in a tale such as this... well, it was a surprise to be sure when Wicker found out a week after her arrival that the princess had eyes only for the horsemaster's daughter, Fallon, who was stocky and strong and as hard-headed as a wood post. Unfortunately there was always a young fellow who thought it a challenge to make one of them fall in love with him; fortunately most of them learned better or grew bored of the chase.

Alas, in the darkening dusk without her watching, the frog had one thought and one thought only – to win himself a princess and his human body back again.

Queen Wicker might have done it, had she still been unmarried, had she been asked; she didn't mind the act, as some did, and quite liked the idea of saving someone without having to leave the castle.

But he won the kiss from the princess sure enough, through quicksilver words and careful silences, through implication of what might happen to her reputation should he go from here without having been helped by the princess who was renowned for her kindness and generosity. *(If ever you ask us what exactly he said and didn't say, we might tell you to catch someone in a lie and listen close to how they try to round its edges so you'll slip into forgiveness.)*

So the frog won a kiss, and we all know it wasn't a good or kind thing.

"stepmother! Oh, please, stepmother!" the princess called, knocking loudly on the door. Queen Wicker unlatched and opened it, keeping hold of the book in her hand. She expected to see a young man, perhaps in a fine green tunic, newly turned from slick to silvered prince with unrequited dreams of marriage to beg of her, but there was none.

"Sweet Grace," Wicker gasped. "Whatever is the matter?"

Princess Grace led her slowly down the stairs, for Wicker was sore of joint and stiff of muscle, and she quickly saw the problem.

"Please help," the princess cried.

Wicker gasped, for there on the ground, sitting up against the stone wall, was not exactly a prince.

Her first thought was to kill it – this green-skinned thing that was not-quite man and not-quite animal – but Grace held onto her arm and pleaded, and Wicker had never willingly hurt anyone in her life.

"Help," the frog-prince rasped. "Help... me." His eyes were caught between blue irises and the yellow-spotted black orbs of his other nature, darting this way and that. His skin was human-dry except for two slimy trails leaking from his eyes.

"Tell me exactly what happened." Wicker removed her shawl, knitted five years ago for her thirtieth birthday by her own stepmother, and tucked it under the frog prince's head. "Every word, every action."

And so Grace did, with some hesitance, and Wicker understood that the kiss hadn't been truly and happily given, for Grace's discomfort was as palpable as a monthly cramp.

"I thought it would turn him," Grace said.

"And that it did." Wicker opened her arms, and Grace accepted the offered comfort with a shaky sigh, both of them regarding the boy warily. He wasn't all there in mind and spirit, it seemed, and she couldn't leave him helpless and alone. Especially not if he was inclined to try to leap back into the woods. "It only works if you say yes to the kiss and mean it, free of detrimental consequence," Wicker said softly, taking Grace's trembling hand. "This is not your fault."

Wicker and Grace quickly moved the boy-frog, who looked a horror, into a small room. His fingers were webbed and his tongue was too long – his lips too thin and hard, teeth too small. She thought of all the tales she'd read of the strong and the brave, the brave heroes of old, because this was surely such a tale. Yet there was no hero amongst the three of them. Those heroes stood up and gritted their teeth, girded their loins, hefted sword and shield and set forth with grim determination. Wicker was exhausted, and had never had the bones of those folk. She had been born tired and sore, with joints that favoured slipping out of sockets. Even as she took up the frog-boy's legs and helped Grace carry him, her shoulders, wrists, and legs ached something shocking.

The boy sobbed. Wicker touched a hand to his brow once they'd laid him down on a narrow sleeping pallet. Both he and Grace looked at Wicker with feverish eyes, not sure what to do, what any of this meant, or how to fix it.

"I'm sorry," the frog-boy murmured, "so... very sorry." He looked to Grace as he said it, didn't break eye contact even when his tongue darted out of its own accord.

Wicker sat in a chair in the corner of the room and sighed. "Well, we know an apology alone won't cut it," she said. "If you're going to ask for a kiss, you must respect the answer."

He blinked, but seemed to understand.

"I thought it would help him," Grace muttered.

"I know. You made a generous decision in the face of a rather ungenerous deal." Wicker cracked each of her finger knuckles, taking comfort from each pop and snap. "Now he is stuck betwixt, neither one nor the other. He has no home here nor in the woods. Your father would see him killed." *(A caring man though the King is, in familial respects, it will be two years yet before he learns that fear does not demand a sword to soothe it. But that story isn't written yet, and exists only in our minds.)*

Grace nodded, knowing the truth of it. "What can I do? I have duties and am expected to show myself daily, and I'm too young yet to travel. Can you fix him? With your knowledge – with all the things folk say about you—" She flushed bright red. "I'm sorry. I know you to be kind beyond measure, beyond even me who they say is kindest of all. Truth be told, I have learned much from you in the two moons since we met."

Wicker gave a tired smile and took Grace's hand in hers again. Indeed she had helped Grace as any mother would, knowing which herbs could ease her bleeding pains and which words could help her when she worried over Fallon's attentions. She was not old, but she was weary. She was nothing like the people she read about in her hundreds of books, who kept getting up and kept going, going, going, ignoring their pain and exhaustion. There was no hero who flared with pain and had to spend a day in bed too tired to weep, like she did. *(You may think she will have to forge and write her own, and you would be right. But the necessity of forging is an overcoming story unto itself, and is a pain different from that of the heroes for whom stories are always written.)*

"I will try to help him," Wicker said, "though I can make no promises."

That night she parsed through her hundreds of books and

the tens of stories within them, searching for an answer. All they offered was a familiar poetic precept: a life must be given for the cause of heroism. It was a mandate woven into everyone's understanding of the world, selflessness which justified death by beast and battle. Heroism, a great and brave act of grand sacrifice, was magic unto itself, and though Wicker would try, she knew of no stories which would allow her to succeed at it, let alone attempt to wield it. It would have to be someone or something else.

* * *

There was nothing to be done about the boy's appearance, only his health. Wicker secretly fed him all manner of things by hand, to see which he could stomach, and in the end he ate bread soaked in milk and honey. All the King knew was that when Wicker touched a hand to his face and kissed him, she smelled as comforting as sweet bread. He loved her unlike any other, but he was still fearful of that which he didn't understand, and for that reason Wicker did not tell him what she was up to nor what had happened to Grace, for it was the princess's story to tell.

It was a danger having the frog-boy in the castle, but he was lucid and aware enough to keep himself quiet and still when people passed by his locked room. When people grew curious and wondered why the new Queen slipped away inside, it was the King who told them not to decry spending time in private with one's thoughts, and for that she was grateful.

The frog-boy found it hard to walk. He couldn't shake the urge to leap when he stood, and it would send him high into the air where he would knock his head against the ceiling. To solve this, he took to crawling, kneeling, and crouching low when he felt the need to move. Wicker encouraged it, knowing he needed to keep up his strength if he was to make the journey into the Wreathwood.

"When will you leave?" Grace asked the Queen one afternoon, when a dozen paces away, the King was preparing his horse for a journey to the neighbouring kingdom. It had been five days since the changing, each one secretive and autumn-hued, languid in their passing.

"Your father will leave tomorrow at dawn and be gone for three days. I will go and return before him, and he shan't know a thing." Queen Wicker smiled at her husband, who caught her eye over the back of his chestnut mare. She had grown up talking to healers and wise-women, and had many ideas on how to protect herself on her quest. The golden ash trees behind the stables were raining leaves, turning the hazy afternoon light yellow and flickering as sunlight glanced off their spinning faces. "I have travelled those paths before. Isn't that what some folk say? That I emerged from the woodland and bespelled your father with uncanny magic. Why else should he want me?" Indeed, all the tales she had read spoke about people like her as though they could only ever be malevolent or miserable, things of dejection or things to be defeated. *(She would have me add that they are also hardly ever wanted, unless they are first an object of pity, a person from whom someone must learn to love.)*

Her step-daughter shook her head. "They say you could fell a chicken with one sharp look, that you collect mushroom caps for poison, and that the apples you give away are laced with it. But I think they say all that because they fear what they don't know."

Wicker hummed agreement. "I wonder what will be said about you, should you ever travel far from here." There are some things that only girls and women understand; some tales spun about them and no-one else, and within those, yet more tales about specific kinds of women, of which Wicker was and Grace was not.

That evening they sat in the main hall for supper, with a storytelling bard on the dais at the end of the room. "There was a blessed, blessed lady who was down to one working eye, the other shot through with an arrow," he said, "and when the creature she came upon plucked out the broken one and licked it, the creature exclaimed…" A dramatic pause. "It does not taste as holy, holey as it looks." Everyone laughed at the hero's injury turned jest. *(Everyone always laughs.)*

* * *

Wicker rose before dawn and sent her husband off with a kiss on the cheek and a wave of her handkerchief, as the Queen was wont to do. Then, under the guise of returning to much-needed rest, she set about oddities even the most suspicious folk never attributed to her.

She caught a wriggling mouse in a trap-cage; she found three crepe myrtle leaves of yellow, orange, and red; carved a face into the body of a swollen pumpkin and strapped it to her front; she wore her shoes on opposite feet; stuffed her pockets with herbal tonics; she turned her and the frog-boy's cloaks inside out before fixing each to their shoulders.

"Come on," she said, and helped him walk. The castle wouldn't come wholly awake for another hour yet, so there was time to walk out free of bother. The air was milky with fog. All about them the wind rustled with damp and tumbling leaves blowing across the cobbles, the trees now stripped bare so only their skeletons remained.

The frog-boy startled at every sound with no visible origin, at every scuff of Wicker's boots on uneven stone. She lifted her feet higher to avoid it. "That's it," she said as they walked far enough that stone changed to hard-packed dirt, then after that, people to plants. At the edge of the autumnal woods, they paused for a sip of water before stepping off all human paths. "Careful now. Don't be afraid." Once inside the treeline, Wicker took the large pumpkin by its curling stem and placed it in the undergrowth, face looking outward so it might warn her if the King came back this way before her. *(It is a dying hearth-magic practice to give a thing eyes, especially in Autumn, though we hope it lives on in whichever time you find this tale.)*

The woods were dark, even with half the trees standing leafless. Their great naked bodies bent at the hip here and there as if reaching for the two travellers, trying to inspect the half-not-quite creature Wicker led by the hand. Something snapped behind them and he startled so greatly that he almost ripped her arm clean out of its socket.

"There, there," she cooed, and sat him down a while. Truth be told, she needed the rest. A fanciful thought crossed her mind, of pain and overcoming, and she wondered if her daily pain, chronic and unrelenting, was enough to make her a hero in her own right. Could this be all? Did she not push herself each day? Did her own tale need a grand moment of almost giving up, when her life had already been full of contempt and disbelief at her invisible illness? She dug a bottle of pain-relieving tonic from her pocket and drank, reminding herself that heroes don't need to sit on damp, mushroomed logs and wait for their herbs to kick in. The mouse in the small cage at her belt made not a peep.

"Afraid," the frog-boy said.

His palms were cold and clammy when she took them in hers again, his green skin so thin as to present his racing pulse to her with the strength of two panic-tapping fingers beneath the surface. "No wolves or ravens will bother us," she said, "they know I've no great patience for their bad manners." *(If you're curious as to how they know, simply ask yourself how a cat knows it's time to be fed; it is habit and pattern that teaches one the ways of the world. If you were not curious at all, then we shall tell you that curiosity is the force that inks this quill, and one must have it in order to write a story which breaks from said ways.)*

He tried to smile, or so it seemed, then stuck his tongue out quick-fast and caught a tiny gleaming fly from the air between them. She did not judge, only led him onward once he'd swallowed. Their shoes worn on opposite feet kept them from getting tangled in the odd paths of the woods which led unsuspecting folk into faery burrows and portals to the otherworld, and the inside-out cloaks protected them from beings who sought to trick them.

She hadn't really known where she should stop, but she knew it when she saw it. A clearing, a bed of fallen leaves, and in the centre of it a naked goddess of a tree. She bade the frog-boy follow her up to it, to bow, and to watch as she took the yellow, orange, and red leaves from her pocket and knotted their thin stems to the branch most comfortably within her reach.

Then they sat beneath the shadow of the ancient trunk. The sun passed overhead into night, and they slept in the crook of the roots, warmed by the life thrumming through it.

"Gracious," said a voice at dawn. The frog-boy leapt up in fright, and Wicker held him down so he wouldn't get lost amongst the branches or bound off and be taken for a wolf's supper. "A frog-fellow and my oldest, oddest woman-friend. How blessed I am."

Wicker stood up straight and met the forest woman's eyes before bowing. "Blessed be the oak."

She conceded a slow nod of her auburn-haired head, chopped as haphazardly as the spikes of a three-pronged leaf.

"I was rather hoping for someone else," Wicker said. "I didn't think an oak spirit would have the chops to help with this befuddlement."

"Dear me," the woman said. 'But we oaken folk are a soft and curious lot. I couldn't help myself. Besides, I may be who you need – even if that seems to have escaped your consideration."

Wicker thought for a moment, and realised exactly what she had done. A poor thing of it too, that she could do to someone else what was often done to her. "I have judged you unkindly. I apologise."

"Mm," the oaken woman hummed. "Now let me see." She

circled Wicker and the frog-boy, poked at his green skin and his clammy palms. *(Take your thumb and lick your forefinger before touching them together; the first press and peel of skin is precisely the feeling. If you did as we said, then know it is as accurate a description as it is playful, and we adore you for your willingness.)* The woman's skin was as brown as the tree she had spirited from, beautiful as anyone Wicker had ever seen, and she patiently waited for her to finish her inspection of them both, wondering what payment would be asked of her. How her lower back felt like a half-snapped twig, sharp edges and splinters digging into her, but she remained still and standing.

She thought of all the heroes whose pain and illness were the consequence of injury after an enemy attack or some grand act, who were given magical implements to render their faults practically non-existent, or healed so they really were. She thought of the others who were not so lucky and died. Having read so many stories, Wicker was inclined to push through her discomfort and the protest of her body, for anything less than that would be considered weak and unacceptable, would not be the act of a hero but that of someone who gave up, who was too frail and unreliable to measure up to the task.

Meanwhile, the oaken woman asked to lick the frog-boy's knee and he consented.

One story stuck out to Wicker then, of a man who had fought for the wrong side in a battle and lost his legs to a bone-weaver, and who was later granted the bones of an aspen upon changing allegiances. He stood up to his enemy, the right enemy, and gestured to his newly aspen-braced legs, proud of the punishment that was his injury. But disability is no divine plan, no price paid for doing moral wrongs, and Wicker resented it. *(Even this frog-boy who manipulated a kiss from a kind girl perhaps should not have been written thus, punished thus for his crime, yet it is the story we are most familiar with and the pattern is hard to escape. We discover this story and its shortcomings as we go.)*

Wicker's bodily state was not the result of crime nor fault of her own, but something which had been part of her existence since she was a babe in the womb, worsened not by herself and her choices, but in fact worsened by people who had ignored and dismissed her.

Wicker did not want to ignore nor dismiss herself, nor did she want to act despite, nor did she want to feel as she had felt at fourteen when a healer had told her she did not need herbal relief for the correcting of her shoulder joint, and who'd chastised her for crying while his apprentice forced her to be still.

She could see it then, the scene which would be written of her: The heroine staggers, having successfully faced her foe and all the challenges, knowing that the frog-boy has been saved. She turns and casts one last, longing look in the direction of home, of her loved ones, at the young boy she has saved, before her body finally gives out under her. And her life, too, gives up.

(If you ask why she might imagine such an ending – is it not overly dramatic? – know that these are taken from the most common stories in existence. Ask yourself in how many tales heroism does not rely on overcoming walls of the mind and body, and in how many tales a brave hero scales these walls by gritting their teeth, by simply wanting it hard enough, as if gritting one's teeth suddenly imbues one with ability.)

"I will sit, if you don't mind," Wicker said, and didn't wait for an answer. She dropped down onto the nearest seat-like root of the oak and sighed.

"You have something for me." The oaken woman held out a slender hand.

"Oh, yes." Wicker gently took the mouse from the little cage and brought it out.

She frowned. "But this is not good enough."

Wicker sighed again. She hadn't thought herself so clever

hat it would be this simple, but she had hoped… "A sacrifice – one life for the boy's. What makes the creature's life less valuable than mine?"

The oaken woman shook her head. "It is ironic you should ask that. The mouse does not want this." She let it go, and the little animal fled into the coiled roots and the shadows between, never to be seen again. "Why should you think this would do?"

Wicker's breath caught; tongue trapped between her teeth. Foolish. What was she but another creature caged, who too would like to flee?

She did not want to give herself up, but all the tales has said it plainly: The hero sacrifices themself. A life is given. The slowest, the sickest – they are the most expendable, and so to earn her place in ink and story, she must not survive. She must suffer, be laughed at, overcome herself, or die. She saw the story threads before her then, and they were almost so real she could feel them tied to her, pulling at her shoulder, her leg, her crooked pinkie finger and her ankle, so hard they all felt like they might tear out of joint. To which thread would she give in? Which threads did she really, truly, have a choice in following?

The pumpkin she had carved with watchful eyes alerted her, with a cotton-like haze over her sight, that people were travelling along the path, entering the trees. She looked to the frog-boy, wide-eyed, unsure of what to do.

This young boy was a manling yet, a prince who had not yet earned his mettle and slain his dragons, giants, or foreign foes. He would see himself as the one inked in those stories. He would see himself as the hero of all those tales. It was, after all, why he had been made a frog – to learn his lesson and return home to applause and tearful waving of his kingdom's flag. If Wicker chose not to give up her life, well, what would that mean?

There were no tales written that way; surely it was not allowed. Surely, for the same reason he had been made a frog –

to conquer limits and challenges, to have a tale to tell – she was being asked to give her life. Who was she to deny what was written? Tales would be told about her, not by her. Wicker only saw herself as the mouse cowering in the oaken woman's hand, too afraid to run and jump for fear of the height of the fall down, down, down into the mess of leaves below. Wicker could not do such a thing in the castle, even with Princess Grace at risk. Her body would allow her no fate but one where she failed to be brave or fast enough, and she would be hailed as the Coward Queen.

Dead, Villain, Coward, Jest... Her heart ached, thick and hard as a bluebell bulb gone to ground for autumn.

All this she knew because of those leather-bound books in her rooms and in her library – that if she could not be a hero, she could be nobody of good consequence to any tale. She wanted more, damn it all. Had she not but recently married the one she loved, and become one part of a family who loved her in return? The bulb of her heart lodged itself in her throat. She was rather helpless, having come to the woods with only the frog-boy who needed her hand to comfort him, and now needed her life to save him.

(As we transcribe this, she would like me to add that she has always had trouble asking for help. When one is often in need of it, asking for yet more can make one feel like a burden, to be sure. But you are not, and you are not alone.)

Wicker realised, in that moment, what a fool she'd been in thinking to come out here alone, to quest as the One True Hero would when she was no such thing and did not want to be.

Since meeting the King and coming to the Kingdom of Wreathwood, she has known the pleasure of friendship and joy, of support, of her stepdaughter and her needlework ladies most of all. The stories she had read told her differently, but she'd known better, and was now in the damp woods paying the price for forgetting that it takes a village to weather a storm.

She knew that no matter how scribes wrote the tales, it was never just the one, singular hero who struck down the evil lords and monsters, it was also the person who forged his sword, and the person who made his armour and the person who strapped him into it and the horse who carried him on its back into danger. *(So you see, everyone shares a single thread, an ever-reaching hand. Asking that someone hold it and keep you warm should not be seen as a burden, but a boon.)*

Without them, the singular hero would have failed, as Wicker was failing now.

Oh, it tasted bitter. Her eyes welled with a salt-sting that made her cry aloud.

The oaken woman had all the patience of the tree she'd sprung from, an ancient thing that had lived longer than Wicker thrice over at least. She sighed and looked at the oak spirit, still unable to talk. Even admitting she did not want to die felt like a betrayal of the very fabric of things.

Suddenly, a trampling sounded in the distance, twigs breaking under several or perhaps only two giant feet. The frog-boy tensed, and Wicker held onto him tightly. She stood, peering out into the shadows of the woodland, and held her breath as though it would do anything against the threat of redcap, trickster, or dragon. The oaken woman had disappeared, leaving the two of them alone. Wicker's back broke into a cold sweat.

From between two yellow-leaved maidenhair trees emerged two women with wide-brimmed hats over their eyes, their hands linked as they approached. They looked up, and Wicker gasped.

"What are you doing here, Grace?" she asked breathlessly. "Your father—" Oh, but it had been Grace that the pumpkin had seen coming this way, hadn't it? She rose to check her stepdaughter and Fallon for injury, but Grace bade her remain seated and came over to her instead.

"I brought friends," Grace said, and from behind her and

Fallon came the elders Edith, Ru, and Robin, still with their needles and spools stuck to their bodices. "We came right away, soon after you left, but we had to take a few breaks, and we got terribly lost."

"Oh," Wicker said, disbelievingly. "Your shoes, quickly. Change them over, left to right."

The oaken woman had appeared again amongst the limbs of the ancient tree and watched on like a cat eyeing a bowl of cream, and though Wicker knew forest spirits such as her could only cause small magic nuisances like itchy feet, she didn't want to risk anything of the sort. As she watched her friends, her heart softened, a blooming peony within her chest.

"The cost is high," Wicker told them. "A life."

Fallon gasped. "A human life?" she asked.

Ru and Robin clutched their chests. "Surely not!" They said in unison, as sometimes twins were wont to do. *(Too late we are realising that the story falls into more trappings, as influenced by the stories we have been inspired by: Twins who are but one person. We apologise.)*

The oaken woman laughed and kicked her feet where she sat in a high branch.

"Grace?" Fallon prompted, looking at the princess with so much care that Wicker was moved by it.

"I don't know," Grace admitted. "This...prince... made me feel like I couldn't say no. And now we must give up something so large to save him? I fear it makes me petty—"

"You? Petty? Hark!" Ru and Robin shook their white-haired heads, and Edith did the same, making her black crow-wig appear to be flapping its wings. "But go on."

Grace shrugged in a way that looked as if she wanted her head to sink into her collar bones. "It is a lot to ask, is all................"

(We are arguing between ourselves, wrangling the plot-beast

with quill and ink. Please forgive the trailing dots, but we have sadly hit the constraints of our imaginations.)

"Women often do a lot for men who would not do the same for us," Ru said dryly. Robin nodded, and the twins rolled their eyes at their husbands, who had been less than generous when they were still alive.

Wicker sighed. A life. A life, for the cause of heroism, for a frog-prince who suffers a consequence of his own actions.

(It appears we have written ourselves into a bind. I do not think we should write the story this way, and my stepmother agrees it is rather unjust and unfair. The plot has been lost down a rather deep hole.)

* * *

Wicker thought about heroism, and holes.

Not because they are words that both begin with 'h' and create a rather poetic effect when written together, but because 'digging oneself out of a hole' is a metaphor for getting oneself out of trouble, and it was trouble that they were in, indisputably. *(I argue that what is disputable is that a hero would let their personal feelings get in the way of doing the right thing, but my stepmother argues that their idea of 'the right thing' is often to slay the beast, burn the witch, or capture and clap the evil person in irons, all of which sits about as right with us as a joint out of socket.)*

Wicker thought about heroism, and healing.

Not at all because they are words that both begin with 'h', but because those things suddenly seem inextricable, even if it isn't often acknowledged. The hero knight does not come home well-rested, nor do the swan-brothers come home without needing time to adjust to human lives again.

Wicker thought about heroism and hmming. *(For this is what we too are doing.)*

'Hmming' in the sense of thinking and talking. Because these were two things seldom done in the face of danger, yet in the woods, the danger was not so present as to force them into a fight. They had time, and space, and Grace had a voice.

"Oh yes," the oaken woman said, sliding down from her tree perch and tapping her temple with a slender finger. "I see the wheels spinning up there."

Grace looked to Wicker, and Wicker nodded for her to say what she needed. "A life must be given for the cause of heroism," Grace said, drawing herself to princess-posture, "could that perhaps mean, instead of sacrificing my life, I dedicate it?"

The oaken woman bowed and flourished a hand, asking her to continue.

"From now until the end of my life, I plant my mind and measure my actions by what they do for the cause. Heroism is bravery and strength, but I think that need not necessitate the swinging of a sword or the brutality of blood," Grace said.

Wicker's eyes welled. Could it work? *(Why not? By the ancient crab-apple, why not? Who writes the rules, but us?)*

The oaken woman, now dancing about the clearing like a fox giddy with full-bellied joy, laughed. "Of course. But what does your bravery and strength look like, young Grace?"

Grace moved to stand by Wicker, took her stepmother's hand, and said, "I think facing what makes me uncomfortable, and what upsets me, is an act of bravery. I think being strong is sometimes remaining generous, open-minded, and open-eared in the aftermath of wrongdoing. Will you help me?"

Quite overcome with pride, Wicker nodded. "Of course."

So the circle of women and the frog-boy formed. Grace, Fallon, and the prince sat cross-legged in the soft dirt, and with her hand on the princess's shoulder, Wicker sat comfortably on a sudden growth of mushroom that would ensure her knees did not trouble her, and the twins shared a log with a gentle flush of moss over their laps to keep their thin bodies warm.

"A life," the oaken woman tutted, merging back with the trees. "It is not often humans think this way." *(Allow us to pat ourselves on the back a little, we beg you. We began writing this story in the early morning, and we now finish it hungry by flickering candlelight, a forging of our own!)*

A rustle of wind, the howl of a faraway wolf. Conversation began with Grace, who explained, with her hand in Fallon's, how the prince had made her feel. To some, it may have seemed such a small thing – what is a small kiss in the face of a curse? – but to Grace it was a wound, and a wound is a thing to be tended with care. Wicker squeezed Grace's shoulder, imbuing her palm with love and pride.

Grace repeated the frog-boy's words back to him, reminded him how he had been careful with his words in order to make her feel guilty and scared of saying no, and how that had meant her 'yes' was not true or freely given. In explaining how uncomfortable she had felt, it allowed the frog-boy to understand what he had done, each truth and detail a leaf falling from a tree, readying itself for new growth.

The frog-boy listened, tongue darting uncontrollably out. He nodded, and blinked, and did not interrupt except to jump when his body was overcome with the need, which all in the circle understood.

"I was wrong," he said, with slightly ribbitish sharpness. "I was... afeared. It is no easy thing to—to be a frog when you ought to be a man."

"It must be difficult," Grace agreed. She looked to the oaken woman, who watched with a flint-spark gleam in her eyes and a curious lilt to her brows. The princess did not quite know what to say from here, and so wordlessly asked her stepmother's help.

Wicker took a deep breath and asked the green-skinned prince, "Is there some other way you might have asked for her help?"

He sloughed mucus, as a man might sweat. "No excuse," he said. "I ought to have asked you kindly. Accepted your answer." He thought for a moment, right leg kicking like a dog with an itch under the scrutinising old eyes of Ru and Robin. "If I had... been honest with you. If I had... truthfully admitted... my fear. Perhaps I could have asked you to help in some – some other way."

"I might have kissed you," Wicker said. She had thought it that very morning, hadn't she? And regretted not keeping a closer eye on the goings on in the courtyard. "I would not have minded, if you had not minded the stories told about me."

"Poison apples. A witchly touch? I was... frightened of that," he admitted. "But I know better now. I am more sorry than I can say – that it took your helping me, for me to see..."

"I also might have kissed you," said Fallon, still holding Grace's hand. "I do not mind getting my hands dirty."

"Kissing is done with lips," Ru said.

"Two of them, puckered, like this," Robin added, miming a laborious and frankly over-dramatic way of kissing, which broke the tension and had everyone laughing through their noses.

"I truly am sorry," said the frog-boy, a little stiller now. And his eyes – they were perhaps a little less yellow than before. "I shall, as you have, be more thoughtful, brave, and sincere."

Grace pressed her lips into a smile as night fell, and the moon glowed over them.

Wicker twisted and popped her lower back, then sagged back down to a more comfortable sitting position. (*My stepmother does this as I transcribe, too, which you can imagine as the sound of a boot on particularly crunchy gravel. We do not write ourselves into the story, only our experiences, roles, and the bodies which we inhabit.*) "And perhaps," Wicker suggested, "we might spread the word across the kingdoms, that other princes who find themselves as frogs might earn their freedom from their curse not through coercion, but through candour."

As stark and honest and ready as an autumn-naked tree bough, he said, "I swear to it."

The princess, with Wicker and Fallon's hands offering steadfast support, as well as Ru and Robin looking at her with love and patience, smiled at him. The oaken woman grinned as well, and, suddenly having turned to air in Wicker's ear, whispered, "I in particular have always thought that sacrificing all you know and think, for hope, is very brave."

The frog-boy's skin turned the milky-blue of a human caught without clothes in the dead of winter. Ru and Robin took their moss blanket and wrapped it about him, and he thanked them with such gratitude that it could only be true and genuine. With the bluest of eyes, he looked at Wicker and Grace, and bowed his head. "You are the sort of heroes I shall endeavour to be."

With hope, Wicker blushed down at the brown leaves beneath their feet, thinking that nothing lasts forever, and that change happens all the time, if only one is willing to try.

(And like autumn, this story comes to an end which foresees a new beginning.)

Ella T. Holmes always dreamed of being a Mad Hatter, Trojan horse, or a cunning princess who is definitely not a witch but reality intervened. Fortunately, she's got a knack for escaping it.

Born and raised around Australia, Ella spends her time avoiding bush turkeys, and drinking enough coffee to bring down the moon. Her work has been published in or is forthcoming in Coffin Bell Journal, Antithesis, and Macfarlane Lantern Publishing Seasonal Anthologies, among others.

You can find her non-fiction work and newsletter over on Substack as 'ella has thoughts.'

HOLLYWOOF

Fiona Simpson

This morning, I got to thinking about Halloween back home in LA. It was always a good time. Big, old, fat, orange Jack O'Lanterns on the doorsteps and balconies. Passing out Hershey's minis and striped candy corn. The neighbourhood kids running up and down the stairwell of our apartment block and screaming, "Trick or Treat!"

Yeah, it was a good time, alright. I met my theatre-producer wife on Halloween four years ago. We were both dressed as characters from *The Mummy* at the adults-only party my agent, Chris, throws for all the clients on his books every year. If I wasn't needed somewhere on set, I'd always try to get back, and take Haven down to it. My wife isn't an actress, but she could be. Even in a room full of actresses and models, she stands out.

I think about home a lot, but Haven and I don't talk about any of that. Like, I can't. We never talk about Hollywood, or movie making, or Chris, or the TV contract that I'm being sued for breaking.

And now we live in a theatre in a tiny, rainy, Scottish town. The irony of Haven and I now living in a theatre, when performing arts is the Number One taboo subject in our lives, isn't lost on me. Living in a sort of temple to acting, I never mention it. I'm too bitter and torn-up inside.

The sitcom is a sore point. We filmed the pilot episode but it never aired. Last I heard, they've recast someone else. Another man, another big smile. My own smile is dead by now. Like a muscle you don't use, eventually it withers up and dies – I haven't smiled properly since we arrived in Scotland.

What is there to smile about, anyway?

Anyway, it's Halloween tonight. This town is small, rainy, grey, cobblestoned. It's like a film set, a miniature toy town. It's barely even on the map.

A good place to run away to.

Haven and I live inside this old theatre we're renovating. It's Scotland's oldest theatre, and our idea is to get it up and running again. It's an aim I hope we never achieve. I open the heavy, red double door at the front of the theatre, peer out into the rain-slicked, cobbled High Street. There's no-one about, and it's only 4pm, but I'm not taking any chances. I close the double doors, bolt and padlock them, then I switch off the lights in the foyer and start to roll down the shutters.

"Making it look like we're not home, huh?"

She really should have been an actress. All 5'3" of her. She's madly pretty, knocks dead any Hollywood starlet I've ever kissed.

"Mm. Heh. You caught me." I kiss her now, there in the foyer, leaning over the pumpkin and the baby between us.

I tap the pumpkin with one hand. It's a big orange Jack O'Lantern – it's funny, the way it almost matches the rounded shape of her abdomen.

"Whatcha got here?" She has carved a face in it. I can see a flashlight inside.

"You know, for the doorstep. Outside." She is so casual

about it. I lock eyes with the lantern's empty, rough-hacked triangle eyes.

"Why?"

"For Halloween, silly."

"Why, though?" A tickle on my neck. I swipe it; it's sweat. Cold sweat. I catch sight of myself in the ancient yellowed mirror behind the ticket booth. I see my frightened eyes, the way the fingers of my left hand are digging into my right shoulder. "Why would we do that?"

"To meet people," says Haven, softly. "Neighbours, locals. To show them that we're open for Halloween. Maybe meet some people. It's been six months and we haven't met anyone yet."

My wife watches my face, and I can see the strain in hers. But our home is *not* open. Not to any strangers, not to anyone.

"Honey?"

I can't say no to her. I can't keep her in this old beast of a building forever, like some princess in a tower. I rake a hand through my thinning hair.

"Ok. Ok." I force a smile. I look directly at her. "Ok," I repeat.

* * *

I head upstairs to wash and shave – my dark beard grows in fast, and despite shaving yesterday, today I'm already giving 'wolf'. Our living quarters are makeshift as heck. We've set up a mattress in a long, narrow dressing room, with three vanity tables along one wall for the actors to apply makeup. The lighting in our 'bedroom' comes from a skylight in the roof, and the small halogen bulbs surrounding each oval mirror.

Rain patters on the skylight. Tonight's full moon hangs in the sky, like a framed picture.

I strip to the waist and take a sink-shower in the small

washroom off the dressing room, and run a razor over my wild jawline. The tarnished mirror seems to lie. Who's *that* dude? There is barely any of the old me in there. No more Hollywood hunk. No more wide, easy grin. I've lost so much weight and I look ten, twenty years older. I shave my face carefully, looking at the stranger in the mirror. He looks... frightened. Really damn scared.

After the home invasion – after we were robbed at gunpoint by three guys and their guns and their dogs – my priority was getting us out of LA. Grabbing my wife, and hightailing it out of the USA altogether, in fact. Moving halfway across the planet and buying into the oldest disused theatre in Scotland – a country where guns are mostly illegal – and ghosting every single one of our LA contacts seemed like the right move. It felt entirely rational, at least to me.

And... it's working out? Kind of, I guess? We're good for money, thanks to all the bank I made working small parts in films. We've holed up in here, restored the public parts of the theatre. Life is not exciting, but it's safe.

Only now, Haven has started asking me when we can open it to the public? She wants rehearsals to start happening. She wants shows. She wants to start letting people into our home.

Strangers. Into our home.

I mean – the answer is never. I keep finding things to do before we're ready.

A deep bark, low in the belly of the building, snaps me out of my thoughts. Getting Chipotle is the second major life decision my wife has made without consulting me in any way, the first being the baby (though I'll admit, I had something to do with that). But the upcoming baby is exactly why getting Chipotle was a horrible idea. Haven rescued this dog from the side of the street or from some dumpster or from a friend – I don't even know, because I shut down when I first saw him standing in my kitchen. He's like no dog I have ever seen before. I think he was last seen guarding the River Styx. The way he's always looking at me, the way he side-eyes me gives me full-body chills.

Haven may have had an idea that I would get used to having a dog around and that would help with my...problems. Some kind of radical immersion therapy, she may have been thinking...or, she just went all gooey when she found him, because that's what she is like, and one of the reasons I love her. She has a place in her heart for all wounded, broken, disenfranchised creatures.

Shaving the final centimetre of my jawline, I make eye contact with myself in the mirror, and catch my wry little smile. Wounded creatures, yeah.

Whatever she was thinking, Cerberus – sorry, Chipotle – is in the back kitchen, which locks from the outside thanks to the new deadbolt I installed as soon as I lost the argument about whether he could stay. He has the run of our yard, which in Scotland is known as a garden, even though it's just a paved yard at the back of the theatre. We don't have a lawn, I mean, it's a 500-year-old theatre, a place of work and entertainment, and was never intended for a family to live in.

I clear my throat like a hundred times, staring at myself in the mirror, at my newly-shaven face, my frightened eyes. Trying to clutch the cracked white enamel of the sink, digging all ten fingertips into it, trying to chill myself out.

Come on, man. Pull yourself together.

Like I said, I can't say no to Haven. So, when evening comes, I find myself being the perfect neighbour.

Haven insisted I should dress up to answer the door to the Trick or Treaters so I'm wearing an oversized wolf costume. It's a huge, moth-eaten thing made of fake fur that we found in the prop room in the wings of the theatre. I'm guessing it's a forgotten relic from a performance of *Red Riding Hood* or *Peter and the Wolf* or something.

It's boiling hot in the suit, and I'm sweating freely in here.

The plastic teeth dig into my human jaw, and you'd think that would trigger my anxiety, my fears. But it's oddly comforting to have this social barrier between myself, to be sequestered from my new neighbours – strangers – in this way.

And it's not... it's not so bad. Of course, I don't let Haven answer the door to strangers – that would be a step too far, unthinkable. But her carefully carved Jack O'Lantern beside the theatre door does the trick, and I'm giving out candy hand over fist to a parade of witches and ghouls and demons.

The wolf costume makes it easier to open the door of my house to strangers, again and again. I feel like a guard dog, which is ironic because of my phobia, and the fact my own hell hound is locked up in the staff kitchen. I can hear Haven laughing and chatting to him, as if he's a person. He's silent except for his deep 'woof' from the staff kitchen, every time a new trick-or-treater bangs on the theatre door.

Trick-or-treaters are called 'guisers' in Scotland. And they don't just holler "Trick or Treat!" – nah, they do a song or crack a few jokes. I'm freaked out at first, standing there with the door open for so many long moments as witches and anime characters stammer out endless bad jokes, but it's weirdly charming.

The guisers come thick and fast. My candy bowl runs out, quickly – I go down to the kitchen twice to refill it, lumbering down the stairs in my wolf suit. I'm not as fit as I used to be, since I stopped going to the gym after that night. I kinda stopped seeing the point. My muscles had not made me able to protect her, so I let them waste away and started eating dirty. I don't look good, but I don't care.

I'm handling Halloween well, until a dog shows up. I look out of the little window and there, giggling in the drizzle of the Halloween evening are two little witches standing with their mom. Rain droplets sparkle in the orange streetlights behind the kids. A full moon, swollen and fat, hangs in the darkness between the spire of the church and a block of flats.

Thing is, they've got a dog with them. An actual living dog, with a face full of teeth – I presume, though I can't *see* any teeth. But I know they are there. The rows of fangs in its mouth. The dog is, I think it's, like, a poodle or a cockapoo type of thing. I can see the crisp curls in the moon and lamp light. The pretty young mom is holding it in the crook of one arm, balancing the kids' candy bags in her other hand. The young witches are standing in front of the huge, locked theatre doors, holding prop broomsticks.

So. I don't open the door. I mean, I *can't,* right? There's a canine out there. The little girls knock on the door over and over, but I don't react. I just *breathe.*

Eventually the family heads off into the night and I sag in relief, my forehead pressed against the window frame, my heart fighting to slow down. It's beating fit to burst, thinking of that dog separated from me and my little family just by a pane of glass and a few planks of wood.

The men that broke into our apartment last year, they had a dog with them. When I came around, it was all I could remember. Not the smashing glass, not the scream of my girlfriend. Just the big dog pacing around the apartment.

Woof.

I ignore the next couple of Trick-or-Treaters until my heart is beating in something like a normal rhythm again. By the end of the night, my third candy bowl empty, I'm done.

I sit there slumped on the faded red foyer carpet, spent, exhausted, leaning against a broken radiator. Bowl empty, social battery drained. It had gone well, sure – but my nerves feel frayed.

Haven comes upstairs and leans against the doorjamb, smiling, with her arms crossed and resting on her belly. My heart thuds for a different reason.

"Hey, look at you," she says, smiling. "Proud of you."

"Thank you, baby."

"Next year you'll be doing the same thing with our cub." Her smile spreads, her eyes dilating. "We can get her a tiny Halloween outfit!"

Fear slices through me, sobering. I don't share Haven's optimism about next Halloween. Opening our home to strangers while my kid is present? No. Just no.

Seized with a surge of anxiety, I scramble to my feet to secure the building. I bolt the door then I lock it all up. Haven watches me, and I know she is exasperated, but she doesn't reprimand me. She probably senses I'm at my absolute limit.

She goes to bed while I check the locks a few more times, circling round the building again and again, triple-checking all my new window bars and their locks and re-checking the chains on the doors.

It gets late, and it's time to peel off the wolf costume. I leave it crumpled like roadkill on the foyer stair carpet. I rinse my face, scrub my teeth, and climb into bed beside Haven. Listening to her deep-sleep breathing, the weight of my responsibility feels like a fist around my heart. I feel grateful and terrified and everything all at once. I get up to check the windows a couple more times.

In the darkness, the room looks greyscale, tinted in moonlight through the skylight. My eyes follow the stars until I'm sleepy. I stay awake as long as possible, listening, guarding, listening.

It's around 11pm when I hear, faintly, something from way downstairs. It's coming from the front door of the theatre. There, again. A soft knocking, scratching. My heart slams in my chest. Instantly alert, I slip silently from bed and grope for the golf club tucked under the mattress. My fingers close around the steel of the 9-iron. My pulse races intensely in my throat.

I tread across the room towards the door. My foot sinks into the carpet. I take another step, and the floor creaks. The hall is dark, and something moves past the little window. Something blots out the light for a fleeting moment.

I'm detached, not in my body, I'm watching this guy from above. He's freezing, he looks thin and vulnerable in the darkness of the hall. I watch myself shivering, holding the 9-iron in both hands, knees bent, eyes stretched wide, mouth tense, neck sinews straining like high notes on a string quartet.

Numb, I can't feel my body, but it signals to me – a deep shiver and I understand it's *me*, I'm here on the stairs, in the dead of night in an unheated building, in just my boxers. So cold.

Lying crumpled at the foot of the staircase is a boneless shadow-thing. It's not breathing and I step closer to it. I crouch, and sink my palm into the fur, my fingers digging down into the unpleasant softness. I don't take my eyes off the window.

I'm not sure why I'm doing this – but it feels right. Like armour. I wriggle into the costume and zip it up to the throat. It doesn't quite fit, because Haven isn't here to fasten it properly – no matter. The wolf skin hangs a little loose, and the musty scent of the old fabric scratches my bare skin, grounding me.

I unlock the door, ease it open and peer out into the street. Inside the wolf costume, no one would be able to tell how hard I'm shaking. There's no one around. No cars, no people... just a cold, rain-slicked Scottish High Street on this Halloween night.

A soft growling rises and falls, directly behind me. My breath and my heart bang to a total halt before my heart races off again.

The growling sounds closer.

Chipotle! How the hell did he get loose from the staff kitchen?

I ease my neck in a half-turn as something hits me below the waist, and I'm falling backwards into the street. My shoulder slams the sidewalk and I moan.

Lying under the lamplight I feel filthy water soaking into my wolf costume at the hips and sleeves. Chipotle's paws are on my chest, as heavy as a full-grown man. He stares down into my face, his jowls hanging loose as he stares with an intelligence in his eyes. They flash oddly in the mixed moon and lamplight, and it can't be, but I fancy I see my own stretched, horrified face reflected tenfold in his hellish eyes.

My breath hitches and I feel a choking urge to scream. And suddenly, suddenly, the pressure is off my chest. The dog is gone.

Chipotle knocked me over. He knocked me over, he got loose. I was right about him! It's all I can think, as I lie there in the dirt – that crazy mutt knocked me clean out of my own front door.

I lie there on the sidewalk thinking about the implosion of my life, how everything we built has just crushed inward like an empty soda can. And I, too, am empty. I'm pathetic, I'm nothing.

I blink, my eyes hot, scratchy. There's danger everywhere – danger, coming for my family. The wind tears crazily like a pinball around the rooftops over my head. Streetlamps seem to sway with the force of the wind. Could they fall on the theatre? Could the metal poles smash right through my bedroom window, enter my home, hurt my family? Hurt Haven again?

Anything could happen. I can't run from danger. I thought I could, but I can't. *Pandemics. Lightning strikes. War.* I roll onto my right side, and maybe I'm crying a little bit. I can't tell; my face is wet from the rainy sidewalk. *Disease. Water shortage. Car crashes.* The rainwater is in my mouth, I spit it out, along with a bit of gravel. *Famine, nuclear fallout.* And most of all, the thing that is *everywhere*, the one thing I can never run from. *Bad guys, bad guys with guns.*

The sleeve of the ridiculous wolf costume has ridden up past my elbow, and my own impossibly-thin arm sticks out of its bulk, my skinny wrist lying on the sidewalk. My hand lies helpless in the moonlight, palm to the sky, gently spangled with raindrops like I'm cradling a handful of stars.

A single bark makes my heart kick, hard against the sidewalk. I lift my head, chin on furry wolf chest. The bulk of the costume's ruff makes it hard to see, but I do make out Chipotle standing by the fast-food shop – locally known as 'the chippy' because it sells fries known as 'chips'. The neon 'CLOSED' sign casts a green glow across Chipotle's back, mingling with his yellowy fur. Kindergarten stuff sparks in my mind, blue plus yellow equals green. Red plus red plus red plus red equals *oh my God don't shoot us, please no.*

My eyes are running, must be the rain because I'm not crying. Standing next to Chipotle flanking him, like henchmen straight from Hell, are two other dogs, each twice his size. All three beasts are watching me. Chipotle barks again, and they turn together, like a three-headed entity, and walk away from me. Like I'm nothing.

Leaving me like I'm some pathetic man that can't defend his family.

Lying there on the sidewalk in the shadow of my home, my wife sleeping upstairs, I am suddenly filled with a pure, righteous rage. I push off with both hands, the gravel digging into my palms. I slip my hands into the huge paws of the wolf suit and I begin to run down the sidewalk after the dogs. I'm barefoot, and my soles feel every pebble and shard of broken glass, but I don't stop, I'm like a madman, head down, sprinting towards the dogs. I don't even know what I'm going to do, I just plan to grab Chipotle and get back inside—

Something hits me in the back and I *oof* to the sidewalk again, smacking my shoulder so hard I nearly black out from the pain. Snarls sound loud in my ears and I feel teeth, teeth sinking deep into the shoulder of the wolf suit.

In the dead of the wet lamplit street, I *scream.*

I holler, I scream and twist. But it doesn't matter, no one can hear me. I'm not being mauled, I'm being dragged. On my back, by the shoulders of the wolf suit. It pulls up over my mouth and nose, almost covering my eyes. The dogs are grunting, whining. My head bumps on the ground, cushioned by the costume but it hurts, anyway. I'm stiff with pure fear.

* * *

Everything hurts.

I open my eyes, too scared to move. I'm lying on my back in a forest, looking up at tall pine trees stretching high into the night sky above me. I blink, stir my sore limbs inside the suit. There are no lights, not out here. It's not dark, though. The moon glows, full and white, almost directly above my head.

I scramble over onto my front and sit up, look around. I'm at the edge of a forest path. I can see bits of litter caught in the ferns lining the path—coffee cups and soda cans. The path is well-trodden, hard-packed earth.

I ease myself to my feet, stand up shakily and breathe in the scent of wet foliage. The air smells of petrichor and a dense, smoky smell that I can't place. The wind shirrs the leaves over my head. I'm not cold; the full-body fur suit takes care of that. Adrenaline is ebbing from me. I turn in a slow circle, taking in nothing but darkness, silence, and the wind shearing softly through the trees.

Something moves in the tail of my eye, and I flail around to face it. A large, pale shape flitting between the trees.

Chipotle? A beat of anger throbs under my tongue again, and I pound down the path in that direction. The pale shape veers into the undergrowth and I wade in after it. After *him*. After it.

Pounding through the trees. I am gasping, enraged. My breath sounds loud inside the wolf costume head. The fur around the mouthpiece dampens with my frantic panting, wetting my face. I struggle on. Brambles snag my fur, but my human skin, deep down inside the costume, is protected. Nature hooks her claws into my thick, fake hide.

I struggle on. Pushing bushes and branches aside with my big paws. A flexible, thorny branch finds my face somehow, scraping and hooking into my cheek and my lip, like a fish hook. I stop, nearly hyperventilating, trying to use my paws to unpick my skin from the tree's talons. Eventually, it pings free and I pause, listening to my own heavy breathing.

I force it to slow down.

The trees come apart like stage curtains, so suddenly that I stumble. Lanterns line a clearing and a slightly uphill track. They're like the Jack O'Lanterns back home and in the town, but smaller, misshapen. Like shrivelled, shrunken heads in some horror B-movie.

I hesitate, hanging back then I take a step and start to walk in between them. The eyes are cut in rough triangles, and from close-up I see they are turnips, not pumpkins at all. Smaller, harder – meaner. The nasty little narrow eyes glow and the smell of singed vegetation spikes the fresh night air.

The crumpled remains of a ruined castle jut out of the forest in a rough clearing. The building is little more than ancient stones, overtaken by time and by nature. Trees burst through the cracked floor and ivy crawls over the dark grey face of the castle.

A bonfire burns in the middle of the clearing. People are standing around it, talking, laughing. Men, women – they are all in various kinds of fur dresses and animal skins, some in wolf masks or realistic-looking costumes complete with paws or gnarled feet. It's... a Halloween party. Here, in the forest, on the edge of town.

My body is sore. Every bone is aching. But I want to laugh in bewilderment, in relief. It's... it's just a Halloween party! I'm even dressed for it! My blood runs sweet with relief. Just the sight of people, human people, is enough to calm me down. I glance around for Chipotle, but I can only see people, no dogs.

A dude around my own age strolls up to me, smelling of bonfire with some kind of meat on the bone dangling from one hand. He has rough, dirty-blond, shoulder-length hair, a red T-shirt, and an amused, friendly face.

"Hi," he mumbles, taking a big bite of what looks like chicken. The flesh strings from his lips to the meat. "Welcome."

I stare at him. He locks eyes with me, pushes a handful of hair back from his forehead. He chews up the chicken, still grinning. And I know him. But how? I don't know anyone here in Scotland, I've made sure of that. So how come he looks so familiar? Maybe he was one of the Trick-Or-Treat dads that brought his kids to my house earlier?

I *know* him. I do.

From where?

The fire cracks loudly, and someone barks with laughter. The group seems to be gathering up sticks, of all kinds, and messing around with them, chasing one another, throwing the biggest sticks onto the already vivid bonfire.

The blond man moves towards me, and rests one on the furry shoulder of my costume. He moves closer, so close, his mouth brushing the edge of my wolf hood.

"You shouldn't worry so much, Hudson," he murmurs. His hair and clothes smell smoky, tinged with the scent of the bonfire. There is a dark smudge across the bridge of his nose.

Shouldn't worry?

"I... I can't help it," I stammer, feeling awkward, feeling like crying out loud. "After what happened back in LA... jeez, man, I'm just so afraid the same type of something could happen again. I... my wife." I glance at him, and colour rushes into my face like a third-degree burn. Why am I spilling my guts to this stranger? Talk about overshare.

The stranger who somehow *isn't* gives my shoulder a gentle squeeze. We watch the bonfire together, and he keeps that hand steadily on my shoulder. It feels nice, that hand. The blond has a frank, friendly gaze, dark brown eyes full of understanding and compassion. The jagged edges of my fear blur, as I look at him, feeling the weight of his hand resting on my shoulder.

"Thanks, man," I hear myself saying.

"No problem," he replies, gazing out at the fire. And I realise with a jolt that he has an LA accent, just like mine.

"Your accent... "

"Valley. Just like you," he murmurs, without looking at me.

Okay, it's official – I am going nuts, for real. We're far from LA now, and I haven't met another American in this town. I know for a fact that Haven and I are the only Americans for miles around.

I look at the party with fresh eyes. *It's weird.*

Everyone here is dressed like wolves. Some just have the pointed ears, some have tails. But everyone is accessorised, in some way, like a wolf-creature. Evidently, the gathering has a theme. But what are the chances? I pick at the sleeve of my own costume, where a loose thread trails free.

The blond man smiles. "Cool costume," he says.

"Thanks?" He isn't in costume. He wears a simple red T-shirt and a tarnished medallion around his neck. He feels so familiar, but I'm just – yeah, this party is *weird.* I'm in a bad dream. Did I smack my head on the sidewalk back in town?

The blond examines his stripped-clean chicken bone, tosses it away.

"I know what you're thinking, man. And the answer is yeah – we *have* met."

"When?"

I notice a woman walking by wearing what looks like a wolf ear headband. She's staring at me, her teeth glinting wet in the firelight. The man she is with is looking at me, too – the one with the fluffy grey gloves that match his fluffy, grey mullet. He licks his teeth and laughs over his shoulder at me.

I flick my eyes around the quieting circle as more and more eyes turn towards me. They are *all* looking at me.

"What's... what's going on?" I find myself asking the blond man. He is a stranger, but somehow, he feels like an ally.

"It's a gathering. Don't be scared, Hudson," he says.

"Hudson. How do you know my name?"

"I just do. Don't be scared."

I *am* scared, though. I've been scared for the past twelve months, I've feared my fellow humans, dogs, guns. Strangers. Breaking glass, unlocked doors. I am *so scared*, all the time.

And now I'm standing in a forest clearing at some strange gathering under a full moon, with these wolf-fanatic people. Everyone seems to be closing in on me. The woman with the wolf ears paces forward, stalks behind me, and I feel her palm running over the fur of my back.

"Back off, give him some space," murmurs the blond man. Someone barks with laughter and I realise everyone is crowding around me, now. I can just make out the tips of their pointed ears silhouetted against the bonfire. These strangers are crowding me, uncomfortably close. I can hear their breathing, smell their animal scent. Intoxicating, frightening.

"If you want us to," says the woman, her voice a low growl, her fingernails like claws digging lightly into my arm through the ridiculous fake fur sleeve – "if you want, we'll bite you." Her eyes are yellowy in the firelight. They almost glow.

Bite me?

"Leave him," growls the blond man. He nuzzles her out of the way and takes both of my shoulders. "Hudson." He shakes me gently and when I look at him, dazed, he says, "I get it, man. I was like you, before. Scared to death. I was homeless, I was alone, I was terrified, man."

He looks over my shoulder, and his expression softens.

"Finding a pack like this... being part of it... it's like being fifty times stronger. I'll bite you if you want, Hud. I'll bite you myself. And by tomorrow morning... no one will be able to mess with you or your family. Not ever again."

I gaze beyond him, bewildered. It seems like there are fewer people at the party now. And a lot more dogs. Huge, wolflike animals flitting around the ruins and the fire. I can see dogs sitting up on the walls of the ruin, I see others dancing and playing amongst the sparks.

"Hudson," says the blond guy, urgently. "I got permission to bring you here tonight to show you. To reassure you, man... you guys are *safe* in this town. I'm with you, man. I got your back." He tips his head to one side, a gesture I recognise, and my heart thumps.

"Oh, my God," I whisper.

"Yeah. I've got your back, man. And so does my pack," he adds. "We're all over this town."

In the moonlight, the changes are subtle. The creatures' lithe bodies dance dark against the blaze. There are no humans here at all. No one except me.

* * *

"You smell of fire," Haven mumbles into my shoulder.

She's right. The smoke lingers on my skin. I lie in bed, watching the bright white moon through the window; its seas and textures, the far-flung celestial mystery of it. My breath is slow, steady. The wolf costume lies discarded on the bedroom floor, and yeah, it does smell strongly of the bonfire. Pieces of bracken and leaves and thorns tangle liberally in the matted fur.

Chipotle lies at the foot of the mattress, bathed in moonlight turning his golden fur to mercury. The red collar is bright against his pale fur, its scratched medallion just visible under his chin. His smell is tinged with smoke from the bonfire, too. I let my hand fall on his soft, warm fur, and close my eyes.

Fiona Simpson, Scottish YA fantasy author, is thrilled to be part of her second *Once Upon a Season* anthology. Her stories explore the myths and legends of her homeland. She currently resides in Scotland while studying creative writing at Oxford. Fiona's writing blends Scottish folklore with magical realism, featuring ghosts, banshees, merfolk, and other aspects of local lore that she is drawn to. She particularly enjoys combining the supernatural with mysterious, lonely characters living life on the fringes of Scottish society.

The Demon at the Door

Caroline Logan

She woke at 3am.

It had been the same every night since she'd arrived at Marl Lodge. The swaying branches outside her window cast shadows over the patterned wallpaper as a phantom storm howled outside.

Scarlet knew she'd shut her curtains before going to sleep. She also knew she'd locked the bedroom door and barricaded it with a chair. But, just like always, the portal was wide open, inviting anyone to spy on her sleeping form.

They always looked in on her, whether it be a cursory glance from the doorway or fully entering the room to stand at the foot of her bed, watching her dream fitfully. She saw them with the veil of sleep still over her eyes. But she never truly awoke until the grandfather clock in the hall chimed three times, an alarm that never failed. That was when she truly saw the house for what it was. And its inhabitants.

She held a palm to her clammy forehead. Images of bruising and blood and dark spaces threatened to devour her.

Remember where you are.

A guest bedroom of Marl Lodge, one of the most haunted historic houses in Scotland. Far, far away from *there*.

Movement in the corner caught her eye.

A single, pale hand curled over the vanity's mirror, poised like marble. Scarlet's mind wrestled with what she was seeing. Was it a doll's hand? A statue?

But three weeks at the Lodge had taught her to stop rationalising. She slumped back against her pillows. "Go on then, get it over with."

It crept out from behind the mirror with hair like seaweed covering its upper face. The wet nightgown clung to its skeletal body as it shuffled towards her. With one rattling inhale, it opened its mouth wide to reveal cracked and rotting teeth.

"Get. Ouuuut."

Scarlet hummed. "You're new. Or, at least, you haven't been awake in a while."

"Get. Ouuuuuuut," said the horror, reaching out with its claw-like hand.

She tried not to roll her eyes. "Here's what you've missed: I'm not leaving." Scarlet swung her legs over the side of the bed, toeing around for her slippers. "If you're going to scare me, you'll have to try harder. I need this job and the house needs cleaned, so it really is in all our best interests if I stay. Now, have you seen Leo?"

The ghost girl seemed to deflate after a beat, staring at Scarlet in silence. Finally, she crossed her arms, hugging her sopping gown to herself. "He's in the kitchen," she said.

"Don't worry," Scarlet soothed, grabbing her dressing gown. "We've got a tour on this evening. Plenty of people there who're dying to be scared shitless."

The spirit gave a rattling sigh. "It's no fun when they want it."

And with that, she faded away until Scarlet was left alone in her room once more.

***

When Scarlet had arrived at Marl Lodge, she'd been told it was haunted. Even if she hadn't been warned, she would have guessed the place was cursed as soon as she'd seen it looming large on the horizon as her taxi drove in.

The windows peered down at her, sizing her up. Fresh meat or a worthy adversary?

The house's no-nonsense caretaker, Mrs Everly, had taken Scarlet for a tour as soon as she arrived.

"The Lodge was empty for a number of years prior to the pandemic," she'd explained as they marched through the wood-panelled dining room and into the hallway. "Many of the rooms are still closed to the public, but the owners want to add bed and breakfast facilities in the future. That's where you come in." She selected a worn bronze key from the chain at her hip and pointed it down a corridor. "As well as keeping the common areas clean, we'd also like you to work on the disused bedrooms. We'd like at least ten to be available by next summer."

Scarlet nodded, taking in the cobwebs that decorated the chandeliers. How hard could the job be? Everything looked in perfect working order, if a little dusty.

Mrs Everly gave her a tight lipped smile before stopping in front of one of the dark stained doors. "Let me show you what you're dealing with." Then she raised her fist to the wood and knocked sharply three times.

Scarlet blinked. "I thought you said the rooms were unoccupied?"

The caretaker didn't answer at first, pausing as if listening for a response. When none came, her shoulders relaxed and she turned the key in the lock with a clunk. "It's best to be polite," she said, finally, as she swung the door open.

Right, thought Scarlet, *because it's haunted.* It wasn't that she didn't believe in the paranormal, it was just that spirits were the least of her problems. Given the choice of staying at home with *her* or putting up with a few creaking floors and banging pipes, she would go with the latter. There were scarier things in the world than ghosts.

The bedroom Mrs Everly revealed was similar to the one Scarlet had been given herself. Green and red tartan carpeted the floor and a four-poster, complete with velvet curtains, took up most of the space. The only difference was the grime and the truly horrendous floral bedspread which looked like it hadn't been changed since the 1950s.

"Piece of cake," said Scarlet, feeling altogether more confident in her abilities. "I'll get started straight away."

"I appreciate the enthusiasm," said Mrs Everly, almost cracking a smile. She looked Scarlet up and down once, her gaze calculating. "What age did you say you were?"

"Twenty," said Scarlet, schooling her features into nonchalance.

The older woman raised an eyebrow but didn't comment further. "You can start tomorrow. Get settled first," she said, ushering her back out of the room. "The kitchen is stocked, so you can make your own breakfast and lunch, but dinner will be catered. Henry, our cook, does a spread for the guests every night so he'll sort you out too."

"Guests? But I thought you said no one stayed here?"

"They don't. But our ghost tours are very popular. You should go along to the one tonight. It's a good chance to learn some of the Lodge's history. And to get better acquainted with our...residents."

***

Marl Lodge creaked and groaned as night drew in, as if stretching from a long sleep. The autumn wind howled as it blew past the windows, but it was a clear and starry night in the Highlands. Back in Glasgow, Scarlet had rarely seen the stars. They were a reminder that she was somewhere else. That she had escaped.

The front doors had been propped open and, despite it still being September, ghoulishly carved pumpkins sat poised to welcome their guests. It was a full house, or so Mrs Everly said. The tours were most popular around Halloween, when spirits and frights were on people's minds.

Scarlet had always loved Halloween. It was a chance to be someone else, even for one night. She would wander the local streets, collecting sweets before tucking herself away somewhere safe to eat as many as she could. She'd hide some more in her boots in an attempt to sneak them to her room. But somehow, *she* would always find them.

"Are you a pig, Scarlet? Should I roast you like one too? Maybe that'll make you squeal."

Scarlet shuddered. *You're safe. You're safe. You're safe.* Marl Lodge might have been a little creepy, but it was a home and a job and, most importantly, they had agreed to pay her in cash. Cash she could use to get even further away one day.

The main sitting room was set up as a base for the tour. Scarlet folded herself into an armchair in the corner, tucking her thick jumper around her toes, and waited as the space filled with ghost hunters. Most were older than Scarlet and came in groups of two or three, laughing excitedly and peering at the paintings and dusty bookshelves. Scarlet made a mental note to clean this room only when October was over; the cobwebs were atmospheric.

Soon, the room was packed and the tour guide took her place in front of the crackling fire, ringing a handbell for attention.

"Evening, everyone, and welcome to Marl Lodge," announced the woman, her blonde bob bouncing as she spoke.

"We have an exciting night of ghost hunting ahead of us. You may hear them through our spirit boxes, communicate via ouija board or even catch some on camera. In the past, some of our guests have felt a hand on their shoulders or spotted a faint orb in a picture. Maybe you'll be one of the lucky ones too. But first, let me tell you some of the history of the house. It was built in 1780 by the Laird of Glencairn, who used it as a hunting lodge. It was sold in 1856 and used as a boarding school for boys —"

Scarlet tried to listen, she really did. But it had been a long day of travelling and the room was warm. Her eyes and mind wandered, taking in the patterned rugs and the plaques on the walls. How many people had lived in this place? How many people had died in it?

A figure in the doorway caught her attention. A man stood hesitating beneath the lintel. He scanned the room in a detached way, observing the other guests in a bored manner. But when his gaze landed on Scarlet, he gave a start, as if he hadn't expected anyone to see him, then smiled. When she returned the grin, he stepped further into the room.

To call him a man was probably an overestimation. He looked to be around Scarlet's age – her *true* age of sixteen – yet his smart clothes marked him as an employee. He wore a pressed white shirt tucked into dark trousers, but his tie was undone, hanging around his collar like he'd just pulled it apart after a long shift. The boy skirted around the outside of the group, working his way closer and closer until she could make out the dimples kissing the corners of his mouth.

Scarlet felt her cheeks heat, realising she'd been staring. *Ogling your new coworker on your first day isn't a good look.* She turned back to the guide, doing her best to tune into what she was saying.

"—it's been with the family ever since. They already own a hotel in town and plan to turn this into another venue. So if you aren't lucky tonight, please join us next year when you can stay in one of our haunted bedrooms!" The guide wiggled her fingers, eliciting *oohs* from the crowd. "Now, enough talking from me. Time to pair up and go hunting. You'll see there's a bag of equipment for each of you, and you can go anywhere in the house that isn't locked. Please don't take anything as a souvenir and respect the house. Otherwise, Marl Lodge's curse might follow you home."

Scarlet watched as the guests assembled themselves, grabbing their bags and heading off into the dark. It seemed like everyone was already in a group. Everyone except the boy who had come in late. She squared her shoulders. There was nothing else for it.

She found him leaning against the grand piano, openly watching her advance. There was an intensity in his eyes, like he was willing her to approach, to hurry up and speak. Scarlet could almost feel the way he was holding himself back, poised like a spring.

"Looks like we're the only two left," she said, once she was close enough.

As soon as she spoke, he visibly relaxed. "You'd better be my partner then," he replied. His voice was hoarse, like he hadn't used it in a while. "I'm Leo. Leo Dunbar. And you are?"

"Scarlet—" She hesitated, reminding herself to use her new name. "—Campbell. I'm the maid. Just started today."

"Well, Miss Campbell, shall we go ghost hunting?"

***

The halls of Marl Lodge grew quieter the further they ventured from the group. Most of the guests had chosen to stay around the main room, but Leo said he knew a good place, so Scarlet had followed him without a thought. Now, alone with a strange boy, she was starting to wonder if she'd made a mistake. The Lodge was so large, she doubted if her screams would carry back to the entrance.

You're fine, she told herself. *He works here too.* To give herself something to do, she pulled her phone out of her pocket and snapped some pictures. The flash illuminated the corridors, revealing nothing but old paintings and the occasional vase.

Finally, Leo stepped into a room off the upstairs corridor. Scarlet's camera flash revealed rows of books lining the walls.

"This is my favourite place in the house," Leo said, touching the antique tomes with a reverent finger. She snapped a picture of him too, then slipped her phone back into her pocket.

"Do you like to read?" she asked, following him into the chamber.

Leo nodded. "I think I've read each of these ten times at least."

Scarlet didn't *think* it sounded like an exaggeration, but how could that be? *Maybe he's just a fast reader. Maybe he grew up here.* "You must have been here for a long time."

"You could say that. And if I were a ghost, I'd definitely hang around a library. Shall we start here?" He rummaged in the sack, producing a black box and setting it on the desk. "This is a spirit box," he informed her, pulling on a silver antennae. "It works like a radio, scanning through frequencies, but ghosts can manipulate them to help them speak."

Scarlet snorted. "If I were dead, I don't think I'd be spending my afterlife fiddling with radios."

He glanced back at her over his shoulder. "Oh really? What would you do?"

"Sneak into movie theatres and watch everything for free." She sank into an armchair, his teasing making her feel at ease. *He's just a teenager, fooling around after a shift.* "Or I'd hang around haunted houses scaring people."

Leo let out a laugh, the sound deep and musical. "So is that why you're here? To be scared by a ghost?"

"I'm not sure I really believe in ghosts. I'm here because I want to get to know the house. And because there's nothing else to do. What about you?"

"Same as you, I suppose." Leo's hand hovered over the button. "Ready?"

As soon as Scarlet nodded, an awful sound filled the library as the spirit box flicked between channels. Voices filled the room, but were cut off before she could make out what they were saying. Hundreds of people screamed their broken words, each like a knife to her eardrums. And amongst them, she could swear she heard *her* voice. The voice that haunted her dreams. Scarlet clutched at her ears, curling in on herself as she tried to block the sound. Her breath came in gasps as a wave of panic climbed from her toes. She was here. She'd found her. She was going to k—

Gentle hands circled her wrists and a thumb rubbed soothing lines into her skin. Scarlet cracked open an eye to find Leo kneeling in front of her, concern on his face. With great heaving gulps of air, she realised the room was silent once more. He'd turned the spirit box off.

"Are you all right?"

Tears pricked the corners of her eyes as she realised the position she was in. She wasn't at her mother's house. This was Marl Lodge and Leo was her new colleague. *God, he must think I'm nuts.*

"I'm so sorry," she wheezed. "I get these panic attacks and—"

"I won't hurt you," he soothed. "Nobody here will hurt you. You're safe. I know it's scary, but..." His eyes widened, and he let go of her wrists. "I'll leave you alone. I'll tell the others too. Just don't—"

"Please," whispered Scarlet. "Don't leave. You didn't scare me."

Leo froze. "But you were terrified."

"I ran away," Scarlet blurted out, the words louder than she'd meant them to be. "Sometimes I forget where I am. I think I'm back there. It was the sound. She used to turn on the TV static really loud when—" Scarlet shivered. "Could we just go back?"

Leo nodded woodenly but bent to help Scarlet out of the chair. He wrapped an arm around her shoulder and led her out of the library and halfway down the stairs before she realised they'd left the equipment back in the room.

"I'll get it later," he said, his jaw set. "The important thing is getting you back downstairs."

"I'm sorry our ghost hunting got cut short."

He chuckled, but the sound was strained. "I think you did a good job anyway."

They turned a corner and the light from the main sitting room glowed like a beacon, calling them home.

"Well," said Scarlet. "If I haven't freaked you out too much, maybe we can try again?"

Leo let her go just outside the door and gave her a warm smile. "I'd like that. You'll see me around anyway. If you want to?"

"Yes," said Scarlet, a little too quickly. She turned away to hide her blush. "Now we just need to explain to the guide why we didn't return their stuff."

But he didn't answer. When Scarlet looked behind her, Leo was gone.

"I guess I'll be explaining myself then," she grumbled. *He probably had to leave for the last bus. Or something. He said you'd see him again.*

Scarlet walked back into the sitting room, still shaking from the panic that had gripped her upstairs. Thank goodness Leo had been there. Being alone, terrified, in the dark, was not a good introduction to the house.

She smiled sheepishly at the tour guide as she approached.

"Sorry, I got frightened and we left your equipment upstairs. Leo said he'd get it for you though. I'm sure you'll have it before tomorrow's tour."

The guide didn't seem annoyed, just confused. "Who's Leo?"

"Leo Dunbar," Scarlet said. "He works here? You must have seen him around. We partnered up for the ghost hunt?"

The guide shook her head. "I was going to catch you to have you join another group but you went off on your own."

Scarlet should have let it go. It didn't matter that the guide hadn't seen him. And yet—

She pulled out her phone, tapping on her gallery app and turning it to show the woman. "That's him. I took his picture when we got to the library. That's where the equipment bag is."

The guide's face had paled, yet she took an excited gasp. "Look at that," she exclaimed, taking Scarlet's phone in her hands. "You caught an orb, and a clear one too. Would you mind sharing this with me? It'll be great for our socials."

Scarlet's brow furrowed. What the hell did the woman mean? But when she turned the screen back to take a look, there it was, clear as day. There were the rows of books; the mahogany shelves. But instead of Leo's face smiling back at her, a bright flash lit up the centre of the picture, right where he'd been standing.

Her stomach sank like a stone.

"Look, everyone," the guide called out to the guests. "Scarlet here has found real evidence of a ghost!"

***

Scarlet woke with a start, her neck aching from where she was bent over the desk in the corner of her now-freezing room. She must have fallen asleep still poring over the internet on her phone's tiny screen. It seemed that the world was divided over what orbs were. Angels? Dust? The camera's flash reflecting on something shiny? If Scarlet had to guess, her mysterious photo was a product of the latter. Ghosts weren't real and, even if they were, you couldn't hold a conversation with one, let alone touch one. Leo had been flesh and bone, just like her. When she saw him tomorrow, she'd prove it to herself.

She checked the time on her phone and groaned. *Today,* she amended. It was three in the morning; she was supposed to start work at nine. *Stop worrying about ghosts and get some sleep.*

Ting ting.

A faint noise echoed from outside her room. A bell? Scarlet strained to hear, holding her breath as she waited.

Ting ting.

What was that? She turned in her chair, finding her bedroom door wide open. That was funny; she was sure she'd closed it. With a yawn, she shuffled to the door and peered out into the pitch black corridor.

Ting ting.

It was probably just a wind chime. No one was in the house but her and she'd made sure to lock up when the ghost hunters left. *You're safe,* Scarlet told herself, swinging her door closed. *You're sa—*

There was someone behind her. Someone there in the dark of her bedroom. She felt the heat from their body, a breath away from hers. Before she could turn and look, the person leaned in even closer and whispered in her ear.

"Get out."

Scarlet screamed, throwing herself at the wall, turning to meet her attacker face on. She threw her hands up, ready to defend herself.

But there was no intruder. Only her dark and silent bedroom, staring back at her.

Scarlet was alone.

***

That was how the hauntings started. Or, at least, that was when Scarlet had conceded there might be such a thing as ghosts after all.

She'd checked every nook and cranny of her room and found no one there, spending the rest of her night with the light on and her back to the corner. When the sun finally rose on Marl Lodge, Scarlet donned her cleaning gear and went to find some answers.

Even in the light of day, Scarlet felt as if a hundred eyes were upon her as she retraced her steps from the previous night. In the library she found the ghost hunting equipment just as she and Leo had left it. Scarlet shivered as she picked up the spirit box, returning it to the sack before surveying the whole room. It was dusty, especially on the shelves. She inspected the books, which looked like they hadn't been moved in years. But hadn't Leo said he'd read them all at least ten times? Maybe he'd been trying to impress her.

Maybe he was trying to scare you. All the talk of ghouls and whispers in the dark could have been nothing but some weird hazing ritual. Cheap tricks to frighten the new girl. If that was true, how far had Leo gone? Had he even found some way to sneak into her room?

That must be it, thought Scarlet, leaving the library at a march. And when she saw him again, she'd be sure to give him a piece of her mind.

When Mrs Everly rang the doorbell at nine, Scarlet was already scrubbing the dining room floor. She opened the door to the older woman, greeting her with a cheery hello.

Mrs Everly's face fell. "You saw them, then?"

Scarlet wiped her hair from her forehead. "Who?"

"The other residents?"

Great, even the caretaker was in on it too. "Listen, I know you probably do this to every new start, but you can cut it out now. It was all very scary, but I want to get on with my job."

"So you're staying?" Mrs Everly's eyebrows rose into her hairline.

"Of course. I really need this job."

The caretaker swept into the house, carrying a bag of shopping to the kitchen. "Most people usually leave after the first night."

Scarlet followed the woman, watching her restock the fridge with the things Scarlet had asked her to buy the previous day. "Does Leo scare them too?"

"Who is Leo?"

"The guy who works here."

Mrs Everly turned and leaned against the counter top, fixing Scarlet with a pitying look. "There is no one else that works here. There's you and I, the tour guide you met last night and Henry, our chef, who brings food up from the other hotel."

"There was definitely a boy here. He looked around my age and he was wearing a shirt and trousers. He said he was a wait—" But with a sinking feeling, Scarlet realised that Leo had never said he was a waiter, let alone that he worked at the Lodge. She'd just assumed he did.

"Will you come with me? I want to show you something." Mrs Everly ushered her into a long hallway, decorated with plum brocade wallpaper. "This is always a good place to start. Over the years, the inhabitants of this house have hung their pictures along this wall. See if you recognise anyone."

Scarlet scanned the frames, watching the clothes change throughout the years of habitation. Family portraits with women in heavy skirts gave way to boys in shorts and blazers. Some were action shots of school children playing sports. Right at the end, a rugby team stood in formation. And right in the middle—

"This has to be another trick."

Mrs Everly placed a hand on her shoulder. "I need someone to clean the house. Believe me, I wouldn't try to frighten you away."

"Right," said Scarlet faintly. She stared at the boy in the picture. Even though it was too grainy to see his dimples, she'd recognise him anywhere.

"But I do understand if this isn't for you," the caretaker continued. "It's one thing to be told a house is haunted; it's another to experience it."

Suddenly, a red hot anger filled Scarlet. If ghosts were indeed real, one had been in her bedroom last night, trying to scare her away. And she was not about to give up her freedom because a bunch of dead people couldn't move on. "Oh, I'm not going anywhere. Whether the people playing tricks on me are living or dead, they're messing with the wrong girl." She set her mouth into a grim smile. "I'm going to haunt them right back."

***

Ghosts hate cleaning, or so the internet said. It was a good thing, then, that it was Scarlet's job. She threw herself into ridding the common areas of dirt and cobwebs from sunrise until the ghost hunters appeared. Every evening, she joined them, hoping to find Leo again; to demand some answers. But he never appeared. That didn't stop the other ghosts, though. They'd shriek and laugh and howl each night, until Scarlet caved and ordered herself some ear plugs. After that, they'd shake her bed, laying their clammy hands on her.

It was like that for weeks, with Scarlet battling through the days to annoy the ghouls while they tormented her at night.

A fortnight in, and it seemed both Scarlet and the ghosts were tired. Whenever the spirits would turn up in her room, she was so exhausted from cleaning that she'd roll over and go back to sleep. And without a reaction, their visits became less frequent. Yes, they'd still come look at her, creeping around in the dark, but it was more like living with some particularly annoying cats than terrifying monsters.

The common areas of the Lodge were fresh and grime free so Scarlet had moved onto some of the sealed bedrooms. She was sitting on a bed, polishing a photo frame when she felt the mattress dip beside her.

"I think they like it, you know. Your cleaning. The others say it smells good."

"And where have you been?" asked Scarlet with a sniff.

Leo grimaced. "I didn't think you'd want to see me. I was trying to, you know, not haunt you? But then I heard the others have been doing it for weeks now..."

She looked him up and down. He was still wearing the same clothes, but his hair stuck out at odd angles like he'd been running his hands through it. "You could tell them to stop."

"They're curious. I can't tell you how boring it is to be dead. It's not like we can leave." He sighed, flopping back onto the duvet. "What I wouldn't give to have died in a theatre or something."

"How did you die?" asked Scarlet. "If that isn't too personal."

"Tuberculosis. There was an outbreak when this was a boarding school. And I thought I'd dodged a bullet when the war ended," he said with a grumble.

"Ah," said Scarlet, setting the photo frame down. "So you're a rich boarding school boy?"

He threw an arm over his eyes dramatically. "And here I am, forever doomed to walk the halls. At least there's no one left to teach me anymore."

Scarlet raised an eyebrow and grinned. "Now *that* has given me a great idea. Maybe learning more about the world is the perfect way to spend your afterlife."

***

Living with the dead was easier than Scarlet had imagined. Now that the house's residents had accepted her, they mostly left her alone in the light of day. And at night, once the visitors were gone, she made it her mission to end their monotony.

That was why she asked Mrs Everly to provide a TV. She'd been prepared to argue her case – hotel guests would enjoy watching movies on rainy Scottish days – but the caretaker didn't argue, just happy to keep her around.

"Whatever you want. You're doing such a great job, I can't tell you how thankful we are."

So in the evenings, Scarlet was determined to expand the horizons of the ghosts and ghouls of Marl Lodge. And if they couldn't leave the house, she'd bring the world to them in the form of movies.

"I can't watch!"

"Leo, this is a kids' movie."

"You said that last night and the lion's father *died*."

First, only Leo joined her, tucked in beside her on the red velvet couch. But slowly, more and more spirits watched with them, some lurking in the doorway and others sitting on the floor. Daisy, a little blonde girl dressed in a white gown, was small enough to curl up under the coffee table with her teddy bear. Ethel, an old woman with black eyes, usually sat in the rocking chair, fading in and out of visibility with each swing. Scarlet even took to writing the evening's movie of choice on the whiteboard in the kitchen so the ghosts could decide if they wished to attend. But every night, Leo was there, offering his commentary and pretending to eat her popcorn.

Halloween was particularly busy with guests looking to be terrified by Scotland's most haunted house. So, naturally, she hid in her room, watching a rom-com with Leo on her new laptop. He had kissed her forehead as the credits rolled and snuck out to perform one last scare before the night was over.

When Scarlet woke the next day, it was with relief. Now that spooky season was over, the Lodge would have a little respite. She decided to make herself some tea before clearing away all the decorations, humming a song about skeletons as she donned her robe and wandered downstairs. She'd just thrown the teabag in the bin when the doorbell rang.

Ding-dong.

"Mrs Everly's early," she said to the house. She'd gotten into the habit of speaking out loud since she knew she was never truly alone. The ghosts didn't come out much in the day, but they were still watching.

Scarlet placed her mug down and hurried to the front door, unlocking it. But before she could fling it open, something stopped her. Whether it was a premonition or paranoia, a feeling of foreboding stayed her hand and had her searching for the peep hole. As soon as she placed her eye against it, she drew back in horror, tripping over her own feet and landing on the parquet floor with a crash.

Not here. Not now. Scarlet clutched at her throat as she backed away from the entrance, never taking her gaze from the door. She couldn't think. Couldn't breathe. She was here. Somehow she'd found her. And she would be angry, so angry and—

"Scarlet?"

She flinched as she backed into a solid chest, but then Leo's arms came around her, holding her to him.

"What's wrong?"

"It's her. My mother."

"Your—"

"Please!" she cried, feeling her stomach rolling. "Please don't let her get me!"

"She hurt you," Leo said, a statement of fact. Scarlet still nodded, unable to stop the shakes that wracked her body. "We'll make sure she never does again." And then he was scooping her up, carrying her into the sitting room. Scarlet tucked her face into his neck and shut her eyes. "You know what to do," he said to someone, before crouching down in the corner of the room, still holding her tightly.

Scarlet gulped, trying to get air into her lungs. "She's going to —"

"No." Leo cut her off. "Once we're done with her, she'll never come back. Trust us, please."

Scarlet nodded and Leo's palm came up to cup her ear. It didn't stop her hearing the front door creak open. Or the call that followed.

"Scarlet?"

But then, with a boom, a door slammed shut and the house was filled with blood-curdling screams. They were guttural, louder than anything she'd ever heard. And with a start, Scarlet realised they weren't all coming from the ghosts.

"You're safe," whispered Leo. "You're safe." He held her, rocking her body to soothe her.

The shrieks grew to a crescendo, echoing throughout the house and in her brain. Only after what seemed like hours, when each wail was permanently etched into her soul, was there another bang, then the yells faded, leaving the house in silence once more.

"It's over," said Leo, letting her go.

"What was that?" Scarlet croaked. "Was that the others? I thought ghosts couldn't hurt anyone?"

He brushed the tears away from her cheeks and gave her a watery smile. "I never said that. I said they won't hurt *you*. You're safe with us, Scarlet. No one will ever scare you again. She's gone."

She nodded dazed. *She's gone.* For sixteen years of her life, she'd been terrified of the woman who had raised her. And now she was finally free.

"Thank you."

***

It turned out the safest place in the world was a haunted house. So Scarlet stayed, even when it became a hotel. Mrs Everly moved the TV to Scarlet's private wing of the house, along with any books she wished for. And when the caretaker retired, Scarlet was there to take up the mantle. Even when she'd finally saved up money to travel, she knew *they'd* be waiting for her return, eager to hear her stories and look at her pictures.

Marl Lodge was her home. A fortress against the pain and horror that had plagued Scarlet's life.

And though she believed in spirits, she did not fear them.

There were scarier things in the world than ghosts. But she was glad not everyone thought so.

<u>Caroline Logan</u> is a writer of Young Adult Fantasy. Her Scottish fantasy series, the Four Treasures, was published by Cranachan Books and is available online and in all good bookshops. Caroline is a high school biology teacher who lives in the Cairngorms National Park in Scotland, with her husband and dogs, Ranger and Scout. She graduated from The University of Glasgow with a bachelor's degree in Marine and Freshwater Biology. In her spare time she likes to ski, paddleboard and play Dungeons and Dragons, though she is happiest with a good book and a cup of tea.

THE THINNING OF THE VEIL

A. J. Van Belle

Sarah's twelve, but she feels a thousand years old. Autumn leaves fly through the air as she gets off the rail car; they whip into a spiral in front of the sign saying *Wellburg Academy for Future Leaders.* More leaves are lifted high in the air currents created by the ventilation system, carried to the top of the dome that keeps the city enclosed in fresh air. The city's abundant plant life balances the human-made structures.

A carpet of gold and crimson leaves covers the walkway leading up to the school's opaque glass door. The trees are only there because the city needs them to provide oxygen – if not for that, city authorities would probably cut them down in a heartbeat – but, to Sarah, the leaves are a reminder the world is alive. And that there is such a thing as seasons. They're not the seasons she knows from books that tell tales from before the world outside the glass became toxic. It certainly never snows in the dome. But things can change: leaves grow, and leaves die. The Earth moves farther from the sun as it hurtles toward winter. And if old cycles can end in autumn, maybe Sarah's life, too, can one day change.

For now, she's late for school. Halloween is just another day on the calendar, not a holiday, and there's no space here for the magic of autumn legends. Her feet crunch the leaves and her smooth, bottle-green reflection looms in the glass doors as she approaches along the catwalk connecting the skypark and the building. She places her palm against the sensor embedded in the wall. The machine inside purrs, and the school doors slide open. Sarah steps into the Wellburg Academy for Future Leaders at 9:10 p.m. Inside, everything is gray, and the smell of bleach stings her nose. She's ten minutes late for her personal start time, so she'll need a virtual pass to enter the learning center.

Behind the semicircular reception desk sits the night secretary, painting her nails a rich mauve. Freshly oxygenated air and mist shoot up in a dozen small jets from the edge of the counter that curves around the desk. The secretary doesn't look up. Two or three minutes pass. The jets waft the smell of ethyl acetate from the nail polish toward Sarah.

"Excuse me," Sarah says, in the smallest voice that will still be heard.

"What?" The secretary still doesn't look up.

"I need a pass. The rail car was late."

The secretary blows on her nails. "You mean you ran behind and you caught a late car."

"No. The car was delayed because of the dome repairs."

The secretary huffs. "Wellburg Link," she says to the school's voice interface with the Net, "were rail cars delayed due to construction this evening?"

"In all directions," says a smooth, androgynous voice. "Would you like a list of all rail lines, scheduled times, and minutes delayed?"

"No. Temporary learning-center access for – who are you?"

"Sarah_06_28_2158."

"You have forty-nine seconds to access the learning center, Sarah," says the Net interface. "Happy studies this evening."

"Twenty-one fifty-eight." The secretary shakes her head. "Can't believe actual human beings were born so recently. You're all such babies. What are you waiting for? Doors won't stay unlocked forever."

Sarah hurries down the hall, past the glass-encased finger paintings done by previous generations of Wellburg students. Established in 1729 as the Wellburg Academy, this is the oldest continuously operating school in the North American Commonwealth.

Sarah opens the door to the learning center just wide enough to allow her slim body and messenger bag to slide through. The door clicks behind her, locking automatically. She walks among the rows of identical cubicles, all defined by four walls of frosted glass. Each one contains a child who spends their days in total isolation.

Sarah stops in front of the cubicle emblazoned with her name. When she tugs the handle, the door opens with a sucking sound, as if there's not enough air inside the cubicle. Alpaca Ted waits for her inside. He is a teddy bear with fur made from real alpaca hair the color of an orange tabby cat. Alpaca Ted is sixty-six inches high if you stand him up, three inches taller than Sarah.

She puts her messenger bag on the desk and gives Ted a hug the way she's been instructed to do every time she arrives for a night of school. She rubs her face against the fur and smiles at the softness of her only companion. The rush of good feeling is only the hormone called oxytocin, but it makes her feel as if Ted is her friend. She knows the lines from the student handbook by heart: *Research has shown that in the absence of human contact, children can maintain adequate emotional and physical health when provided with a soft surrogate item. Hugging something fluffy and pliable stimulates healthy brain chemistry and proper release of growth hormones.*

She pushes Ted to the back of her chair, leans against him, and swipes the glass wall in front of her to request an accelerated version of the fourteen minutes she's now missed. The system gives her the lesson at double speed until she's caught up, which occurs at the twenty-one-minute mark. They're learning about DNA replication. Science is one of her favorite subjects, and she watches, rapt, as a sub-microscope recording plays. Sparkling with sub-micro phosphorescence, nucleotides are added to a holographic image of an unzipped DNA helix as a polymerase travels the strand.

Illuminated letters in the corner of her cubicle continually remind her of her stats. She and all the other students are retested every year and the results calibrated to give the most accurate and up-to-date assessment of potential. Sarah hardly sees her percentiles anymore; they are background, like the ceiling, like the air jets scattered throughout the building. "Verbal: 99.997[th] percentile. Quantitative: 69.021[st] percentile. Spatial: 73.423[rd] percentile. Recommended education tracks based on aptitude and interest: (1) Medicine (Recommended Subfields: Neuroscience or Genetic Oncology). (2) Bioengineering. (3) Renewable Energy Innovation."

The filtered air smells stale. In a nearby cubicle, someone coughs, a muffled, mortified sound. Students at the Wellburg Academy for Future Leaders are expected to be silent.

As the first hour of lessons draws near its end, Sarah's cubicle chimes to announce a three-minute stretch break. These occur after every fifty-seven minutes of instruction. She stands so the cubicle will detect her compliance. She retrieves a slim, yellowed volume from her messenger bag. *Well-Bludgeoned: A Memoir and Exposé of America's Oldest College-Prep School,* by Felicity Sanchez. The cover bears an old photograph of the school's facade, the way it looked in the days when the building's foundation had roots in grassy earth, when a U.S. flag flew in a clear sky above its flat roof and a sign made of wood and metal displayed the words "Wellburg Academy." Sarah shifts her weight from foot to foot and holds the book in both hands, with reverence. As the cover promises, the book is an exposé, not an ode. But it is Sarah's window into a different life.

Felicity Sanchez died in 2070 at the age of ninety-seven, thirty years after giving the world the memoir that changed the face of education in the North American Commonwealth. Felicity's book, published when the author was nearly seventy, describes events from her childhood. It opens when she was eleven years old, in 1984.

A soft chime marks a warning: the next lesson will begin in thirty seconds. Sarah presses one palm against the book's front cover and another against the back, holding it as if in prayer. She learned a phrase from the book that hums like a litany in her thoughts: *Personal failings*. Sarah has not experienced personal failings. She looks at her hand, pale and perfect, with blue-green veins. As clean as the bleach that sterilizes the school between every study shift.

When the cubicle chimes to signal Sarah's lunch break at midnight, she hugs Alpaca Ted again as required and exits her cubicle. Lunch breaks are staggered by a few minutes for each pupil so they never see each other. She uses one of the private bathroom stalls at the back of the learning center. When she returns to her cubicle, she takes a sip of electrolyte-infused water and retrieves the flat sandwich from her messenger bag. As usual, she has an absorption-optimized fungal protein spread on whole-plant bread made from thirty-seven nutrient-dense green vegetables and herbs. As she chews her first bite, she opens *Well-Bludgeoned*. The book has no heat signature. The cubicle won't detect it. For all the school administrators know, Sarah merely daydreams as she eats her sandwich.

The well-worn spine allows the book to fall open to her favorite page. It's fascinating. It freezes Sarah's face in a rictus of entangled empathy and joy. And at the same time it brings Sarah to life. The events on the page took place in March 1985.

* * *

A cold wind whipped the other girls' hair across their eyes. They looked like wild horses standing there under the sky, untamable and unknowable, their manes beautiful and free. Hands jammed deep into my windbreaker's pockets, I leaned against the school's brick wall and watched the boys far away on the other side of the athletic field playing an informal soccer match. The ball made a satisfying thock each time they kicked it, and even though I knew those boys despised me, even after everything they'd done to tear me down, I wished I could play with them. They ran free in the wind, their cries as savage as ravens' caws. But I never asked to play, knowing what the answer would be.

* * *

Sarah knows that further down the page, the other children will call Felicity terrible names. That's what children do in groups, and that's why the Wellburg Academy for Future Leaders ensures its pupils are never subjected to each other's cruelty. But Sarah reads the passage about wild horses and ravens over and over. She feels a charge in her veins like the rumbling of distant thunder clouds. It never rains in the dome, but storms sweep the outside – especially in autumn. When they do, she feels their voltage build tension in every atom of the air, even inside the dome's protected space. She breathes the same electric air when she immerses herself in Felicity's tale.

This book inspired research on school bullying that revolutionized the educational system. Felicity Sanchez' classmates taunted her all day, every day, for years. Decades later, Felicity gathered stories from scores of other students who endured similar abuse at the Wellburg Academy before the school was rebuilt, renamed, and its teaching system restructured.

But Sarah thinks being called a few names would be a small price to pay for running in the wind under a cloudy sky, for the freedom to choose what to do during recess as her feet pound the grassy soil.

She puts the book away and daydreams about another Halloween, long ago, when she wasn't stuck inside this sterile school building.

* * *

The year she was 10, Halloween fell on a Saturday. Sarah was off school, her mother was off work, and her mother took her to an alley at the edge of the domed city, where they looked out at the world beyond.

Lightning snaked through the purple sky, the wild electricity fracturing into a spider's web of white brilliance over the dome's surface. The land outside the protected city was an expanse of rolling hills, untamed and vast in its utter indifference to human life, just as Sarah had always been taught. But she thought she saw a hint of green out there in the darkness, somewhere on the sandy knolls. Strange, since everyone knew nothing grew out there anymore. The air was too polluted, and now green things only grew in special greenhouses, with fresh water pumped up from natural reservoirs miles deep in the earth.

Whatever was out there, it was beautiful. It made Sarah's heart beat in a drum-like patter with longing to go somewhere, do something, someday.

Her mother squeezed her shoulders. "When I was a little girl, my mother told me the traditions she learned from *her* mother. She said there used to be a belief that on Halloween, the veil between the worlds was thin, and you could communicate with loved ones who'd passed on."

Feeling the rare warmth of her mother's hands on her shoulders, Sarah looked through the glass into the gorgeous light show of a storm and tried to imagine what it would have been like to know her mother's mother. What it would be like to be able to talk to her grandmother now, even though she'd died before Sarah was born.

Now, thinking back, she has a hard time being sure if what came next was a memory, a dream, or wishful thinking. She remembers seeing movement behind the faint reflection of her own face, but not feeling startled – not even a little unsettled. Somehow, the movement felt natural. Even comforting. Beyond the glass, floating somewhere in a limbo realm between the calm reality inside the dome and the raging storm beyond, a face came into view. The face of a woman who resembled Sarah, and her mother too, but older, and with a light in her eyes Sarah had never seen in any living person.

Grandma? she thought at the image.

Her grandmother's face, a face both there and not there, smiled. *Don't believe them when they tell you there's only one way to live.* The words clearly came from the spirit of her grandmother – if that's what this was – yet they whispered their way silently into Sarah's mind. *Protection has its place, but so does the freedom to enter the unknown.*

Sarah reached out and was about to touch the glass when her mother pulled her back. "Never touch the dome," her mother reminded her. "You know that."

Sarah did know that, but she'd never known why. Even now, she still didn't know. Maybe that rule was just a way to instill fear in people – so they wouldn't look too closely, wouldn't wonder why there was a hint of green in the distance in the world outside.

* * *

After lunch, the cubicle displays a French lesson. The vocabulary word of the day is *ennui.* The ironic weight of an empty world upon one's shoulders.

Sarah smells artificial dust in the air, fine particles from the synthetic filters used in the HVAC system to keep contaminants out of the building.

The day's end is staggered by a minute or two for all students, just as their lunch breaks are. Her dismissal time coordinates with the arrival of a rail car that goes to her part of the dome. But when she walks into the school lobby and stands on the platform in front of the big glass doors, the usual rail car does not arrive.

She checks her smartscreen. There's an alert: her usual car has been canceled due to the construction. The next car will not come for two hours.

She goes back into the school, where the morning secretary now sits at the reception desk. He is absorbed in his tablet screen, and gray light bathes his grim face. He does not notice Sarah. She walks past the reception desk and toward the stairs at the end of the faculty hallway.

Sarah enrolled at the Wellburg Academy for Future Leaders five years ago. She remembers the day as clearly as a vivid dream, and she knows that at the termination of the hallway that houses the faculty offices, she will find a stairwell. It leads down into the bowels of the building to physical education centers where older students, those ages sixteen through eighteen, are permitted limited daily contact with one another. For half an hour a day, they begin to learn interpersonal communication skills.

The faculty offices remain locked, frosted windows eternally glowing green. The rooms are always closed. But these stairs are not blocked, not guarded. And the stairs do not only lead down. The stairs *up* from that uninteresting and unlocked stairwell lead, she recalls being told when she first enrolled at this school, to an unused attic.

Because Sarah hopes to go undetected until the next rail car comes to take her home, she mounts the steps.

The open stairs are made of metal, with a railing painted bright red and steps painted grass green. The walls are painted butter yellow. At the top she finds an old-fashioned door. She stands gazing at it for a long moment, imagining it's not just a door to a boring attic, but rather a door from her current reality into somewhere else. Into a liminal space where her grandmother might still exist. Where the days and nights aren't all the same, aren't all lonely. Where, by some miracle, something exciting might happen. Today is Halloween, after all.

If the old stories Sarah's mother told her are true, this is the night when the veil between what *is* and what *could be* grows thin.

When anything is possible.

The brass knob feels warm under her hand. It turns loosely, and the door opens with a creak. Sarah walks into the attic and finds herself among pale shapes illuminated by the light of a late-rising moon spilling through a long row of windows in one wall. The air has a smell she has never encountered before but she thinks it might be *real* dust, the scent of old things and mold and memories. She lifts the corner of a sheet draped over a round shape. Underneath is a ball perhaps three feet in diameter, its surface rough, leatherlike. She knows this object from Felicity's book. A Swiss ball, they called them then, and this old-fashioned kind weighed as much as twenty pounds – not like the light, purple plastic exercise ball Sarah's mother uses for Pilates. Sarah kneels next to the ball. Presses her whole palm against its surface. Generations of children played games with this ball. Some were hit and hurt by it, then recovered and played again another day. She can almost feel a silent hum through the ball's skinlike surface, the vibrating echo of generations of children playing. Fighting. Jousting for dominance, a concept she did not know existed, until Felicity spoke to her down through the decades. She stands, lets the sheet fall, and walks among the other draped sheets.

Something shuffles in a far corner of the room. Sarah freezes. There's no one here. She sees no HVAC vents. She waits, but there is no more sound.

She lifts another cloth that forms an irregular shape. Folds it back with care, revealing a desk attached to a chair. The seat looks too small for her, intended for a younger child. The wooden desk top has a long, narrow depression that, she knows from *Well-Bludgeoned,* was intended to hold pencils so they wouldn't roll off the desk. Deep scars and old writing mar the dark golden wood of the desk's surface. Names written and scratched out. Deep grooves worn by pencil tips. *Life sucks* in spidery handwriting. *No it doesn't* in a different script. The first writer: *Yes it does.* The desk is everything her own spotless cubicle isn't.

"Beautiful," she murmurs.

When she replaces the sheet and lifts her gaze toward the far side of the room, a pair of wide eyes stare back at her from within a brown, oval face framed by a mass of curls. The face belongs to a little girl a few years younger than Sarah. The child crouches behind one of the cloth-draped objects, her back to the wall.

"Hi," Sarah says, awed by the rare sight of another girl. The veil must be thin indeed tonight, to allow the two of them to meet. It feels like magic.

"Hi," says the girl. "I heard you." She stands up. Moonlight rims her in a silver glow. "I wasn't going to come out, but then I heard your voice and I knew you weren't a grown-up. So, hi."

"I'm Sarah." Sarah takes a step forward. Liquid moonlight caresses her shoulders. "What are you doing here?"

The girl smiles as if at some secret joke. "I live here. Well, as of yesterday, I do."

Sarah moves another step closer to the girl. "Don't you have to go home?"

The child's smile twists, mouth half up and half down. "My father's in the hospital. He had a stroke, and they say he isn't going to be able to come home. If I go back to our apartment, the building superintendent is going to send me to a group home."

"You're just planning to stay here? What do you eat?" Sarah asks.

"I brought food." The girl frowns. "Well, it's all gone now."

Sarah blinks and sees a vision of the child after weeks up

here, skin stretched over sharp bones. She pulls a flat, leathery nutrition bar from her bag. "Here. It's not much, but you can have it."

The girl almost reaches for the snack, then draws her palm back toward her chest. "That's okay."

Sarah drops the bar back into her bag. "I'll keep it here in case you change your mind." She searches for something else to say. What was it Felicity said when she met someone for the first time? "What's your name?"

"Charlotte_03_14_2162."

Sarah smiles and pulls words, heavy as molasses, from memories of her reading. "Nice to meet you, Charlotte." Charlotte's birthdate contains pi to the first two decimal places, but Sarah doesn't point that out. The numbers would reduce Charlotte to a single date. And Charlotte is a real person, not a number. "But you can't stay here forever."

Charlotte's face contorts. "I can't go to a group home. That would be like being here at school, except all the time. My father and I used to play games together. There won't be any games in a group home."

"You mean he watched you play your prescribed learning games?"

Charlotte's head shake whips her curls back and forth. "No. We played games like Scrabble and Monopoly. Even Dungeons and Dragons. My father inherited a game master's manual from his grandfather."

"I have a real paper book I inherited from my grandmother." This spills out unbidden. "No one knows about it except my mother." Sarah grins. "And now you."

"And we played games in the infinity pool," Charlotte says.

"Your father swam with you during your exercise time?" Sarah asks.

"No. We played catch with an inflatable ball. And we tossed in spoons and forks and dived to pick them up from the bottom." Charlotte looks down at the floor. "A group home would be an alone home. I'd rather be up here. It's peaceful."

An impulse sings through Sarah's bones. "You could come home with me. My mother would take care of you." A second jolt of voltage runs through her. "She said she always wished a second child was permitted."

Charlotte shakes her head. Her eyes look sad, wise beyond her nine years. "The dome authorities would catch her." She brightens. "But there's a back way out of the school. I've been watching the rail tracks that run past these windows. The track right here connects to another track that passes over a roof. There are three minutes between rail cars. We would have enough time to go out the window and walk to the other building. From there, we could climb down to the street."

"Why not just go out the front door of the school?" Sarah feels her eyebrows draw together.

"Then they might see me." Charlotte's expression says, *Duh.* Sarah only knows the word from Felicity's book, but she recognizes the sentiment when she sees it. "I'm a day student. I'm supposed to be in my cubicle soon."

"Sorry if I'm holding you up."

Charlotte swings her small body out from behind the cloaked objects, comes to stand in front of Sarah, looks up at her, and shakes her head. "You're not holding me up. I'm not going to school."

"You're staying here all day? With nothing to do and nothing to eat?"

Charlotte smiles, and Sarah sees sadness in the younger girl's brown eyes, as if she pities Sarah for her slowness. "No. I'm not staying here. I'm going. *Away.*" She rubs her chin. Something inside her seems to sparkle as she studies Sarah. "You should come, too."

"I'm just waiting for the next rail car. So I can go home." But even as Sarah says these words, she feels the sparkle of a truth beyond what the eyes can see and the ears can hear. On this morning after Halloween night, the impossible can take concrete form. She can break through the skin of what she sees on the surface of things and find a deeper reality on the other side.

"Do you *want* to go home?"

Sarah feels the outline of her book through her messenger bag's fabric. She would like to see her mother, but her mother works during the day, and Sarah does her exercise and homework units in the mornings while her mother is gone. She's asleep when her mother comes home each evening. She's alone nearly all the time, and it will be the same every day until she graduates from high school. "Where are you going?"

Charlotte's shoulders twitch. "I told you. I'm going *away*."

"But away to where?"

Charlotte reaches into her pocket and pulls out a folded piece of paper. Sarah almost jumps in surprise. She rarely sees paper except in the small collection of inherited books she and her mother share. The younger girl unfolds the crisp, cream-colored note page. "Here. I'm not supposed to show this to anyone, but you're not just anyone." She holds it out to Sarah, who reads the neat, slanted printing on it without taking it from Charlotte's hand.

Charlotte Luciano-Johnson

318 Hudson Avenue

Old Haven, Massachusetts

"Is that an address?" Sarah asks.

Charlotte smiles and her eyes take on a knowing look. "That's how they used to write addresses. And that's my grandmother. I'm named after her. She lives outside the dome.

She doesn't know my father had a stroke. I'm going to go tell her. Do you want to come?"

Sarah glances out the window at the moonlight reflecting from the sinuous curves of multi-layered rail tracks. "People can't survive outside the dome."

"Of course they can, silly. My grandmother lives out there. The domes haven't been needed anymore for years, but the city authorities don't want us to know. My dad says that if people knew we could leave, maybe the city authorities would be left alone here, with no one they could order around. But I know we can leave, and now you know it too. So first we figure out how to get outside the dome. Then we figure out where Old Haven is."

Sarah takes a deep breath. This is the longest conversation she's had in as far back as she can remember. "Okay. We can try. I'll come with you."

Charlotte's eyes shine. "You will?"

Sarah nods. The celestial glow of moonlight that surrounds Charlotte is also in Sarah now, making her feel like she's glowing from the inside.

A rail car zips by the attic windows, interrupting the beams of moonlight for a heartbeat before sliding on its silent way through the city.

"There's our opening. We have three minutes." Like a mystical sprite, feet hardly touching the floor, Charlotte moves to a window, twists the latch, and slides the pane up. She puts a knee on the windowsill. "You're coming?"

Leaves swirl past the window. Outside, trees glow lemon yellow and deep auburn in the pre-dawn light.

Sarah lifts her messenger bag's strap over her head so the strap crosses her body and the bag hugs her hip securely. Charlotte climbs out the window, her step as light and sure as a squirrel's as she places her feet on the flat, two-foot-wide rail.

Halfway out of the window, Sarah takes one look down at the hundreds of feet of empty space between her and the dome's concrete foundation. She closes her eyes, fills her lungs with cool air, and lifts her chin. Opens her eyes again and looks up at the moon, which is fading to pale blue as the sky lightens.

She does not know if Charlotte is right that some people survive outside the dome – but when she remembers the vision of her grandmother's face on a previous Halloween, she knows there's more to the world than she's been taught to believe. And now that she's met Charlotte, she knows she won't go back to her cubicle. Not ever.

She climbs onto the rail and crouches, clinging to the slick metal. Ahead of her, Charlotte prances along the rail with a light, sure tread. But Sarah hesitates. It's a long way down. If she falls, she'll die.

But if she doesn't fall, and if they find a way out of the dome, she might finally have the chance to truly live.

Charlotte's form grows smaller, gliding above the soulless city without a misstep.

Behind Sarah, in the room, dozens of misshapen lumps sit under sheets in the darkness. She imagines the learning center below the attic floor, with its harsh grid of cubicles. Those cubicles are now filling with day students, each alone with a teddy bear and a video screen in a disinfected coffin.

Sarah rises to her feet, balanced on the narrow rail. She might fall. Or she might not. Either way, for this one moment, she's alive. Behind her, the window stays open, leaking Wellburg's filtered, humidified air into the dawn. She follows Charlotte over the rail, arms out at her sides for balance. The air outside the school smells like autumn. Like leaves turned, like old things ending and new ones beginning.

She's twelve years old, and she feels like a newborn.

A. J. Van Belle is a nonbinary writer and scientist, living on Vancouver Island with their husband and two dogs. A Best of the Net nominee, they've penned short fiction and essays that have appeared in journals and anthologies from 2004 to the present. Lauren Bieker of FinePrint Literary represents their novels. They're on Instagram at ajvanbelle and Bluesky at ajvanbelle.bsky.social.

Mirror, Mirror

M. J. Weatherall

"Stare too long in the mirror and you'll get sucked in," her grandmother had warned her.

She never listened to anything her grandmother told her. Eating carrots will help you see in the dark, don't swim until an hour after eating, don't put new shoes on the table; it was all nonsense.

Quinn looked at herself in the mirror for a few more seconds before exhaling deeply, plucking her toothbrush from its holder on the sink and squeezing the last of the toothpaste onto it. She desperately needed to go shopping, but her bank account was empty and she was running on fumes. In more ways than one.

Desperation was the theme of the year. It had been the worst year of her life so far; she was thirty-three years old and usually optimistic, but even she couldn't imagine it improving any time soon. It was nearly Halloween and she was in debt, alone, and unemployed. It couldn't be going more wrong, she thought. Halloween was usually her favourite holiday of the year, but this year it heralded the end of her life as she knew it. Unless she could prove that she was turning it around, that she could pay the next month's mortgage payment, then the bank would repossess her house and she'd have to be out by November 1st. That gave her six days. Six fucking humiliating, useless, bastard days.

She brushed her teeth and thought about the job interview she had lined up for that morning. Another job that she was overqualified for. The majority of her rejections were because of that, but she couldn't get the jobs she was qualified for, either, so it was a never-ending circle of shit. She met her own stare in the mirror and tried to smile. The toothpaste foaming over her lips wasn't the most obscene thing about her appearance lately. She was gaunt, with low-hanging bags under her bloodshot eyes, and her black hair was dry and lifeless, looking more grey than black. She needed the job. She plucked a stray eyelash off her cheek and stared at it.

"I wish I could get this job," she whispered, before blowing the eyelash off her finger.

She gathered her hair behind her head and spat toothpaste into the sink, savouring the smell of fresh mint. She didn't look back in the mirror, so she didn't see the surface cloud over with smoke, or the flash of brilliant red eyes following her out of the room.

Soon, a voice echoed, *you'll see.*

Quinn didn't hear the disembodied voice, but the hairs on her neck stood on end as she left the bathroom. She swiped them down with her hand and continued to think about what outfit she was going to wear this time. It was her thirteenth interview and she was running out of clean clothes. She chose a plain black pantsuit with an ivory blouse. Respectable enough, she thought, picking pink fuzzy lint off her shoulder. Pink was Pearl's favourite colour; everything she'd owned was pink. *Was.* She hated thinking of Pearl in the past tense.

Quinn drove to the interview in her banged up old Fiesta, hoping that she had enough petrol to get her there and back.

It was all her fault, of course; she'd lost everyone she ever loved, her job, and her cat in all one fell swoop. Her cat had disappeared at the same time her ex-husband did, leaving her with the house and all the debt. It wasn't all that simple, but that pretty much summed it up. Yes, there was a restraining order and the divorce, but no-one could actually prove she did those things. They didn't find a body. She hadn't served any jail time. But she had been all over the news, which was probably why she couldn't get a job. People had long memories for stuff like that.

No one wanted to hire the woman who might have killed her stepdaughter.

***

Pearl sat down with Florian. She couldn't bring herself to trust the cat completely. She had seen him disappear for days on end and return with some foreign object, proof of a portal. All that proved was that the cat was fine to move between worlds, but was she? She wasn't even sure how she'd got to the mirror world in the first place. The last thing she remembered was her father and Quinn arguing...

Quinn had screamed, "I wish it was just the two of us!" and Pearl had disappeared. Florian had too. He was Quinn's cat from before she'd married Pearl's father. They'd ended up in the mirror world, Pearl and the cat. She didn't know how long they had been there, but she felt the life being sapped out of her every second she stayed.

***

Quinn had her interview – it went well, she thought as she drove back home and changed into comfier clothes. All she could do was wait. The interviewer had said they'd be in touch, but they hadn't said when. Quinn had just smiled and shaken their hand, all the while dying to press them for a real answer. She knew she was too pushy, so she'd tried to suppress that part of herself, at least until she had the job.

She made herself relax. Everything was riding on this

interview. Her whole life was in pieces, and this job would be the glue to stick it back together. She couldn't afford to think about what would happen if she didn't.

She decided to give herself a facial, to try and breathe some life back into the withered husk that used to be an attractive body, so she sat cross legged on the floor in front of her full-length bedroom mirror and tried to smooth away the stress of the last few months.

Suddenly, the mirror clouded over, like a storm was amassing behind the glass.

"What the hell?" she exclaimed, backing away from the mirror.

Your time has come, Quinn, a voice echoed.

"Time for what?" she asked.

Time to pay the price.

"Price? I don't understand," she begged.

We got rid of your little problem, and what have you done with your second chance? Nothing. We've come to collect our payment.

"What do I owe you? What little problem? I don't know who you are."

Quinn stared hard into the mirror, trying to work out whether this was all some elaborate prank. But she couldn't see any wires or speakers. It seemed like magic.

Your kind couldn't survive looking at our true form.

She looked closer and saw the edges of a humanoid face floating like a mask in the centre of the frame. Quinn backed away from the mirror, all the way into the hall, and slammed the bedroom door behind her.

"That had to be some kind of hallucination, right?" she asked herself. "And talking to yourself isn't normal either." She went downstairs, figuring that her blood sugar was a bit low.

The smell hit her as soon as she reached the bottom of the stairs. It was acrid and caught in her throat. She gagged, covering her mouth with her hand. Mouldy oranges festered in her fruit bowl, fat flies circling hungrily around them like vultures.

She knew at that moment that something terrible was going to happen. That a demon was in her house.

And another thing her grandmother had told her? Don't make a deal with a demon.

Was the voice right? Had she made a deal with the mysterious mirror-dwelling creature? Quinn ran back upstairs, racking her brain, trying to remember everything she knew about demons. They had to be invited in? Or was that vampires? She was spiralling. She had to get rid of the mirror. All the mirrors.

Without a care for the house's aesthetic she pulled the bathroom mirror off the wall and wrapped an old t-shirt around it. What else had her grandmother told her? Something about mirrors... She closed her eyes and tried to remember. Break a mirror and you'll have seven years of bad luck. Quinn wondered how many mirrors she had broken to get to where she was today. Careful now to neither break or look into it, she took it out to the front yard. She would make a sign: 'Free to a good home, definitely not possessed.'

She carried a blanket to the bedroom and held it up as if to protect her from the demon inside her mirror. Was it eye contact? Or was that something else? It didn't want to turn me to stone, just to take my soul, she reminded herself.

Quinn wrapped the blanket around the long mirror and hauled it downstairs. Just a few more steps and she would be free – never able to look at her reflection again, but free.

It was just her luck that as she was crossing her yard, the blanket slipped down and she stepped on it. As if in slow motion, the mirror was falling. Quinn was falling along with it, and the blanket was fluttering to the ground. Quinn was going to land on the mirror; she was going to be ripped to shreds by broken glass. In front of neighbours that loathed her. It was just her luck.

But she didn't shatter the mirror. She didn't get ripped to shreds. She would have preferred that over what actually happened.

Like it was a doorway, Quinn fell through the mirror and landed with a winded thud on the other side. If she hadn't seen it happen, she wouldn't have believed it. She would have assumed that she'd missed falling on the mirror and landed awkwardly on the ground.

When she walked into her house it was the same as before, but flipped, like looking in a mirror. Everything was the same but sapped of life and colour: the pile of bills she couldn't pay stacked on the kitchen side, the mouldy oranges in the bowl, the pathetic assortment of items she owned.

"Oh god, this is the mirror world," she whispered, remembering tales her grandmother had told her.

She didn't know what to do next. She could try to find the mirror and see if she could return home that way, or she could find the demon and explain that he'd made a terrible mistake. Although she wasn't sure how well that would work.

Quinn walked around her house, half expecting her ex-husband to be around every corner. He wouldn't be, but even if he were it felt like it wouldn't be the weirdest thing to happen to her that day. She looked out of her living room window and watched her neighbours, something she had done hundreds of times before. Just twitch the blind open and watch.

They seemed ordinary, but not quite right. Mrs Jones usually limped on her right leg after her skiing accident, but now her limp was on her left side. Patty Smith was getting into her car, on the wrong side. Of course, everything was flipped! She'd fallen through her mirror into another dimension.

The only question now was, how the hell was she going to get back? She couldn't imagine it was as straightforward as getting there.

***

Pearl felt the rumble of a doorway being opened. She could almost smell the fresh air of home and taste the freedom she so desperately wanted. She knew she wasn't the only one who felt it. The Huntsman would be here soon.

***

Quinn felt the shiver rack her whole body, the warmth leaching out of her. She reached for her phone, hoping to have at least some comfort, but it was dead. She wasn't surprised. Next, she was going to try and find a mirror. She walked outside to where she'd deposited the offending items in her own world, but they weren't there.

With hands on her hips, she looked around. Her neighbours were still being weird. She wasn't going to try and talk to them. Quinn headed upstairs to her bedroom, hoping that the mirror would be there. She was half expecting it to have disappeared too, but there it was. She looked at her reflection, which must have been a reflection of her reflection, because she was in the mirror world – confusing, now she thought about it. She looked upon her true image.

"So, this is how people see me then?" she asked herself, turning to admire herself from all angles.

Conceited and self-absorbed, yes. The demon's voice had returned.

The mirror clouded over again and she saw the same floating mask-like face.

"What do you want from me?" Quinn asked, balling her fists.

I'm so glad you asked, the demon said, grinning maliciously.

It reached forward with a shrivelled, clawed hand and plunged its gnarled appendages into Quinn's chest with a sickening crack and squelch.

Quinn suppressed a scream. Her whole body froze.

The demon rifled around in her chest cavity for what seemed like an eternity until it finally exited her with a triumphant yank. Its clawed hand closed around something.

"What the fuck? WHAT THE FUCK?" Quinn yelled, grasping at her chest.

The demon cackled. *Nice doing business with you,* it taunted as it opened its palm to reveal a pea-sized black marble. And as quickly as it had arrived, the demon was gone.

Quinn collapsed to the ground.

***

Pearl couldn't imagine what it would have been like for her, if she hadn't been taken in by the Seven. They were the only other people here that weren't echoes of the real world – at least, the ones that were friendly. So, discounting the Huntsman. She wondered whether the door opening was someone new joining them in the mirror world. She wondered if she had the guts to try and save this one.

"Crabby?" she ventured.

"What?" Crabby answered, looking uninterested already.

"The door opened."

"And?" Crabby snapped.

"Should we see if we can find them?"

"No."

"Why not?" she complained.

"You know why," Crabby replied, turning his back to signal the end of the conversation.

Pearl gave up with Crabby and decided to ask one of the others.

The Seven had found Pearl when she first came to the mirror world running from the Huntsman. They'd lived together ever since in a nice little house on the outskirts, where the Huntsman didn't like to go. The Seven had been in the mirror world for most of their lives; they'd entered as children and been cursed to stay in their childhood bodies ever since. It was one of the reasons Pearl felt sorry for them: being adults trapped in children's bodies.

She found Jock instead. He was usually in a better mood than Crabby and had more time for conversation with Pearl.

"Jock, the door, can we go see?" she asked, trying to contain her excitement.

"What did Crabs say?"

"What? No fair," she complained.

"You only come to me when you want to get your way, and I'm assuming that Crabby said no."

"He said no, but it could be important, they could help us get out of here!"

"I wish I could believe that, Pea, but we have been trying for decades," he said sadly.

Pearl hated seeing Jock like this. Every day he lost a bit more of the sparkle that made him, well, him.

"Fine," she huffed, pretending to drop the matter.

"And don't go asking any of the others either, I don't want anyone else getting the Lou treatment," he winced as he said it. Lou, short for Loopy, had once had a close encounter with the Huntsman and had never been the same since. He often sat staring into space and giggling to himself.

"Fine!" she repeated, stomping off like the petulant teenager she was supposed to be.

She'd made up her mind already. She was going to see what was happening with the door, she was going to see who the newcomer was, and she was going to get them all out of their mirror prison. First, she just needed to find Florian. Where was that damn cat when you needed him?

***

Quinn woke to the sound of footsteps approaching. Her head was fuzzy and her chest ached. Was she having a heart attack? She was too young to have a heart attack, surely? She snapped herself out of her spiral in time to see the figure stomping up the stairs towards her. He swayed and loped like a Neanderthal. Panic rose and caught in her throat.

It was just her neighbour Ted.

"Oh, Ted, thank god you're here. I think I'm having a heart attack," Quinn babbled.

Ted ignored her.

"Ted, come on now. I know we weren't on the best of terms but are you going to leave me here to die? Call an ambulance!"

Ted continued to ignore her. Instead, he looked around the landing, and after spying the bedroom door ajar, sneaked into Quinn's bedroom.

"Oi, you old perv!" she squawked, her face turning a dark rouge. She tried to pry herself up off the floor, but pain flooded her chest again and her ears started ringing.

Ted didn't acknowledge her on his way out, either, after he had checked every room. She assumed he was still pissed off at her for the divorce. He'd always preferred her ex-husband, and when he found out she'd got the house instead, he called her leech and a succubus. She'd never quite got over that, choosing to ignore him completely when passing. She certainly hadn't sent him a Christmas card that year.

Quinn lay on the floor for a long time after Ted left, wondering what was happening to her, wondering if anyone would come to help her. But no one did. She was alone in the world, and she had no one to blame but herself.

Once she regained control of her body, she returned to the living room, plotting her next move. She flicked the television on, hoping that the background noise would kickstart her brain.

She made a mental list of all the things she knew for certain. She was in the mirror world; the demon had taken his payment – although she couldn't quite work out what it was. Her neighbours couldn't see her, and she was alone.

Quinn paced the living room. If the demon had his payment, then he wouldn't mind her leaving, right? She decided that she would try to talk to him, maybe make another deal. She ascended the stairs to her bedroom again and made a beeline for the bedroom mirror.

She cleared her throat, not knowing what to say. "Erm, hello, Mr Demon?"

No answer.

She waited, wondering what to say next, until the mirror clouded over and the mask-like face appeared.

You have nothing more I want, the demon said, sounding bored.

"That's good. Then maybe you won't mind letting me go back to my own world?"

The demon laughed. *Locate the doorway and slip past the Huntsman, and you can have your freedom.*

"Thank you!" Quinn breathed with relief. "Wait, what's the Huntsman? And what doorway am I looking for?"

***Who** is the Huntsman, you mean? I can't give you all the answers,* the demon retorted, giggling slyly as the mirror returned to its usual state.

Quinn cursed. She had to get out of this damn mirror world. People would soon notice that she was missing, and then they would assume she had skipped town to avoid the bank repossessing her house. No one would care. No one would assume that she'd been kidnapped. She wasn't even sure it counted as kidnapping, but she was being held somewhere against her will and that was enough for her. No one would ever believe her.

She had to find the doorway.

"There have to be a thousand mirrors here. Which one is it?" Quinn whispered to herself. She rested her head in her hands and explored her brain. The demon had said she had to slip past the Huntsman, whoever that was. "If I was a mirror door to another realm, where would I be?"

***

Pearl slipped out of the back door with Florian at her heels. She knew where the Huntsman lived, so she knew which direction he would be coming from; she just had to work out where he was going before he killed her latest chance at freedom.

"What do you think? Where is our new friend?" she asked the cat, not expecting an answer.

Florian opened his mouth and gave a sharp meow, curling his body around her calves.

"That's nice, but it doesn't help me much," she replied, bending down to give him a gentle scratch behind his ear.

It looked like the cat was about to turn back inside to the comfort of his own bed when a breath of wind caught his attention. It shouldn't have been possible for the cat to look confused, but he did. Pearl ignored him, thinking that he was about to leave her to hunt for whatever it was he ate in the mirror world.

Florian batted her retreating calf with his paw, made another sharp meow and jogged ahead, turning after a few strides to see if she was following – a look of triumph appeared on his feline features when she was.

"Follow the cat – not the strangest thing to have ever happened to me," Pearl mused, skipping to keep up with the possessed puss.

If only she knew what he did; if only she had a keen enough sense of smell to have picked up on that expensive perfume floating on the wind, as fresh as the day she last saw her.

Florian wished humans weren't so stupid.

***

The streets were confusing Quinn. She knew this neighbourhood like the back of her hand in the real world, but she couldn't for the life of her figure out where everything was in reverse. Even the street signs were backwards, making navigating even more frustrating – not that she knew where she was navigating to.

Quinn had made it out of the estate and onto a usually busy A-road. She hadn't seen any more of her neighbours; it was like they had disappeared after she went back inside. Never mind, she thought, she could manage just fine by herself. She just had to figure out where she was going and what she was going to do once she got there.

Time moved slowly. Quinn didn't feel the hunger or worry that plagued her waking moments in the real world. She almost felt like she could stay here, if she wouldn't die of boredom. All of a sudden, things became a lot less boring for Quinn as she spotted the High Street, empty and calling her name. The large sign unmistakably advertising the shopping centre shone in the otherwise bleached landscape, a diamond in the sand. She made a beeline for the most expensive shop she could see.

Maybe she would be happy here after all, she thought.

***

If you were to hunt humans, where would you set your traps? Where would you go to observe them in their gorging, greedy glory? Like a moth to a flame, like a fly on flypaper, like a human at the shopping centre. The Huntsman knew his game.

***

Following the cat was easy. Pearl knew the roads they walked, and she knew the only danger was the Huntsman, that she would hear him on his Harley coming from miles away. She knew that she was safe. For now. What she didn't know was what she was going to find at the end of Florian's wild cat chase, whether it was the new arrival or just another tasty snack that he wanted to share with her – although he should know by now that she doesn't have the same appetite for mice as he did.

So, she followed, along the streets she used to know, the ones she had walked with her father when they'd moved to their new house with Quinn. Quinn, who was always too busy for her, who was always too self-absorbed, who probably didn't care that she was missing. She tried not to think about her father and stepmother. It made her gut wrench and tears sting her eyes; it made her want to do something rash and stupid. It made her blind and deaf to her surroundings.

Florian was yowling at her from under a nearby parked car and she snapped back to reality. A low rumbling was getting louder and louder, closer and closer. Pearl squeaked. If she hadn't been so distracted then—

There was her old house. She ran towards it, crashing into the unlocked door with enough force to wind her. The door flew open, but she didn't allow it to hit the wall. She didn't need to draw any more attention to herself.

"Flor!" she hissed, tapping her thigh encouragingly in the direction of the parked car and the cat cowering underneath. Florian just looked at her with petrified, slitted eyes as she closed the door and slid the bolt. He would be fine, she told herself. He was always fine.

The rumbling, guttering noise of the motorbike was so close Pearl swore she could smell the exhaust. The Huntsman would have a field day with her, she thought, since she still had her soul – unlike the other unfortunate people he hunted.

Pearl held her breath as the Harley barked on the road outside, the noise reaching its pinnacle, spluttering as if it was about to halt, then passing and getting quieter, further. She sobbed, her breath bursting from her like a cough. She had come so close to getting caught, so close to ruining all the work the Seven had done to save her, to care for her. She vowed that she would never be so selfish again, that she would go straight home and listen to Jock and Crabby forever.

She waited, not wanting to leave the sanctuary of her hiding place even though being inside the house of her father and stepmother was painful. She wondered what had happened to Florian, whether the Huntsman had seen him, or whether he was safe at home now.

***

Finding the shopping centre was the best thing that had happened to Quinn in a long time. She went into every shop, trying on clothes and loading up a trolley with her stolen goods. She was having the time of her life, no longer burdened by thoughts of impending homelessness. As Quinn rounded the circular ramp to the higher level she noticed something. A tug in her chest, like anxiety, like something was missing. She couldn't ignore the feeling. So, putting her trolley safely to one side she began searching for the cause of the tug.

Her chest was leading her: more pain meant she was further away, less pain meant she was getting close. Close to what? she let herself ask.

A maintenance corridor. That was what her longing chest was driving her towards. Not the dress shops or the expensive shoe shops; no, the maintenance corridor. With one hand on the wall, she let herself walk almost on autopilot down the corridor. At the end was a single door, closed but not locked. Quinn couldn't help reaching out and pushing the handle. She didn't know why she was feeling so anxious now, after her illegal shopping spree, after seeing no-one since the spectres of the real world had faded.

What Quinn had failed to do was look at the ground – she

rarely did unless she was wearing a particularly nice pair of shoes. If she had, she would have seen the thick tire tracks winding up the ramp and down the corridor to the door, like a trail she could have followed without the pain in her chest. But Quinn had been poor for months, so she wasn't wearing nice shoes, and she didn't see the Huntsman's trailing trap leading right into his lair.

***

Pearl waited for what felt like a lifetime. She didn't want to leave the safety of her hiding spot, but she knew that if she didn't go home soon the Seven would come looking for her, and she didn't want to put them at risk unnecessarily. She crept towards the window and looked out onto the street. No sign of Florian or the Huntsman. She let out a deep breath; she would go straight home and tell the Seven what she'd seen.

Quietly, Pearl opened the front door and took a step out, looking around each corner in case he was lurking there. Another deep breath of relief. As she took another, more confident stride forward, a large leather-clad hand clamped over her mouth and another seized her around her middle.

"I've been looking for you, poor child," a voice crooned in her ear.

Pearl's blood went ice cold as she realised that he had come from behind her; he had been in the house too.

The world went black and Pearl collapsed into the Huntsman's arms, her ebony hair hanging limp, her blood red lips parted slightly in surprise, her snow white skin already looking the colour of death.

The Huntsman chuckled at the sight.

***

The walls were lined with cages, racks of weapons, and shelves filled with ominous looking jars whose contents Quinn didn't dare think about.

"What the fuck?" she breathed, her hand still tracing the wall.

Another doorway off to the side had a softer light oozing from under the door. Quinn went towards it, hoping the room on the other side was less macabre than the one she currently stood in. The door opened slowly, as if hardly used, and revealed a bedroom. A king-sized bed stood in the centre with an obscene sized TV hung on the wall opposite, games consoles and DVDs stacked around it like a funeral pyre.

"What the fuck?" Quinn said again, louder this time.

She didn't hear the rumble of the Harley coming up the ramp, or the clinking footsteps of biker boots behind her.

"It's my lucky day," a velvety voice said in her ear.

Quinn only had time to spin around before his hands were on her. She struggled, pushing backwards to avoid his embrace. She flopped on the bed and he landed hard on top of her, a gloved hand stifling the noise that escaped her – a noise that was not completely one of fear. It had been a long time since someone had thrown her down on a bed like that.

He must have seen it in her eyes because he paused, looking her up and down as if thinking about it himself. The Huntsman's face was covered, a motorbike helmet hiding his features from her. It was the last thing she saw before everything faded to black and she lost control of her body.

***

It was Crabby who noticed Pearl was missing first.

"Eh, Jock?" he called across the cottage.

"Hmm?" Jock responded, not looking up from his book.

"She's not pestered me for a while," Crabby said flatly.

Jock paused for a second, his eyes glazing over. "Little shit."

Crabby shook his head and collected his gear, whistling for the others to join him.

"I'll go with you, but the others should stay," Jock protested, folding his book down on the coffee table.

"The others will want to help her, and to be honest, we need all hands on deck against the Huntsman," Crabby replied grimly, swinging his baseball bat over his shoulder.

Less than fifteen minutes later, seven children toting an arsenal of weapons trudged down the High Street with thunderous expressions.

***

Quinn returned to consciousness inside one of the cages she'd seen in the main room. She groaned and clutched her head, the drug wearing off slowly – too slowly, making her feel groggy and heavy with it.

"Good morning." The velvety voice spoke teasingly.

Quinn looked around for the source of the voice. The helmeted biker seemed to blend with the darkness of the room; he sat in a chair opposite the cages, just a figure in the blackness.

"Who the fuck are you? And what's with the cage kink?" Quinn replied, with enough poison to make the Huntsman twitch in his seat.

"I might keep you," he purred, leaning forward so she could see his face. "They never have any spunk. They always beg."

The Huntsman shocked Quinn. She'd been expecting some sad, ugly loser with psychopath vibes, but he was ... gorgeous, with curly dark hair, olive skin, chocolate brown eyes, and tattoos. Tattoos everywhere, spreading up his hands and arms to poke out of his shirt at the throat.

"I never beg," she quipped, holding his hard stare with intrigue. She didn't know who this man was, or why people begged him, but she certainly wanted to play with him.

"Tell me," he said, standing and coming close to the bars, "why I was following your scent but found a little girl instead? And then found you here, snooping through my things?"

Quinn whipped her head around. A little girl? She thought, not seeing the small figure crumpled in a dark corner of another cage. "I have no idea what you are on about. Following my scent? I'm going to pretend that's not as creepy as it sounds."

"You really have no idea what is going on here, do you? I am the Huntsman, the demon's soul collector and butcher."

Quinn almost hissed. The demon, of course – she had forgotten about the masked weirdo in her shopping euphoria. This gorgeous creature was the keeper of the door she was meant to find.

"There it is," he crooned, dark curls falling over his brow seductively. "The penny finally dropped."

She was about to respond when a groaning from the next cage stopped her.

"What do you want?" she asked, focus returned to the Huntsman, hands fisted around the metal bars.

The Huntsman leaned forward, close enough to taste her if he wanted. "Everything."

She lowered her eyes. Back in the real world she'd wanted everything too. Everything that she had lost the moment she made a deal with the demon.

"You understand." He blanched, taking a step back from the bars.

"When the demon took me, ripped out my pathetic, black little soul and dumped me here, I had nothing – I was on the verge of homelessness, alone, hated and bankrupt. I wanted everything and ended up with nothing," Quinn said quietly, more honest than she had been with another living being in her life. More honest than she had been with her ex-husband when they were fighting to save their marriage.

"And now?" he asked.

"Before you caged me, I was the happiest I had been in a

very long time," she answered.

The Huntsman thought for a moment.

"Quinn?" a small voice groaned.

Quinn retreated to the side of the cage. She thought she recognised that voice, but it couldn't be, "Pearl?" she asked, hoping more than anything that she was wrong.

The small figure stood and lurched into the light, tiny porcelain hands gripping the cage bars. "Quinn!"

For the first time in her life, Quinn's heart broke. A sob escaped her lips as she held the gaze of her missing stepdaughter. She turned back to the Huntsman. "Make a deal with me. You let her go through your door to the human realm, and I'll stay here, be whatever you want me to be."

The Huntsman's brows raised while he contemplated her offer, but at that moment, the Seven came barreling in, weapons raised, with a shrill war cry. The Huntsman flicked his wrist and a crack sounded by the Seven's feet; a plume of gas erupted around them. Seconds later, their tiny forms crumpled to the ground.

"No!" Pearl yelled, pulling against the bars as if she could do something.

"Quiet," Quinn hissed, her eyes pleading.

"Quinn, you can't stay here with him. He's a monster."

"It's my fault you're here. It's my responsibility to get you out," Quinn said, the words sounding foreign in her ears.

"He took out your evil soul," Pearl theorised. "Now you're good. I need a good stepmother. My father needs a good wife."

"Enough," the Huntsman snapped, grunting as he dragged each of Pearl's seven companions into another cage.

"You have a soul. I don't, and I don't belong," Quinn hissed at Pearl, some of her old personality returning.

"I don't need to take your deal. I have nine marks in one day," the Huntsman said, his chest puffing out.

"And what? Your demon master will give you a gold star and then you're alone again?" Quinn snapped urgently.

It could have been the light, but she could have sworn the Huntsman's eyes flashed red, reminiscent of the demon's crazed eyes, making her stumble back in her cage.

"You have nothing, you fill your days with meaningless things." Quinn doubled down, waving her hand towards his bedroom and the large TV inside. "Working for a demon who couldn't give two craps if you do your job or not, so take the deal."

"What do I need you for?" The Huntsman hissed, pain in his eyes.

"Company, companionship, other things I can't say in front of children," she teased, not taking her eyes off him, not wanting to look at Pearl in case she broke her resolve.

"The girl goes. You stay and be my bride. I kill the rest," the Huntsman said levelly, and Quinn could feel the deal take hold – a rushing in her blood, a fullness in her chest.

"No!" Pearl screamed, looking to the cage beside her, full of the softly breathing bodies of her child-guardians.

The Huntsman took the ring of keys off his belt and jangled them in front of them. "Too late, little girl." He unlocked Quinns cage first, looking her up and down hungrily with his almost black eyes.

"Let me," Quinn said, clasping her hands around his. "You open the portal door – I have to say goodbye."

The Huntsman looked at his betrothed, suspicion flashing in his eyes for a moment before relenting. He headed to his bedroom, where the portal door sat disguised as a built-in wardrobe. He placed his hand on the chipped white paint and magic thrummed through him into the door.

Quinn rushed to the Sevens' cage first and unlocked it, kicking the nearest child without guilt – trying to wake them quickly – before making a big deal of finding the right key to open Pearl's cage door.

"You can't do this, Quinn," Pearl stammered, her body shaking with emotion, rattling the cage door and stirring the small figures in the neighbouring cage.

"Your father hates me, everyone hates me, I lost my job, my house... There is nothing for me through that door, Pearl." Quinn looked at her pointedly and almost shouted, "Go through the door, go home," which was enough to rouse the rest of the Seven and have them crawling out of their cage towards her.

"I'm sorry, Quinn," Pearl sobbed, hugging the waist of the woman who had never been kind to her, the woman who had wished her away and made a deal with a demon, the woman who was saving them now.

"I know," was all Quinn said as she hugged her stepdaughter back, her arm still around her as she steered her towards the door, hoping her own larger figure would be enough to shield the Seven from view.

"Hurry now," the Huntsman ordered, his hand outstretched.

Pearl let go of her stepmother and leaned towards the Huntsman, feigning a fall on her way. He stooped down to catch her and didn't notice the seven small figures darting past Quinn and through the portal.

"Tell your father I'm sorry," Quinn said, as Pearl took her final look back towards her and disappeared through the door.

The Huntsman snapped it shut behind her, his magic sealing it as quickly as it had opened. He turned towards her, his hunger palpable as he closed the distance between them and threw her down onto the bed. Oh yes, Quinn thought, this will do nicely.

M. J. Weatherall is one of those people who loves writing but always struggles to write about herself. She always feel like she's bragging (which in and of itself sounds like a brag according to her).

She is a young author from Sheffield who moved to the Lake District to get her BSc (Hons) degree in Outdoor Adventure and Environment. More recently she has qualified as a primary school teacher and is now fulfilling her calling as an educator.

M. J. loves climbing, kayaking and spending all her spare time in nature. A lifelong bookworm, she takes pride in growing her book knowledge (an asset to any pub quiz team to be sure!). She likes to think that she's a fun person to be around...at the very least, her cat seems to think so.

Swans Upon a Time

Adie Hart

By the time the carriage dropped me outside Wendlebury Castle, I'd worn a hole in the letter, right in the middle of the word "help".

As a District Witch, I was used to envelopes appearing in my satchel bearing instructions for my next case. That was standard procedure. And if it had been a normal case request slip that had summoned me here, I'd have read it, signed it, and magicked it back to Dispatch to signal that I was on my way. But this *wasn't* a normal case request slip, and that was the reason I kept pulling it out of my pocket to unfold it – more and more carefully as it disintegrated – and scrutinise it again.

It didn't even look like official stationery. It was just a scrap of parchment torn off of something else, with a few words scribbled on it. It said:

"Pen, I know you hate me, but I really need your help. Case gone bad at Wendlebury Castle. It's important. <u>Please.</u>"

The only other thing on there was a squiggle that, if you squinted, could just about read "Dare".

I folded it up again.

Sighed.

Tried to make myself knock on the door.

Sighed.

Pulled the letter out again.

What was bothering me was that I didn't know what I was walking into. I hadn't seen Alexander Cobham in a decade, nearly to the day, and quite frankly, that was perfectly all right with me. Right out of the Academy, freshly graduated and freshly broken-hearted, it had seemed easier to request postings that would naturally keep us at a distance. I'd tackled avalanches in the north-most mountains of Nivena, knowing how he hated the cold; I'd wrangled a wizard illegally breeding wyverns in the Kisian forests, since Dare had never really gotten over his aversion to flapping things. While I was building a reputation as a witch who could solve any problem, no matter how messy, Dare had made a name for himself with the softer side of District work, becoming the diplomatic star our professors had always expected him to be. So as we'd aged, it was only natural that we rarely bumped into each other, wasn't it? We had different specialties. No one could question that.

And if I avoided events at the Academy so I wouldn't bump into him, so what? I didn't want to be there anyway. I'd turned down an invitation to the Autumn graduation ceremony only a few days ago; it wasn't that I didn't support the new cohort of qualified witches – I went to the Spring graduations whenever I could – it was just that it was too painful to see them, bright-eyed and full of hope under their hats decorated with autumn leaves, as *I* had once been.

Ten years of effort to avoid Dare, and now I was walking straight towards him. But I couldn't ignore that "please". Not as a District Witch, sworn to help those who needed it, and not as Penelope Reed, who'd once thought Dare Cobham hung the stars in the sky. I couldn't leave him in trouble.

I just hoped he wouldn't rub it in too hard.

I let myself have one more sigh for good measure, folded the letter up again, and raised my hand to knock.

A harried-looking maidservant answered the door. "Oh, thank goodness," she said breathlessly, taking in my uniform with a smile. "You must be Mr Cobham's assistant."

I bristled at that. "I'm not Mr Cobham's anything."

"I'm so sorry, miss, I didn't mean..." Her face fell, and I realised that probably all she'd known was that he'd said he was calling in some back-up. It wasn't a comment on me or my relationship (non-existent) with Dare, and there was absolutely no need for me to have been so rude.

I pasted a standard issue smile on my face and tried to sound a bit more professional. "Sorry. I know what you meant. Let's start over – yes, I'm here to help Mr Cobham. Penelope Reed, District Witch." I shook her hand, and was reassured to see her smile return. "Er, actually, what *does* he need help with? He didn't say."

"The swans, miss. It's chaos."

"...Swans?" Swans were mostly quite placid birds, weren't they? You saw them on rivers and in moats and things, sailing along gracefully. They... migrated in autumn? That was about the extent of my swan knowledge. What could possibly be so bad about them that it would make Dare send such a panicked note?

The maid grimaced. "It'll be easier to show you. Mr Cobham's out by the pond now, if you'll follow me?"

***

"Pond" was a little bit of an understatement for what was clearly the defining feature of the castle grounds. The gardens sloped down towards it in elegant terraces; the trees on the far side were dainty little matchsticks full of orange leaves which I was certain had been specifically planted to bring out the picture-perfection of it all, if you liked that kind of thing. There was a wooden dock with three skiffs bobbing, too, and I was pretty sure if you could boat on it, that moved it fully out of "pond" status and into "lake".

It was also entirely full of swans.

I don't mean that there were several swans, or even that there were a lot of swans – I mean it was *full* of swans. So many swans you could barely even see the water. It was white feathers and trumpeting from shore to shore. Kind of mesmerising, but definitely not right.

And there, peering out at the honking horde – just to add the finishing touch to the chaos – was the man I'd been avoiding for the last ten years.

"Bloody hell," I said.

"Indeed," said Dare Cobham without turning round. "You see why I requested back-up."

"And you couldn't just have asked Dispatch like a normal person?" I asked archly.

At that, he did turn round, and my first sight of him in ten years was somewhat marred by the way his bronzed face went ashen. He looked different, ish. He'd grown into his angular face slightly more, and there were whispers of lines around his eyes and where his smile lurked. He was still devastatingly handsome, was the main thing; my traitor heart fluttered.

"*Pen?*" he whispered. "What are you doing here?"

"I... got your note?" Worry made my voice uncertain. Had I somehow misinterpreted the letter? It had seemed pretty clear, but perhaps... I fumbled the ragged paper out of my pocket and held it out to him. "You asked me to come."

He spluttered. "I certainly did not!"

"It's your writing."

I wiggled the note and he took it, careful not to brush my fingers as he did so, and peered down at it. He hadn't found a solution for that wayward bit of fringe in the last decade, it seemed, because it flopped right down into his eyes the way it always had.

"It is my writing, but..." He looked up at me with those big dark eyes; I tried not to notice they were full of concern. "I didn't write this, Pen, I swear. I'd never... I wouldn't ever ask for you."

Ouch. "Oh, because you couldn't bear to work with me?"

Frustration flashed in his eyes, overwriting the concern. "No, because *you* can't bear to work with *me*. You've been avoiding me ever since graduation."

I scoffed. "Since you dumped me, you mean, and disappeared to the other side of the kingdoms?"

"I didn't dump you – I was giving you space! You dumped me! I distinctly remember the letter you did it in!"

"Yeah, well, I didn't exactly have the option to talk to you, did I? You'd already made too much space," I said flatly. "Space to grow, space to start your marvellous career without your Academy girlfriend holding you back."

"It wasn't like that, Pen."

Petty anger flared in me, and I said coolly, "It's Penelope, now. You lost the privilege of pet names a long time ago." If only I could force myself not to think of him as Dare.

He flinched at that. "Penelope, then." He raked a hand through his hair as he always used to when he was puzzling out how to talk to someone; how funny, to know someone's every gesture so intimately even after years, and to be on the receiving end of it as a stranger. He gathered himself and said quietly, "You know I never wanted to break up with you, Penelope. I just thought that if we were assigned as work partners, as well as choosing to be romantic partners, we'd regret tying our lives together so thoroughly, so young. We'd just graduated; we were taking our first cases. We needed time to learn to do things on our own."

"Firstly, as I said at the time, that's nonsense and you know it. We'd done enough solo cases to pass. Why wouldn't we be partners when we were such a great team?" I'd always specialised in hands-on, practical magic, where Dare had been wonderful at winning confidences and smoothing conversations. Between us, we could cover anything. "And secondly – more importantly – at no point did you actually give me a chance to decide. I came down to Dispatch the morning after graduation all ready to set off with you, and had to find out from Professor Carter that you'd requested another assignment, and more importantly, that you were *already gone*. That felt pretty breaking-up-ish to me." I'd woken up that morning cold, with nothing in my bed but the dead leaves we'd decorated our hats with the day before. I still cursed the naivety I'd had not to realise what that meant.

Dare was quiet for a moment, worrying his fingers into knots. "I'm sorry. The new case they assigned me needed someone right away, and I was nervous that if I didn't go, you'd convince me otherwise, and..."

"And we might have lived happily ever after," I said tartly. "What a shame."

He gave me a sad smile. "Or we might have ended up treading on each others' toes until we hated each other. At least this way we grew into our own people. You look good, by the way." He gestured at me. "I like your hair long."

"Fancied a change," I said. "You kept yours the same, though. You're thirty-two and you still have the hair of a boy who can't sit still for the scissors."

"You always said it suited me," he laughed.

"It does." It did. I'd loved the way it waved over his forehead like it was begging to be touched, loved to feel it brush it across my shoulders when we– "Well, that's enough catching up. Are you going to tell me what's going on with all these swans?" I paused. "The swans *are* the case, right?" There was every chance this was just the home of a royal who really, really liked birds; I'd seen weirder.

"Wait," said Dare. "You mean you're staying?"

"You asked for backup, didn't you?"

"Yes, but... I can request a new partner from Dispatch. They'll send someone else, and you can go back to, you know, not seeing me."

I sighed. "You're the one who wanted us to grow into our own people – well, I'm all grown up now, and I assume you are too, so let's be adults about this. I'm here now, and I can help. I won't walk away from people in need because of a decade-old wound." I chewed my lip. That sounded like I was still hurting. "Especially since it's fully healed."

He looked taken aback, but smiled tentatively. "Right. Friends, then?"

"Colleagues, Cobham." I held out my hand for him to shake, and pretended not to feel the buzz of memory as his skin touched mine.

"Colleagues," he repeated. "In that case, let's go find the kings and get you filled in."

***

I perched on the edge of an extremely uncomfortable sofa in a sitting room that dripped with gold and silver, as far away from Dare as I could manage, as he introduced me to King Peter, King Ilya and Prince Siegfried, the latter of whom it transpired was no relation to either of the kings, but the betrothed of their daughter Odette.

"And will I meet the princess?" I asked politely once introductions had been made, and titles (thankfully) dropped.

"Ah, no," said Ilya somewhat sheepishly. "You see, that's why we called in the District."

"She's missing?" That wouldn't be a terribly unusual case for us to handle, but it was certainly one that should have been within Dare's solo diplomatic skills.

"No, no," Ilya said. "We know exactly where she is."

"She's in the pond," added Peter.

"With the swans?" I asked.

"She *is* a swan," wailed Siegfried, dissolving into a prince-shaped puddle of brocade, blond hair, and tears.

I ignored the eyebrow Dare raised at me; I'd always had a nightmare keeping a straight face in classes when he gave me that look, but I just about managed to keep my professional demeanour. Fixing my eyes on the kings, who at least had the dignity to look faintly embarrassed by Siegfried's outburst, I asked, "So the princess is part of that flock?"

"It was a bit of a mistake," said Peter, grimacing. "We were trying to help."

I suppressed a sigh. "With the greatest of respect, could someone just tell me what happened from the beginning? I won't judge anyone's motives or actions, but I have to know the details to know how to proceed."

"Of course," said Ilya, setting a comforting hand over his husband's, then handing Siegfried a handkerchief to snuffle into. "Our daughter Odette is our pride and joy, but she's..."

"Headstrong," finished Peter.

"Yes," said Ilya. "She must be married before her thirtieth birthday in order to begin preparing for the throne, but she kept saying she'd get to it in her own time."

That didn't sound quite right. "Did anyone ask her if she actually wants to get married? Not everybody does."

"She's always said she didn't object to the concept, but she wasn't ready yet," said Peter. "But she has to be. So we thought long and hard and selected young Siggy here as the most eligible match."

Ilya looked fondly at his husband. "An arranged marriage can blossom into the most wonderful love, you know. It did for us."

"So you... selected Siegfried. What happens next?"

Ilya smiled. "Well, it's tradition for the incoming spouse to perform a great feat at the Autumn Festival to prove their worthiness."

"I had to empty a lake with a thimble," said Peter brightly.

It was rather a great feat of my own not to roll my eyes. Nothing about this case required me; betrothal tasks were the diplomatic bread and butter of the District Witches, and far more Dare's wheelhouse than mine. I'd always found the whole idea rather silly – if you loved someone, why not just be with them? People were always making it more complicated than it needed to be.

Ilya continued, "Spring is for lovers meeting, but autumn is the time for marriages, for commitments before the long winter ahead. The idea behind the feat is to ensure that there's a strong connection between the two betrotheds. Odette had a look at the books and came up with the idea that she'd get the court sorceress to turn her into a swan, and then Siggy would need to pick her out of a group of seven identical swans."

Siegfried sniffed, interrupting him. "Something about knowing her regardless of her looks, she said? I think?"

"It sounds like a nice idea," said Dare reassuringly.

It sounded like the foolishness these things usually were. "So what went wrong?" I asked.

Peter sighed. "The transformation went well, and then we had the spell to summon some other swans. Only, they started coming, and then they kept coming, and now we have this situation."

"Two hundred and forty-three swans," said Ilya. "They won't go home; the spell is too strong. And the worst part is, some of them are magical."

"How do you know?" I asked.

"I'm allergic to magic," Siegfried said sadly. "They make me sneeze."

"Oh, so at least it would have been easy for you to pick Odette out of a flock of regular swans," I said.

"Huh? Why?" Siegfried's eyebrows crinkled in puzzlement.

"...Because of the transformation spell on her?"

His eyes widened. "Oh. Wow, yeah, you're right. I didn't think of that."

At my side, Dare let out a small huff of laughter.

Oh dear. This was going to be a tiring case.

"Well," I said, putting on my most reassuring smile. "I'm sure we can get this all sorted out for you in no time."

"In four days?" said Peter hopefully. "For the festival?"

"We'll do our best." I certainly hoped this wouldn't take any longer than four days. I didn't care about their festival, but the equinox was the anniversary of Dare leaving, and I wanted to be long shot of him by then. "We'll need to have a look at the summoning spell," I continued, "to see what went wrong, and then we'll tackle getting the swans back to where they need to be. Cobham, have you spoken to the court sorceress yet?"

"Yes," he said, "but we haven't made much progress on working out why the spell went haywire."

"I think talking to her should be my first job, then," I said.

"Shall I send for her?" asked Peter.

"No need," called a new voice from the doorway behind me. "I'm here. Sorry I'm late."

Footsteps clacked across the floorboards and I turned to see a tall woman in a long black dress hurrying towards us. I blinked. Surely it couldn't be who I thought it was.

The sorceress stopped dead as she caught sight of me. "*Pen?*"

My heart dropped out of the bottom of my feet.

This was a test. This was a nightmare. This was an elaborate practical joke set up by someone who hated me. There had to be some kind of explanation for this other than my enormously, colossally bad luck, because it seemed that the Wendlebury court sorceress was none other than Vonda Rothbart.

My *other* ex.

I shot to my feet. "I have to... I need to check something in... I'll be right back," I jabbered over my shoulder as I grabbed wildly for the ornate door handle and let myself out into the equally ornate, blessedly quiet, miraculously ex-free corridor.

***

A passing footman took pity on me and showed me to the library to wait while he had a room made up for me. The sheer number of books would have made it a relaxing space, were it not for the fact it looked directly onto the pond; as such, it was impossible not to find yourself drawn to the window by the endless noise and flapping.

I didn't hear the door open over the cacophony, so I was still contemplating the swans when I felt a slim hand settle on my shoulder and jumped about a mile.

"Oh, I've startled you again, sorry," said Vonda. "I've been looking for you everywhere. It's nice to see you, darling."

I didn't read too much into the 'darling'; Vonda had always addressed all her friends with it, and I'd gotten used to it well before we started dating. I hadn't seen her for a few years, but she'd maintained the habit, apparently. She kissed me on both cheeks, then pulled me in for a hug.

"Uh, it's nice to see you too," I said hesitantly, not sure what to do with my hands, and then abruptly aware of everything I *had* done with my hands, and then even more not sure what to do with them now.

Vonda leaned back, hands still on my shoulders, to examine my face worriedly. "Oh no, darling, are you mad at me? I thought we left things on good terms?"

We had, actually. Not all my break ups were world-shattering. Sometimes you and the incredibly hot sorceress you'd teamed up with to lift a village's curse just fell into bed, enjoyed each others' company enough to stick around for a year or so, then realised you were ultimately better suited as friends. I had no hard feelings about our relationship, and it seemed neither did she.

"You surprised me, Von, that's all," I said, returning the hug with a little more feeling when she leaned in again. "I wasn't expecting to see you after so long, and I certainly wasn't expecting to see you right after I just ran into Dare Cobham for the first time in ten years. It's a lot for a woman to take in."

"It *is* your Dare!" She clapped her hands happily. "I thought it was, but you know, he introduces himself as Alexander now."

"He's not *my* Dare," I said defensively.

She waved a hand at my objection. "You know what I mean. Your first love, the one who got away, all of that business. *That* Dare. The one who broke your heart."

"I wouldn't say he—"

"Darling." She gave me a reproving look. "You cried on my shoulder enough about it."

"Well, I'm starting to wish I hadn't," I muttered. "Look, enough about Dare. It's a horrible coincidence, and I just want to get through this case as quickly and efficiently as possible and then put several kingdoms between the two of us again."

"Actually, about that horrible coincidence..." said Vonda, biting her lip.

Oh, that sounded bad.

"Von, what did you do?"

She winced. "Will you come and sit down so I can explain myself?"

I plopped myself down in one of the wingback chairs by the window and raised my eyebrows expectantly. "This had better be good."

Vonda peered around the bookshelves before sitting down across from me and twisting her fingers into an intricate loop. The trumpeting of the swans silenced immediately.

She slipped me a small smile. "I don't want anyone overhearing while I bare my soul to you."

"How bad *is* it?"

"Oh, nothing awful," she trilled, and then rushed out in a single breath, "I just sort of abducted the princess and then summoned a few hundred swans and it's all got out of hand and I can't get Siggy to leave and the kings are really mad at me for messing up the betrothal and so they sent for the District to help fix it all and now I might be fired and also I might have ruined everyone's life."

I snorted. "Is that all?"

She worried at her lip. "I also might have intercepted Dare's letter to Dispatch and altered it to make sure it was you who came here."

"Vonda! You *know* I don't work with Dare." I was certain I'd complained in detail to Vonda, several times, about how hard I had to work to keep myself out of Dare's orbit after graduation. She knew exactly how difficult a task she was asking me to do in coming here – which meant, perhaps, that things were even worse than she was telling me.

"I'm sorry," she said. "I really needed someone I trusted on my side."

This was giving me a headache. "So why didn't you just write and ask me openly? And come to think of it, why were you so shocked when you saw me?"

"Ah. That's the awkward part." She paused; she was going to wear a hole in that lip. "I couldn't ask you to come openly because Dare had already shown up – it would have looked suspicious if I hired my own District Witch when we already had a District Wizard on the case. I had to make it look like it was an error on someone else's part. And as for the acting... I kind of need you to pretend to everyone that I had nothing to do with any of this."

"Wh—"

A movement flickered in the corner of my eye, and I looked up to see Dare enter the library. He was mouthing something, and when Vonda flicked her fingers again, the trumpeting restarted and I heard him say "—in here?"

"Yes, we're in here," answered Vonda smoothly, as if we hadn't just been deep in conversation about her secrets. "What can we do for you?"

Dare looked a little flustered at that *we*. "I wanted to check on you, Penelope. You looked terrified, and I wanted to make sure you were all right."

"I'm fine, Cobham," I said, ignoring the feeling that pricked through my chest at the way his eyes searched my face. "I was just surprised to see Vonda."

He blinked. "You two know each other, then?"

"Intimately," purred Vonda before I could reply.

"We're old friends," I said quickly.

Vonda laughed. "Darling! We were more than that. Old lovers," she said with a conspiratorial wink at Dare.

"Oh. Oh!" His eyes widened. "Should I... leave you to it?"

"No," I said, at the same time as Vonda said, "Yes."

Dare looked like I felt, like a bird caught in the path of a broomstick; Vonda was the only person in the room who was enjoying herself.

Before any of us could break the stalemate, there was a high-pitched yelp from outside, followed by an almighty splash. We all rushed to the window in time to see the swans rippling outwards from an empty space in the centre of the pond – well, empty apart from an overturned skiff and a blond head bobbing morosely up and down.

"Siegfried!" I cried, though I doubted he could hear me across the distance and the swans. "Hold on, I'm coming to help!"

I scooped up my satchel and made for the door. Vonda offered me a gallant arm as Dare stretched his elbow out to escort me; I rolled my eyes at them both and swept past them. I didn't claim to understand what was going on with either of them, but I could certainly manage to walk on my own.

***

It was somewhat daunting, rowing through the swans to get to Siegfried. Vonda had refused to get her dress wet to help "that big blond idiot", as she called him, so Dare and I had commandeered one of the remaining skiffs and were inching towards the centre of the pond, but it was slow going. The birds weren't hostile, but, as I'm sure they say somewhere, you can't shove your way through a couple of hundred swans without rustling a few feathers. Luckily, although it didn't seem Siegfried could swim, he'd at least had the presence of mind to flatten himself out to float on his back, so he wasn't going anywhere.

We rowed in silence until a wing clipped Dare for the second time, making him flinch, and I threw a shield spell around the boat, giving us both a bit of breathing space.

"Thanks, Pen," he said with feeling.

Oh no, I couldn't handle that grateful smile and what it did to my insides. "You were getting out of rhythm, that's all," I said tartly, to make up for it.

"I thought we were being cordial?"

"I *am* being cordial."

He wrinkled his nose. "Bitter lemon cordial, maybe."

A laugh bubbled out of me. Only a small one. "That's such a stupid joke."

"I haven't forgotten those are the ones that get you," he said, and suddenly the atmosphere inside the shield bubble felt charged with all the things *I* hadn't forgotten: the sparkle in his eyes when he made me laugh; the way he pushed that ridiculous hair out of his eyes with his long fingers; the easy back-and-forth pull of our bodies as we worked together seamlessly on the task at hand.

I shook my head to clear the memories. "Change the subject, Cobham."

"Sure. So what about your old lover?" he said conversationally. "You two seemed friendly."

Not to that, I wanted to scream, but I summoned up the confidence to say, "Why, are you jealous?"

He shrugged. "A little."

I looked at him in shock; I'd meant it as a joke. "It's been ten years. You didn't think I'd spent the whole of it pining for you, did you?"

"Oh, not of Vonda," he deadpanned. "Of you. She's a beautiful woman."

Ouch. "I do have good taste sometimes, you know."

"Touché. Should I keep my eyes out for more of your exes, then?" His voice sounded casual, but his eyes were intense.

"It's not like I have them stashed all over the kingdoms," I said. "It's pretty much just you and her, for the big ones, and I'm in my own personal hell right now, so can we focus on the case?"

He grinned. "So you're not seeing anyone at the moment?"

"No, not that it's any of your business."

"Interesting," he said, that intensity changing slightly, and before I could think of a retort, added "We're here."

We had, in fact, broken through the last of the swans, and I hadn't even noticed, I'd been so focused on deciphering that strange emotion in his eyes. Prince Siegfried floated alongside us, eyes closed, looking for all the world like he was out for a pleasurable dip.

I pulled down the shield and poked him with an oar. "Siegfried, do you want to get in the boat?"

He opened his eyes and immediately lost control of his float position, thrashing his limbs about in a way that achieved nothing but soaking us as badly as him.

I looked at Dare. "Net?"

"Net." He nodded and held out his hand to me.

I only hesitated slightly before slipping my hand into his. It more than doubles the size of the net spell if there's two of you doing it, and you need that connection to make it work; I just had to focus really, *really* hard on the spell, and not at all on the way Dare's hand still felt so right around mine. He had new calluses, ones I didn't recognise, but the feel of his fingers curled so warmly around mine was so familiar, I could almost be back at the Academy, holding hands under the desk, oblivious to what was coming.

The net. Right.

We slid the invisible ropes under the flailing prince and hauled him up into the skiff. I dropped Dare's hand like it was on fire, and set to patting Siegfried firmly on the back.

"Thanks," he spluttered.

"You get your breath back," said Dare, "and then we'll get you home and dry."

"What were you even doing out here if you can't swim?" I

asked.

"I was looking for Odette," he said. "I thought if I fed all the swans, I might get an Odette-y feeling off one of them."

"And did you?" asked Dare.

"No," he said mournfully. "They all just make me sneeze. That's why I fell in."

"Ah," Dare and I said at the same time.

"And now my bread is ruined." He produced a soggy bag of soggier bread from somewhere about his soggy person.

As kindly as I could (since he looked like he was about to burst into tears) I said, "You shouldn't feed swans bread, anyway. It's not good for them."

Siegfried looked baleful. "It's not? But then how am I meant to get close to them?"

"Try asking the cook for some peas. And maybe try feeding them from the shore next time."

***

The journey back to shore was a lot easier than the way out had been, since the swans gave Siegfried a wide berth. We only had to deal with his sniffles, which were more annoying than anything. You couldn't even tell if they were related to his allergy, his general moroseness, or whether he was getting a cold from his impromptu swim.

Once he'd been safely delivered to the footmen waiting for him on the shore (it seemed Vonda had done something useful while we effected our rescue), the three of us remained by the edge of the water, staring out at the mass of swans. The sun was beginning to set over the pond, lighting their pale feathers with the kind of rich pinks and oranges you only got on warm autumn evenings like this. We stood side-by-side, Dare to my left, Vonda to my right, each of us keeping our eyes fixed on the water. I don't know who was feeling most awkward, but I had a strong feeling it was me.

"That really is a *lot* of swans," I said to break the silence.

"Two hundred and forty-three," said Dare with a shudder. "That's four hundred and eighty-six wings."

"Still not over the flapping thing?" I asked, remembering the way he'd flinched back in the boat whenever a stray swan had entered his personal space.

"Ugh, never," he said. "Things with wings are just wrong."

"What do you do about creature cases, then?" asked Vonda.

"I request backup," he said wryly, with a shrug of his shoulder at me. "It usually isn't someone who hates me."

Vonda said very disingenuously, "Oh, do you two know each other?"

Dare looked at her in surprise, then at me. Was he *hurt?* "Did... did you not tell her about me? While you were... you know..."

She grinned at him. "Having all that phenomenal sex? It didn't come up."

I tutted. "Von, don't tease him. Yes, Cobham, I told her about you."

"All bad, I assume?"

"Yes," said Vonda, over the top of my "No".

I wheeled around so I could see both of them at once. "Right," I said in the firm tones I usually reserved for particularly rowdy goblin infestations, or my sister's incorrigible twins. "This *isn't* my idea of fun. I don't know what I did to get stuck here with the two of you, but we are all going to be professionals, and we are going to sort out this swan problem, and then we are going to go our separate ways. There will be no teasing, no bickering, and no hair-pulling. Got it?"

"Not even a little bit of hair-pulling?" asked Vonda with a dramatic pout. "His hair looks really pullable."

It was, but not in the way she meant— No, I could *not* think about that right now.

"None," I said. "Can we agree to get along for the next few days, please?"

Both Dare and Vonda opened their mouths, but if they were going to argue, they were cut off by a speeding white streak of feathers that swooped down over their heads. The most enormous swan I'd ever seen settled into the pond with a hiss.

"Two hundred and forty-four," said Dare with a huge sigh. "I'm going to bed."

I stifled a yawn. "I think I'll join you."

Two pairs of dark eyes flashed with surprise.

"In the act of going to bed," I said, then realised that sounded worse. "Going to our own beds. Alone."

I strode off towards the castle, pretending I couldn't hear either of them giggle.

***

I always sleep badly when I'm worrying about a case, so when someone slipped into my room around midnight, I was bolt upright before they'd closed the door.

"Who's there? I warn you, it's a bad idea to sneak up on a witch," I said.

"It's me, darling."

A soft light grew until I could see the intruder.

"Von?"

"Ooh, who else were you expecting?" She perched on the end of my bed.

"No one," I said, panicking slightly, "but I certainly wasn't expecting you. I hope I didn't give you any signals, because—"

"Oh, keep your hat on, Pen. I'm very happily taken, I'll have you know."

Well, that was interesting. "So you've woken me up to tell me you have a new girlfriend? Wow, thanks."

She swatted my leg. "No, darling, I'm here because we were interrupted earlier before I could spill all my secrets."

Oh, that made more sense. "So spill."

"You say that like it's so easy..." She paused, then chuckled. "Okay, I suppose I have woken you up to tell you about my girlfriend."

"Von," I groaned.

"No, it's relevant, I promise. It's Odette."

"Odette the *princess*?"

"The one and only," Vonda smiled. "It'll be two years in a couple of weeks."

Vonda and I had only parted ways about three years ago, so this wasn't just a fling. "That's great, Von. I'm happy for you."

She pursed her lips. "It is and it isn't. It's very much a secret at the moment - so please don't tell anyone. Especially not Peter and Ilya, or Siggy."

"Bloody hell," I said. "The betrothal. Why didn't either of you say anything?"

"Odette wanted to, but I don't know, Pen, it seemed... I'm just a witch from the Dales, whatever my title is now. It's not right - have you seen how fancy everything is here? It took me six months before I could let myself lie on the bedspread instead of folding it up carefully on a chair every night. I can't be Queen!"

I rolled my eyes. "Oh, because a very talented, very attractive witch in the highest position in the kingdom is such a lowly person?"

That got a small laugh out of her. "Can I keep you around for pep talks? But seriously, Pen, I can't just weasel my way into the royal household and sweep the heir to the throne off her feet!

I'd never get another job."

She wouldn't need one – judging by the amount of gold that dripped from every surface in this castle, Odette was loaded – but I bit my tongue. This was obviously a sore spot for her.

"But how did they pick Siegfried? Her fathers didn't know her preference for women?" That seemed odd, given their own relationship, but I supposed it was possible.

"Oh, no, she's like you, darling, she likes everyone. Just not Siggy. Don't get me wrong, he's not horrible. A bit dim, but kind, even if he is dramatic—"

"Says you."

"—and his mother's queendom's right next door, so I think if it weren't for me, it wouldn't be an awful match, on paper. It's just that there's absolutely no one in the world I think could be less interesting for someone as brilliant as Odette."

I smiled. "So if she doesn't want to marry him..."

"Right," said Vonda. "That's where the plan comes in. The kings told you about the test, right? It's a stupid tradition, but Odette's idea was pretty brilliant. There's no way he'd be able to pick her out of a bunch of identical anything; he doesn't know the first thing about her."

"And then there's the magic allergy." I was catching on.

"Exactly! So he'd instinctively steer away from the one that made him sneeze, pick another swan, fail the test, and head home, no feelings hurt." She clicked her fingers. "She'd be free."

"But wouldn't Odette's fathers just choose another betrothed after that?"

She nodded. "That's where it all went a bit wrong. We realised we needed more time to think, so I've been stalling. I had a spell ready to summon six swans from a nearby lake and bind them to the castle grounds till we needed them, and I shoved a whole lot more power into it, hoping it would take Siggy a lot longer to go through them all if there were even more. That way, even if he found her, they couldn't get married at the Autumn Festival, and the kings would probably postpone until next year. They're big on tradition like that."

I could see the logic, sort of. "But you didn't mean to bring this many swans?"

"Not quite so many. And not enchanted ones! That's what made the kings decide to call in the District. We can't be stealing people's magic swans." She paused. "Actually, some of them probably *are* people, and we definitely can't keep those here."

"I see. And where's Odette?"

"Hiding out in Wendlebury. One of the barmaids at the Black Swan wanted a week off."

"So she's not even a swan like everyone thinks?" This case was such a mess. "How have you been keeping Dare off the scent?"

"Mostly pretending I don't know what happened, burning my notes and so on, but it's wearing thin. And I miss Odette, and, oh, Pen, I don't know how to fix this so we can be together."

Tears glistened in her eyes in the low light, and I reached out to hug her. "We'll get this sorted out, Von. Don't worry."

She sniffed. "Thank you, darling. You don't know what it means to me that you're here."

"You can thank me by getting out of here so I can sleep," I teased.

"Oh, I think you'll get a better reward than that," she said, but where once that would have been an innuendo, now there was nothing lascivious in her voice, only a smile.

I would have asked her what she meant, but she was already slipping out of the door, and I was too tired to follow.

***

In the morning, Dare and I set up an open-sided gazebo by the edge of the pond and began to make a plan to triage the swans. Odette might not be among them – though nobody but Vonda and I knew that right now – but regardless of that, we still needed to sort through the rest and make sure they were either restored to their original forms, returned to their original owners, or otherwise sorted out in terms of the spells they were under. Any one of those would have been a pretty standard case for a District Witch or Wizard, but two hundred-odd at once would require us to be extremely organised.

"Right," said Dare. "I've made some flyers for Dispatch to distribute through the usual systems – how does this sound?"

I looked down at the piece of paper he offered me.

SWANS FOUND, it read. *Are you missing a swan or multiple swans? Apply to Wendlebury Castle with identifying details to be reunited with your feathered friend(s).*

"Looks good," I said. "There's probably plenty of people wondering where their swans have got to, and it'll really help us if they can come and pick their own, as it were."

He nodded and sent the paper off to the Post Room with the usual spell. "Let's hope they all get claimed quickly."

"We have three days till the Autumn Festival," I said, and felt a pang of guilt that I was ruining Vonda's postponement plan. I still had time to come up with a better idea, though, so I needed to do what I could to appease the kings in the meantime. "For now," I continued, "Vonda's turned off the part of the spell that kept them coming in, so the number can only go down, though they're still bound to the castle grounds."

"That's a good idea," said Dare. "If they're all free to go, we could lose Odette too—"

Oh yes. It was going to get very tricky to keep Dare in the dark, if I didn't find a way to get Vonda to come clean soon.

"—and anyway, there's bound to be a bunch of curses and misfires in here. We'd only be making more work for some other witch or wizard to rescue them in future, if we let them disappear."

"True," I said. "So, let's start checking each swan over and removing any spells that are easy to do. If that yields any transformed humans, hopefully they can tell us themselves what they need to get where they should be."

"And if we find Odette while we're working, we can always hold onto her until the festival."

I swallowed hard; it felt so wrong to lie to him. "Yep, good idea. And for any that stay in swan form, I've asked Peter to provide us with some enclosures we can use to separate out the ones we've checked. They should be putting up the fences now."

Dare grimaced.

"It won't hurt them to be kept captive for a night or two," I said.

"No, it's not that. It's... I'm going to have to touch them, aren't I?"

I resisted the urge to cup his face to smooth the worry from it. "Only to begin with," I reassured him. "Hopefully after today you can do your diplomacy thing with the newly-human ones and any claimants that arrive."

"But that leaves you to do all the magic," he protested. "That's a lot of work – it's hardly fair on you."

"Oh, believe me, I'd rather untangle twelve thousand curses than have to schmooze with anxious relatives and so on. You'd be doing me a favour."

"You still hate the talking part?"

"Says the man who's still trying to get out of dealing with birds."

He chuckled. "We cover each others' weaknesses so well."

"We always did make a good team," I said, and instantly regretted it when his eyes softened.

"We did," he said quietly.

Bloody hell, it was hard to shove down all the old feelings that came bubbling up when he looked at me like that. We'd been *such* a good team, and not just in the practical splitting of tasks, but in the way we could bounce problems back and forth between us until we came to the solution together. Our professors had often joked that they should graduate us as a pair on one certificate. I'd always enjoyed that sense of belonging, of being essential to someone else; it had been strange, in a way, learning to do it all on my own after graduation. I was perfectly capable of it, of course – a District Witch was prepared for anything – but there was a loneliness in those first couple of years that I couldn't shake. A sense that I was missing the joy of the moment a tricky puzzle clicks into place, without someone to celebrate it with.

It didn't matter. This was a weird fluke, and we weren't going to be a team again once we'd dealt with this case.

"Come on," I said to Dare, who was still looking at me with a softness in his eyes that made me want to throw my arms around him and nestle into the spot below his chin where I'd always fit. "Let's go catch us some swans."

***

That first day, we made it through eighty-nine swans. Many of them were just regular birds, caught by Vonda's summoning spell as intended; these we set into one enclosure until I could ask her to reverse the spell and let them fly home of their own accord. There were four swan-maidens, all friends from the same bevy, who were more than happy to doff their wing-cloaks and take up temporary residence in the castle's guest rooms once Dare had promised not to try to steal their garments in order to marry them. They were understandably wary of men, so I tasked

Vonda with keeping them away from Siegfried – I wasn't worried he'd try anything, only that he gave off a sort of feeling of "looking for a wife" that I thought might unnerve them.

Sixteen of the swans we'd checked, amusingly, were ducks in glamour.

"Some royal must have felt like their moat wasn't prestigious enough," laughed Dare as he handed me a glass of wine.

He'd knocked on my door after dinner for a debrief, which was perfectly within the normal bounds of colleague-ship when working a case together, and the wine was just a friendly gesture. I could drink wine with Dare in a professional way. It didn't need to remind me of anything.

"There's a market in that, probably," I said. "Castle Fancification for the Royal on a Budget."

"Give your moat some quackitude!" laughed Dare.

I groaned and threw a pillow at him. "Bloody hell, Dare. That was terrible."

"No need for fowl language," he said with a wink. "I can't help it if I quack you up."

The giggle escaped me before I could force it down, and I grabbed another pillow. "You'd better *duck* and cover." I faked a toss, catching him around the head with it as he bobbed back up.

"Oh, masterful duck-nique," he said, "but I'll have you know, I'm poultry in motion."

When I swung again, he caught my arm in mid-air, knocking the pillow from my grasp and holding me steady, half-out of my seat. One moment we were laughing, and the next, all the breath had gone out of my lungs as he searched my face with those soft brown eyes.

"Pen," he whispered, and if I could have breathed, I would have murmured his name too. He flicked his gaze down to my lips, up to my eyes, into my heart. "I've missed this, you know," he murmured. "I've missed you."

There was barely a space between us anymore. It felt so familiar to be here like this, laughing and joking and feeling... *Feeling whole,* my traitor mind whispered. I let my eyes fall closed, savouring the feel of the moment before I pulled away. I was *going* to pull away. Any moment now.

"Well, what's all this then?" came an amused voice it took me a moment to recognise.

I leapt back from Dare, wrenching my wrist from his grasp. "Vonda? What are you doing here?"

"I did knock, darling," she said, eyes shining with humour. "I thought you and I could take a little trip, but you seem awfully busy."

"No," I said quickly. "We were just debriefing." I very deliberately did not look at Dare.

Vonda snorted. "Is that what they call it these days? Anyway, I'll come back later. I was going to ask if you wanted to go into the village on an errand with me." She widened her eyes at me significantly. "The errand we talked about last night?"

Dare stood. "I can go if you two want to be alone. Penelope, you should have said something."

"Thanks a bunch, darling," drawled Vonda.

I sighed heavily and caught Dare's arm. "Wait. Listen, Vonda, I think we need to bring Cobham into this. I can't keep being pulled between the two of you."

"Oh, no no no," he muttered. "You two are consenting adults and we broke up a long time ago and whatever you do is your own business. I'm... um... I'm flattered, but I don't want... I'm not going to be... I don't want to be second fiddle in... um... this." Dare's bronze skin usually hid most of his blushes, but now he was redder than I'd ever seen him.

I was probably the same colour.

Vonda cackled. "We're not inviting you to *bed*."

"...You're not?"

"Men." She rolled her eyes. "If we wanted to have a good night we certainly wouldn't need you. No, Pen wants me to come clean about the swan thing."

"Oh," said Dare quietly. He sat down again, looking intently at his boots.

"And are you going to?" I asked, eyebrow raised. "It will be a lot easier to get this sorted out if we're all on the same page."

"Fine," she said. "If you trust him. Grab your cloaks and meet me at the kitchen door in ten minutes."

***

Odette, as Vonda had hinted, was hiding in plain sight as a barmaid in the Black Swan Inn. Once we were safely tucked away under a soundproofing spell in her attic room, Vonda removed the glamour from her. I watched in awe as her long, straight black hair lightened into soft blonde waves; her brown eyes shifted into a sparkling olive green, and her ruddy skin brightened to a perfect porcelain. I'd never even have known she was in disguise, but the difference was like night and day.

She fell into Vonda's arms immediately; Dare and I perched awkwardly on the end of the bed and looked awkwardly around the room to give them a little space to reunite. Eventually, they separated and Odette shone a beautiful smile at the two of us.

"Thank you so much for coming," she said, snuggling into Vonda's side. "We've been at our wits' end with how to fix this mess we're in."

"That's what we do," I said. "Well, I fix the problems. He smoothes it all over afterwards so no one's mad."

"The perfect team," smiled Odette, which made Vonda chuckle.

"Don't I know it," I muttered, which made Dare elbow me.

"Ignore her," he said. "Just so I can be sure I've got this straight – you two are in love, but Odette's betrothed to Siegfried. You're stalling the wedding by spoiling the betrothal task with too many swans, but now that Penelope and I are here, that's not going to work anymore because we're sorting out the swans, so we need a new plan to get the wedding called off so you two can be together. Have I missed anything?"

"That's about the size of it," said Vonda.

"Okay. Nobody bite my head off," he said with a cautious smile, "but Odette, have you actually tried telling your fathers that you want to marry Vonda, not Siegfried? They seem like they want you to be happy."

Vonda grimaced, and Odette patted her hand. "I would, but Vonda doesn't think it's a good idea. She's worried they won't accept her because she's not a royal."

"It's not that, exactly," Vonda said. "But Wendlebury is so traditional, with their betrothals and trials and protocols. The kings aren't going to take kindly to an upstart commoner stealing their daughter, let alone teaching me to rule alongside her."

"I still think you're being ridiculous—" I began, but Dare shot me a warning glance.

"I understand your feelings," he said, which I had to admit was a little less inflammatory. "What if we can get rid of Siegfried – could you formally apply to the kings as a suitor and undertake a trial of your own? They like you, it seems. There's every chance they might say yes."

"That could work," said Odette.

"I don't know," said Vonda. "The whole system is set up for suitors to prove they're worthy of Odette. They could pick anything they wanted to make it look like I'm not."

Odette cupped the sorceress's face. "I can't think of anyone worthier," she said. "Surely *I* should decide that."

Something in the way she said it made the piece fall into place for me. "Wait. Von, what if you proved your love *before* you applied to the kings?"

Vonda raised an eyebrow. "How?"

"By completing Siegfried's trial," interjected Dare. "Pen, that's brilliant! Vonda, what if we whittle the swans down to the seven you originally wanted, Odette included—"

"—but then we make sure Siegfried gets stuck," I continued, excited that he'd picked up my thread of thinking. "And oh no, even the District Witches are stumped, what a shame, maybe we'll never find the princess. But look, here comes the brave and clever Court Sorceress, Vonda Rothbart, to the rescue—"

"—and you pick her out of the line up of swans—"

"—proving it's *you*, and only you, who knows her better than anyone."

"Who can argue with true love, proved fair and square in front of everyone?" finished Dare. "The kings get their spectacle for the festival, and you get to win the princess in a highly official, backed-up-by-tradition way."

Vonda and Odette exchanged looks, and smiles crept over their faces.

"It's perfect," Odette said. "We can finally be together."

"Oh, darling," said Vonda, and swooped in for a kiss.

When they didn't show much sign of stopping, I grabbed Dare's wrist. "Let's give them some space," I whispered. "They've not seen each other in a week."

"Ah," said Dare, and let me tug him to his feet and towards the door.

I didn't remember to drop his hand until we were halfway down the stairs.

***

The next morning dawned drizzly, that particularly *wet* kind of weather that makes you wish there were proper raindrops, and not just this cursed autumnal dampness that seeps into your bones. It made me restless, itching to get on with our task but not particularly keen to spend the day out by the pond.

After breakfast, when I really couldn't hold it off anymore, I hovered in the doorway, looking out at the grey squelch of it all. Just as I'd made up my mind to brave it – thanking the District for the standard-issue waterproofing on my boots – Dare appeared at my elbow.

"Still don't like the rain?" he asked.

I rolled my eyes. "I don't think that kind of thing changes as you grow up."

"Good thing I have a new trick, then," he grinned, and stepped out into the drizzle.

"Dare, you don't even have a cloak—" I began, but he... wasn't getting wet? The rain bounced around his shoulders, splashing on something invisible and running off, leaving him perfectly untouched.

"Would you care for an escort?" he asked, holding out a hand to me.

The bubble, or whatever it was, stretched with his movement – not a plain umbrella spell, then – and when I slipped my hand into his, it was dry. I felt a shiver run over my skin as the magic slid over me, and he pulled me out into the open.

"This is marvellous!" I beamed up at him. "How did you do that?"

"I didn't, actually," he said. "Vonda did it for me this morning, but she said she'd show me how later. You... we have to be touching for it to cover you, though. Is that okay?"

I was surprised to find that actually, I didn't care in the slightest. "If it would keep me dry, I'd hold hands with a wyvern," I said.

"Oh, nice to know I rank about the same as a horrifying creature."

I'd squeezed his hand before I realised it. "At least you don't smell of sulphur."

"Such a compliment," he said. "Come on then, monster-tamer."

***

By lunch, we'd identified twenty-three more normal swans, six more swan maidens, and ten more glamoured ducks. I'd uncursed four birds who refused to be separated, revealing the most aged and decrepit humans I'd ever seen, before realising there was yet another layer to their curse; once Dare and I had unpicked *that*, we were left with a quartet of siblings barely out of their teens, who immediately began planning how to save their father from the wicked stepmother who'd transformed them.

We'd also had a very encouraging response to our flyers; people were streaming through the castle gates in varying degrees of pomp and pageantry. One little girl arrived with an armful of sparkling necklaces, only to be swarmed by six swans as soon as she approached the lake. She slipped a necklace over each long neck and disappeared beneath a pile of older brothers.

After that, a king arrived in a huge golden carriage and instantly picked out a large male swan he claimed could make anyone stick to it – I was glad we hadn't got to that one yet – but somehow, he wasn't even the most dramatic entrance. I was particularly impressed by the knight who arrived carrying a small boat on his back, painstakingly selected six of the heftiest swans, and harnessed them up with a set of golden chains to the front of his boat.

Dare was in charge of dealing with these claimants once their swans had been restored, settling them into the guest rooms of the castle until the holding spell could be undone, while I kept records as best I could. This was mostly easy, except for the boat knight; when I asked him his name, he took great offence and tried to flounce away, ordering his swans to soar off with the boat. Unfortunately for him, the spell caught his team at the edge of the castle grounds and all seven of them plus boat came tumbling down to the ground.

I was quite grateful Dare was on hand to sort that one out. I still wasn't sure what I'd done wrong.

It did, unfortunately, leave me dealing with Siegfried, who had taken my recommendation to stick to the shore in his perusal of the swans, and, in his own words, was "getting some very Odette-y vibes" off one particular bird.

"I really think it's her," he insisted through heavy sneezes.

I was entirely certain it wasn't, but I couldn't let him know that. "All right," I said, handing him a handkerchief. "Let's keep her to one side for the festival."

Siegfried teared up, making his sneezes even wetter. "But she'll be so sad and cold in the pond."

I bit my tongue, resisting the urge to point out that swans were literally designed to live in ponds, but his sad eyes bored into mine. I sighed. "Fine. I'll see if it's her."

Unsurprisingly, it wasn't.

But surprisingly, it *was* a transformed young woman, one with long dark hair and rich brown eyes that strongly reminded me of someone. Odette's barmaid disguise, I realised with a start; she couldn't have looked more similar to the face Odette had worn at the inn.

The only reason she didn't notice me staring at her was because she herself was gazing into the watery blue eyes of Prince Siegfried.

"Thank you," said the woman to Siegfried, quite ignoring the fact that he hadn't done anything. "I quite liked the idea of being a swan when that sorceress suggested it, but swimming about all day doesn't half leave your legs sore."

"Well, you can rest now," said Siegfried valiantly, somehow entirely missing the part of her sentence where she'd almost given up our secret. "I'll have them make up our finest room for you, Miss..."

"Oh," giggled the woman. "I'm just Odile. You mean I get to stay in the castle?"

"But of course," he said.

I could practically see his heart beating out of his gaze, and hers wasn't far off. This was... an interesting development.

"I'll need to take your name and details for our records, Odile," I said, but Siegfried waved me off, tucking his jacket around Odile's shoulders to protect her from the rain.

"Let her get warm and dry first," he said, and swept her up into his arms.

I stifled a snort. Well. So much for his supposedly unbreakable bond with Odette. That would make our jobs a lot easier at the Autumn Festival.

As Siegfried carried Odile up to the castle, Vonda came out to the gazebo under her own umbrella spell.

"Oh, hello," I said. "I thought you weren't helping?"

She plonked herself down into the chair next to me and helped herself to my notebook, flipping through the lists of names. "I wasn't, while it was in aid of Siegfried marrying my girlfriend," she said wryly.

"Well, yes, but you could have come down now we're all on the same side," I said. "I just transformed your barmaid, actually."

"Oh, Odile? How did she like her holiday? She's been pestering me to let her try being an animal for ages, so she was very happy to let Odette take her place for a bit if it meant she got to be a swan."

"She said her legs hurt. Then she fell rather spectacularly in love at first sight with Siegfried."

"With *Siggy*?" She looked incredulous.

"Occupational hazard of District Witchery," I shrugged. "Something about untangling spells and wrangling mysteries sets people falling in love all around you. It'll be handy if we can use it to convince him to give up his suit before the festival. Speaking of which, where have you been? We've been run off our feet!"

She smiled wickedly. "But you looked like you were having such a nice time, darling."

"I mean, I do like my job?" I shrugged. "It's fun, solving so many curses and things at once."

"Aha!" she cried, jabbing a finger at me, making me jump.

"What? I'm not allowed to have fun at work?"

"Oh, don't be obtuse, darling. Two days ago you were all 'oh no, I can't work with Dare, don't make me work with Dare, I wouldn't work with Dare if he was the last person left in the District' – today you haven't even complained once! You just admitted it, you've had a nice day. Working with Dare."

Oh, bloody hell. She was right, actually. I hadn't spent any of today thinking about memories or awkwardness or how horrible this whole situation was. I'd just been working – working well with Dare, like we always used to. It was comfortable, moving the pieces of a case around beside him, trusting him to have my back, chatting and joking and getting things done. He'd had a pencil ready the moment I snapped mine, annoyed at some stupid hold up; I'd surprised him mid-morning with the ginger biscuits I always kept in my satchel (not mentioning that I'd never dropped the habit of carrying them after many years of dealing with his pre-lunch peckishness). We'd slipped back into old habits as if there hadn't even been a break of ten days, let alone ten years. And I *had* had a nice day.

Vonda waved her finger at me again, circling around my face.

"You see? I say again, *aha.*"

I sighed. "We always were a good team, Von. That part was never the problem."

"Yes, I know, it's all his fault," she said. "The thing is, darling, what happened to the two of you ten years ago was rotten, but it might not be a grudge you need to hold forever. Not if you want to be happy. You have a chance to work out your feelings, now the two of you are in one place."

"What's brought this on? Why are *you* suddenly his number one fan?"

"Oh, this and that," she said vaguely. "I'd best be getting back to my work." She rose and started to walk off, but stopped, turning back to me with a small smile. "He's surprisingly decent, you know. I've tried very hard to hate him for you, darling, but I can't."

I waited until she was halfway back to the castle before I whispered to myself, "I can't, either."

***

By the morning of the festival, we had just twelve swans left. It had been frustrating to stop so close to the end of the flock, but by sunset the day before, both Dare and I had been physically and magically spent. We'd each argued the other needed to take a break, and then we'd come to the conclusion that probably, we were both right. The festival wasn't until midday. We had time.

The pond looked almost serene; a heron ploshed through the water on the far shore as if to reclaim its territory. The rain had eased off in the night, leaving everything basking in a cold grey glow, as if summer was making its final farewell. It was beautiful.

It was also, unfortunately, shortly before sunrise.

"This way," I yawned, motioning the girl to follow me through the castle's back door.

She'd arrived in a panic, thumping on the door with an

enormous brown sack over one shoulder, red welts lacing her forearms. The night porter had taken one look at her and brought her to me; I'd taken one look at her and brought her to Dare. Now the three of us were trailing sleepily (on our part) and frantically (on hers) down to the pond.

She didn't reply. She hadn't replied to anything we'd said, just shaken her head with her lips flattened into a line before thrusting one of Dare's flyers at us. From that, we figured she probably wanted to look at the swans.

As we neared our gazebo by the shore, the swans came sailing over to us, a silvery-white phalanx so calm even Dare couldn't object to them.

"Wow," I breathed, as each of the swans stepped gracefully out of the water and made their way to surround the girl on the bank. She kissed each of their heads in turn, then burst into silent tears.

One of the swans pulled at the ties of her sack; another wiggled its head inside and began pulling out...

"Shirts?" asked Dare incredulously.

The girl's head snapped up, and she nodded furiously, grabbing the closest swan and starting to push the green garment over its head. She waved us over and thrust a shirt at each of us.

"Ouch," I said. The fabric was prickly, and now I looked at it closely, very poorly knitted, with great gapping stitches and lopsided hems. My hands started to itch. What was this *made* of?

The girl shoved me towards a swan and, getting her meaning, I tentatively held out the shirt. The bird ducked its head, as politely as any courtier, and I slipped the collar down over the long white neck. It hissed, quietly, and helped me wrestle its wings into the sleeves.

When I turned back to look at the girl, she made an urgent "continue" motion and pointed at the horizon, where a pastel glow was beginning to creep across the sky.

"Dare, I think we need to get the shirts on all twelve swans by sunrise," I said, smiling when the girl nodded again.

"I'd gathered," he said, eyeing his nearest neighbour.

"Oh." Of course. His hesitation wasn't because he hadn't understood; it was that old fear again, the thought of wings rooting him to the spot.

I leapt into action. "Okay, you pass me shirts and I'll get them on swans," I said, grabbing the itchy bundle he held. "Bloody hell, what even *is* this fabric?"

"Nettle, I think."

"Who would make shirts out of nettles?" I cried, shoving it over a swan and holding out my hand for another garment.

"Someone under a curse," he said, and the girl nodded. "And if you made a noise while working them, it's all ruined?"

More nodding.

She enshirted her fourth swan; I managed my third shortly after.

"Of course," I said. "This whole thing is a curse."

Four swans. There was a rhythm to this. Head, neck, wings. Five. Six. I punched the air as I got the final wing through and turned to check on the girl's progress. She had five swans covered, and was staring in horror at the sixth. It was wearing a shirt – but one wing was still halfway bare, a loose thread trailing down against the white feathers. The girl raked her hands over her face, aghast. She looked ready to scream.

Dare and I hit her with silencing spells at almost exactly the same time.

"Oh no," I said. "I think if it isn't covering its wing, it won't work."

"We don't have time to knit!" said Dare.

He couldn't anyway. My sister Sara had tried to teach him at the same time as she'd taught me, and he'd never taken to it.

Thinking of Sara and her impeccable knitting skills gave me an idea. "Wait!" I ran to the sleeveless swan and, dislodging the girl, pulled the shirt back over its head. Then I legged it to the water and dove in. "Knitting stretches if you get it wet," I spluttered back to Dare. "Tell her not to worry."

In the water, I tugged and tugged at the half-sleeve until it gave, stretching and pulling and measuring against my own arm until I had a decent length. The enormous stitches worked in my favour; it might have had more of a fishnet look by the time I was finished with it, but it would cover the whole wing.

"Pen!" yelled Dare. "The sun's coming up!"

It was. The tiniest sliver of light was just appearing at the horizon. There wasn't going to be time to climb out, run back, and wrestle this onto the swan.

"Dare," I called. "Catch!" I flicked the sopping shirt into the air and cast a spell to send it flying towards him. In any other situation I would have found the resulting *splat* hilarious.

He ran, thrust the soaking bundle towards the girl, and stepped back as she shook it out and tried to get it over the swan's head. I watched in dismay as the wet fabric tangled and caught around its neck, got stuck on its wing.

"Dare," I called again, intending to tell him to dry it with a spell, but he simply held up a hand and said, "On it."

He plunged forwards, well within wing-beating distance, and helped the girl to wrangle the final wing into place. He caught a buffet or two from the swan's flailing wings as it struggled, but didn't falter. My heart soared.

So did the sun.

As it lifted into the sky, implacable and uncaring, the beshirted swans shivered and a great silver fog rose around them. I lost sight of them, the girl, and Dare for a moment, and when the air cleared again, there were no swans to be seen on the bank, only twelve astonishingly handsome men wearing horrible green shirts.

"Talia," the tallest of them said. "Darling sister. You saved us."

The girl nodded, silent tears leaking from her eyes, and then seemed to remember she could speak again. "Yes," she whispered. Her voice was scratchy and hoarse from disuse, but the swan-brothers cheered as if she'd made a full proclamation. They buried her in their embrace, everyone talking at once.

Dare appeared by my side.

"Good job, Dare," I said quietly, still watching the siblings.

He chuckled. "Good job yourself, Penelope."

"Pen," I corrected. "I think you've earned it."

"What we've earned," he said with a smile, "is a rest. Come on, they'll be a while. We might as well sit down." He offered me his arm.

"Sounds perfect," I said, and let him lead me to the gazebo.

When the castle servants came to clear the shore for the festival stage, they found us sleeping hand in hand, propped in the chairs we'd been working in all week.

I couldn't bring myself to care.

***

As Ilya and Peter opened the Autumn Festival, I thanked my lucky stars that my part in the whole thing was nearly done; all I had to do now was get through the inevitable speeches about love and commitment without rolling my eyes too hard. There were seven swans arrayed behind the kings – we'd grabbed six at random from the enclosure of normal swans, and Vonda had snuck Odette into the mix when no one was looking. Dare and I had glamoured all seven of them to look identical – since if we'd learned anything in the last three days, it was that there was a surprising amount of variation in swans – and we'd made sure to do it in front of the kings, so that there could be no suggestion later that anyone had had an advantage. All that needed to happen now was Siegfried's failure, and Vonda's triumph.

Ilya beamed out at the crowd as he finished his speech. "And now, I declare, the festival is open and autumn is here! Let Prince Siegfried approach the stage!"

Dare and I exchanged worried looks as Siegfried strode out to meet the kings; Vonda wrung her hands at the edge of the stage. A lot was riding on Siegfried's choice, and there was still a chance he might choose Odette – a slim chance, given how poorly he'd done at finding Odette so far, but a chance nonetheless.

"Many of you remember thirty years ago, when my dear Peter completed his marriage feat to win my hand," Ilya boomed. "Today, we continue the tradition for our darling Odette. If Prince Siegfried can identify his betrothed even in swan-form, then truly, they must be meant for each other!"

Wild applause rang out and both kings beamed, but Siegfried looked just as concerned as Vonda. He worried at his lip as he strolled up and down the line of swans, pausing to consider each one and sneezing discreetly into a golden handkerchief as each glamour touched him.

He stopped in front of Odette.

My heart flew into my mouth and I grabbed Dare's arm. "We can't let—"

"Knock out spell?" asked Dare out of the side of his mouth.

"A bit dramatic, but we have to do something if he doesn't move on." I slid my hand down his arm so our palms were touching, and felt the power build as we both began the spell.

On stage, Siegfried raked a hand through his hair, sneezed, and said, "I choose..." Another sneeze interrupted him, and another.

Dare and I raised our hands, ready to cast.

"Oh, enough with this," Siegfried groaned, throwing down the handkerchief. "Your Majesties, I apologise, but I'm not going to choose a swan."

Gasps erupted from the crowd; Peter clapped a hand over his mouth.

"I have no sodding idea which one is Odette," continued Siegfried, "and quite frankly, I'm not that concerned about it."

"What do you mean?" Ilya said. "The feat requires—"

"I don't want to marry Odette," said Siegfried, bursting into tears. "I want to marry Odile."

"Who the hell is Odile?" asked Peter, but she was already mounting the stage, and Siegfried swept her into his arms.

"I love her, Your Majesties," said Siegfried, "and I believe she loves me too."

"I do," said Odile.

Peter and Ilya exchanged glances.

"Well," said Ilya. "That puts rather a damper on the whole marriage thing. Siggy, you fool, why didn't you say anything?"

Siegfried sniffed. "You were so excited. I didn't want to disappoint you."

Peter smiled fondly. "As if we'd want either of you to be unhappy. Come, let's talk this through in private." To the audience, he said, "It looks like there will be no marriage feat today. Please, do enjoy the rest of the festival and—"

Vonda stood up. "Excuse me, Your Majesty, but there *will* be a feat today. *I* will find Odette, and with your permission, *I* will claim her hand in marriage." She paused. "We have been partners for two years," she added quietly. "This is not a surprise for her."

The kings stared at her in shock; the audience murmured

before breaking into cheers and applause. Vonda stood firm, hands on her hips, eyes fixed on Odette's fathers, but I knew her well enough to know she'd be quivering inside. Let them say yes, let them say yes—

Ilya and Peter murmured to each other for a moment while the crowd whooped, and then Ilya held up a hand, silencing them. "You believe this will make our daughter happy?" he asked Vonda.

"More than anything in the world," said Vonda, with her heart in her voice.

"Very well," he said, smiling softly, and Vonda's tension dissipated, her chin coming up and her eyes shining. "Our daughter is an excellent judge of character."

I felt that same sense of sheer relief drop through me like the swoop of a broomstick as Dare squeezed my hand. "This is it."

Vonda wasted no time dithering over the other swans as Siegfried had, but marched straight to Odette and laid her hand on the soft white head. "This is my beloved," she said, and cancelled the spell.

Between one blink and the next, the swan's white form disappeared and, with no sparks, no fog, no drama, Odette stepped into her lover's arms and dipped Vonda in a deep, passionate kiss.

"Well," said Ilya. "Who can argue with that?"

The crowd burst into hollers and cheers, and I couldn't help but join them, shouting my happiness into the general din. Dare scooped me into a hug and I suddenly realised that this – this moment when everything clicked, this joy of a job well done together – was back, where it had been missing from so many cases before. There was no time to examine it, though, as we were swept along into the celebrations. Ilya and Peter were embracing Odette and Vonda was beaming and someone had struck up a tune and we were dancing, all of us, euphoric at the sight of true love.

***

Some time later, once we'd danced till our feet ached and grinned till our cheeks hurt, I found myself sitting beside a bonfire with Dare, drinks in hand, orange leaves woven through our hair, as the first true sun of autumn dipped below the treeline. Vonda and Odette sat across the fire from us, lost in their own world.

I nudged him with my elbow to look at them. "We didn't do a bad job this time, did we?"

"Probably one of our best," he said, then swallowed, hard. "But Pen, I don't think—"

"Don't," I said, putting a finger over his lips. "Don't spoil it. I'm happy right now. This is the first time I've enjoyed an autumn equinox in ten years."

"You don't even know what I was going to say," he complained.

I tried very hard to keep my voice steady as I said, "I've heard you say it every night in my head for ten years: 'Pen, I don't think we should be partners anymore.' Believe me, it's burned into my brain. Let me enjoy tonight and you can ditch me again in the morning."

He chuckled, softly. "Actually, I was going to say that I don't think I want to do this without you anymore."

I stared at him. "What?"

"Look, I'm not going to say that I was wrong. I was wrong to disappear in the night, yes – that was pure idiocy, and I'm sorry – but us being apart? We have no way of knowing that, of knowing if we would have made it, but what we do know is that we're here tonight, and we're an even better team now than we were at twenty-one, and I've never felt so happy. So I wasn't wrong, but I wasn't right either."

"That's the most infuriating way you could have put it."

"But right now I don't really care if I was right or not, Pen. Either way I missed out on ten years of knowing you, of waking up with you, of loving you – and don't look at me like that, because I never *stopped* loving you, I just sort of shoved it into the background so it stopped hurting so much."

Well, that was the most romantic thing I'd ever heard anyone say. "Me too," I whispered.

"And now we have something we would never have had otherwise," he smiled. "Now we get to know each other all over again. The Penelope standing in front of me is *incredible,* you know. So much better than the Pen who dumped me ten years ago. You're an amazing witch and a wonderful woman and what I'm saying, Pen, is that the more I talk the more I'm trying to convince myself that there was some point to all those days and nights without you, because right now I'm so thought-consumingly in love with you, every piece of me is screaming at me to grab you and never let you go again."

Oh. No. *That* was the most romantic thing I'd ever heard anyone say.

"Okay," I said. "Prove it."

His kiss had the force of a lost decade behind it, and I met him memory for memory, joy for joy, heart for heart.

A triumphant whoop rang out from across the fire, and I stuck two fingers up at Vonda without opening my eyes or breaking the kiss, prompting a burst of laughter in its place. I wasn't going to let anything interrupt this feeling, this wholeheartedly, wonderfully *right* feeling.

"You know what this means?" I asked, when we finally came up for air.

"What?" His eyes were shining in the flickering firelight, his hair was mussed, and his breath was coming fast. I'd never seen anyone more beautiful.

I grinned. "You *were* wrong."

He rolled his eyes, but there was a fondness in it. "Does it matter anymore?"

"No," I said, winding my arms around the man I'd fallen in love with all over again, letting the memories of that autumn long ago drift away with the sparks from the fire. "No, it doesn't."

Adie Hart is a lover of stories and the words behind them. With a background in the history and literature of the Ancient World, and an abiding love of classic fairy tales, she writes fun and fluffy queer-norm fantasy rom-coms, many of them set in her District Witch world.

When she's not writing, she can usually be found reading, knitting, or trapped under her large cat! Check out her website at https://adiehart.wordpress.com.

Shadows of the Fall

R. A. Gerritse

No sky above, no ground below – the dancing flame remained his sole reality. *Perhaps I never should have lit that cursed thing,* Caleb thought, but banished that notion as quickly as it popped into his head. *You know why you're here,* he admonished himself reflexively and hated himself for it. As if he needed any reminder. As if he could forget. As if he wasn't knee-deep in shit and dead-center in chaos, hanging by his fingertips, struggling to climb out of the darkest recesses of his past, determined not to let go of *her.*

Physically, he knew himself to be sitting comfortably in the rocker on the porch of his cabin in Jackson, Wyoming. At least, he assumed he still was – comfortable, that is, but what did he know? If he were being honest with himself, Caleb had no idea how much time had passed this time, locked away in this realm of nightmares. The thought sent a shiver down his spine. Robbed of most of his senses and desperately lost in what had undoubtedly been *his* initiative, time seemed fleeting.

When he began this painful journey, he promised himself that he could stop at any time, but what a self-delusion that had been. As if, as if... Along the way, Caleb had gathered too many of those to turn back now.

I should be cold, shouldn't I? He didn't know if it was a side effect of the storm lantern's magic or if he'd descended too far into the damned thing's labyrinth of shadows. All he knew was that he no longer felt the bite of the autumn winds pierce his quilted flannel – at least, not during these little intermissions between his dives, back in the lantern's vestibule. Still, a small, stubbornly repressed voice kept nagging at him that he should probably have lit the lantern indoors, safe from the unseasonably cold October weather, comfortably on the couch by the hearth, fire hazards be damned. *Or, you could have waited for clearer skies, you impatient dumbass.* Could have, should have, wouldn't have worked – not with these stakes, he'd already wasted too much time on doubts and regrets.

This damned lantern... why had he even ended up with it, who had sent it? He never had find out. The thing just stood on his porch one day – no box or any other kind of wrapping, with only a typed little card attached to it. "May it return you the spark of joy you've lost," it had said. *Well, all it's brought me so far is more pain. Thank you so much. Couldn't you just have left me to my grief?*

Caleb mentally grunted as he strained to keep blocking out the flame. He had to, or all the darkness he had willingly endured would have been for naught. Not that there came any damned instructions with the lantern, but he just *knew*, so he fought. It was excruciating, inhumanly taxing. Through the cracks in his volition, the light seemed to scream at him, beg him to take notice, embrace and let go, and take the easy road, the intended road, the way of light. He was still unable – no, unwilling – to submit to its desperate calls for reason. *I'm not done here yet, you bastard. Not until I've got what I came for or have died trying.* His world held no value without *her.*

Still, while willing to sacrifice everything, he felt that seemingly inevitable moment of defeated submission creeping closer, like the icy breath of a hellhound sending chills down his spine in anticipation of the inevitable strike. Or was that just the autumn wind punishing his recklessness? Either way, time was running precariously low – he could already see most of his bridges burning or long since in ashes.

Gathering his quickly dwindling strength of will from amidst the frayed ends of his shattered nerves, grabbing hold of one of the few remaining shadows from the edges of the ever brighter burning flame, Caleb closed his mind's eye and *pulled*.

Once more into the breach. I'll never let you go. I'm coming, Tabby. I am coming.

* * *

Veiled in the barest ghost of a cloud cover, the muted sun stood in the ashen blue September sky as if softened with a pencil eraser. Caleb eyed the sky with a building sense of dread. He thought he'd noticed it on his last few descents into the lantern's shadows, but there was no mistaking it now. The sun was dimming, and something told him that could only mean one thing - his time had almost run out.

A cold wind struck Caleb, rustling his messy, too-long hair as he turned away from the sun, blinking, his eyes still adjusting to the light, trying to find his bearings. How many jumps had he made to this day, this town, this cursed moment in time? He had lost count, but for some reason, he never quite landed on the same spot or at the same moment of that fateful autumn day, almost ten years gone. But here that day was again, as vivid and alive as the first time he lived it. *After nearly a week of reliving this damned day through the lantern, I still don't understand how I could possibly be reliving it in places where I was not at the time,* he thought but shook it off. The mechanics of the lantern's time magic were a complete mystery to him and probably always would remain as such. Sure, Caleb had passed through this small Idaho mountain town en route to Tabatha's sister's wedding, but until the accident, he'd never set foot here. It felt so strange that now the town and the lives of its residents seemed all too familiar to him and held almost no more mysteries. *But since I am here once again, there must still be some.*

Without needing to look at the clock tower, he knew the time of day down to the minute, for across the street, he could see the widow Johnson loading the last of her groceries into her rusted Chevrolet Belair. As always, when seeing her while reliving this day, Caleb had to swallow. In seven mere hours, she would pass him and Tabby in the opposite direction to pick up the cornflakes she forgot, making her the last person to see them before they crashed their car through the guard rail. She had been the subject of the first dozen or so shadows Caleb had grabbed in his search through the past for better futures, but if there were any, none of those started with Em. Any meddling in her timeline had only resulted in different, still horrific, equally fatal endings, where she usually ended up simply not being a witness to their fall into the ravine on the outskirts of town. Still, Caleb never stopped wondering.

With a sigh, he pulled up his collar, put his hands in the pockets of his long coat, and stepped onto the sidewalk, knowing that a delivery van was about to rush around the corner where he stood. And right on cue, Billy Corben came racing onto Main Street with his windows down, blasting his AC/DC songs at an inconsiderate level. At least, that was what Caleb expected. The music drifting from the van was not the song "Hell's Bells," the track that should have been playing, nor was it any of the other two dozen rock anthems Billy always had on repeat. No, there were melodies. Violins, brass instruments... There were choir sounds and an orchestra – it sounded nearly angelic.

Before Caleb could focus on the music's details, Billy had already floored the gas pedal of his yellow Buick van and raced out of earshot towards Maple Drive, the next stop on his delivery route.

Caleb stood nailed to the sidewalk. What was that song? Something very familiar tickled his memories but remained just out of grasp. "Billy does not listen to classical..." he muttered.

This had never happened on his previous runs – it was not *meant* to happen. Things never changed. A foreboding chill ran down his spine as he unsuccessfully tried to shake off his shock. After so many runs that started out as nothing but scripted and predictable – at least, until Caleb acted to change things – he felt his presumed control suddenly slipping and did not like it one bit.

Uneasy and jumping at shadows, even the overly familiar ones, he forced himself into motion until he reached the corner of Third Street, where he stopped to first peek around the corner, his eyes nervously scanning both sides of the busy street for anything out of the ordinary.

Caleb's nerves calmed somewhat when everything on Third seemed to be as he remembered it. The three housewives were happily gossiping at the Paris Café, as usual, over a spiked fancy coffee drink. He had learned that fun but useless bit of trivia on a previous disappointing run after tasting one of the drinks, grabbing it from the hands of one shocked Margreth Johnson. He smiled at the memory, scolded himself for being paranoid, and rounded the corner, greeting the ladies in passing.

The dog sat in front of the butcher's window, the city worker was collecting dead leaves from the little park across the street, and the asshole cyclists were still blocking traffic, riding three abreast towards Main Street – all as expected, all on cue. It was the usual serene eve of Tabby's apocalypse, as it should be, with all players in their normal positions.

Back to business, Caleb. Find your shadow. He knew the thread he'd pulled from the lantern must be somewhere.

Over at Mr. Harrods' tobacco shop, the owner's wife, Melany, was already busy dressing the store up for Halloween, happily humming a song while decorating pumpkins and skeletons with plastic cigars even though there was still over a month to go until the holiday. Even the wooden statue of a Native American smoking a peace pipe hadn't escaped the Halloween treatment - it looked like Count Dracula, had the vampire been from the Wild West instead of Transylvania.

Morning, Mrs. Harrods, Caleb thought to himself as he passed her, then stopped dead in his tracks and felt the blood rush from his face. He turned around and watched her for a long moment in disbelief as she finished decorating a trio of gangster pumpkins and listened. She was humming the same melody as had been playing in Billy's car! Caleb felt like he was losing it. What was up with this song? Where had it suddenly come from, and why the hell did it feel so familiar?

He couldn't control himself anymore, so he grabbed the older woman by the shoulder and swung her around. "That song," he almost yelled at her. "What is that song? Where did you hear it, and why are you singing it?" Caleb immediately let go of her when he saw the shocked expression on her face as she clutched a handful of the fake plastic cigars to her chest. He had nearly given her a heart attack, it seemed.

"S-sorry, s-sir? What's that?" she stammered with a trembling lower lip, immediately making him regret his impulsiveness.

Caleb, as a rule, did not interfere with town life – not unless he had a targeted plan to change the outcome of something that might help him save Tabatha, or if he found himself on a particularly bad run, or if he failed at what he set out to do, or if his mood turned sour. Looking the visibly shaken Mrs. Harrods in the eyes, he realized that finding exceptions to the rule had become the status quo during the last few dozen runs, and he shivered.

Get yourself together, Caleb. What the hell are you doing, man? he thought as he raised his hands and gave Melany an apologetic smile. "I'm so sorry, ma'am, I never meant to frighten you. I am just having a horrible day." *On repeat,* he mentally added. "That song you were humming just now sounds so eerily familiar, but I cannot seem to place it. Could you tell me what tune it is?"

Melany carefully emptied her hands and straightened her

dress, never taking her eyes off him. Caleb could almost see the mental gears inside her head turn, trying to determine whether to trust him – which made perfect sense. He must have come across as a madman.

"Well," she finally snapped at him after taking a deep breath, "I guess you're not much of a fan of Halloween, are you?" Her tone and expression told Caleb that she seriously suspected him of pulling some practical joke on her, which puzzled him.

"Halloween? Eh, no, not particularly, ma'am, but what does classical music have to do with the, ehm, spooky season?" Caleb gestured at the growing forest of decorations around the store.

Again, there was no answer but silence and that suspecting look. "You could call 'The Monster Mash' a classic, I guess," she said before carefully taking a few backward steps away from him. "I suggest you look it up on those inter-webs, sir; it's a great song. But do pardon me – I need to get back to work. Have a nice day." And with that, she hurried back into the store and almost slammed the door behind her, leaving a flabbergasted Caleb behind.

The Monster Mash? That was not the Monster Mash. The memory of the melody she was *supposed* to have been humming clicked in place. Caleb had heard a few notes from her before but had never taken much notice of what song she'd been humming. *What the hell is happening with that cursed classical melody? Why is it suddenly everywhere?*

And just like that, his panic was back – in overdrive – and he ran from the store toward Market Street, crossing the street without checking his surroundings. There sounded a horn and a set of screeching tires, and then Caleb's world spun. The fading sun was the last thing he saw before white pain and utter darkness claimed him.

* * *

Caleb awoke in a bed in an almost freezing, dimly lit space and instinctively pulled up his blankets while his foggy mind tried to figure out where he was or what had happened. It was quiet except for the echoes of several sets of steady beeps coming from the machine next to him and those next to the other beds in the large room – each bed occupied, judging by shapes and shadows.

Am I in a hospital? No, Tabby, the shadow! I need to save her! How long have I...

"Welcome back, Caleb," a calm, soothing voice said somewhere on his left, just out of sight, interrupting his reigniting panic before falling silent again.

Holding his breath, Caleb waited several heartbeats for more, but nothing came. He tried looking behind him to see who had spoken, but a flash of pain made clear that he probably should not make sudden movements or turn his head too far. "W-who's there?" he finally croaked, his throat dry and sore. "Who are you, and how do you know my name? Sh-show yourself."

"I cannot, Caleb," the voice answered. "We are already breaking far too many rules as it is. But then again, we have never met anyone as determined to break the rules as you, either."

"You are not a doctor, are you?" Caleb said after what felt like minutes of silence.

"You know I am not."

"You are of the flame, then?"

More silence followed – lots more, to the point Caleb began drifting off to the rhythmic sounds of the heart monitors, shivering under his blankets. He almost became convinced he'd gotten lost in a hellish dream until a hovering light started glowing and growing and growing at the foot of his hospital bed. When it reached roughly the size of a pumpkin, its hue changed to a burnt orange, and a small human figure became visible at its center, sitting on the polished iron bars of Caleb's bed frame, its waving and flickering hair almost the embodiment of a flame.

"What's a few more broken rules, so close to the end?" the figure said solemnly. The wavering light radiating from his fiery appearance was reflected in the frame's metal, bathing the whole room in moving ember shadows. "You may call me Tres."

Caleb stared at Tres in wonder, lost for words. Just for a moment, his panic, his pain, his troubles were forgotten – he had never seen anything as magical as this radiant little person smiling down at him, and it drowned out the world. "You are the voice of the storm lantern," he whispered in complete awe.

"I am," Tres said. "And why did you not listen?" He shook his little head, sending a fresh batch of shadows over the ceiling. "Never mind that, though. It's too late for that, anyway. But I must admit that I am curious. What did you think the lantern was for?"

"Too late?" Caleb asked. "Too late for what?" Saying it out loud brought back all the details of his last run with the lantern's shadows. His eyes drifted to the curtained windows to his right, where no light shone through the cracks. "It is night? But... Tabby!"

Tres looked at him with so much sadness. "It's been five days since your accident, Caleb. You have been in a coma. Like all these poor souls around you are. That last shadow you pulled... involved you."

Five days? Five... days... That means... Caleb started crying, the tears cold on his skin. "She still died, didn't she?" he sobbed. "I failed again. But how am I still here?"

"Before I answer that, please enlighten me and try to respond to my earlier question. What did you think the lantern does?" Tres crossed his little legs and leaned forward, resting his head on his palm.

"It... changes things for you," was all Caleb could think of between his now-uncontrollable sobs, and he closed his eyes. He cried for what felt like an hour, until he felt nothing more than emptiness. When he finally opened his eyes, Tres still sat there, looking at him.

"You clutched at the shadows, thinking you could change your past," Tres said, "but dear Caleb, in life, you cannot change what has already been written. Could you really not see that after your first few failed attempts?"

Caleb stared at the lit figure and just nodded. He knew. He'd always known, but Tabby had been his everything. "What good is the damned lantern then, when it cannot give me what I desire most?"

Tres sighed and straightened. "This is not a fairy tale lantern. We are not genies – we are Sparks. We have been the watchers and the keepers of seasons, guardians of life in all its shades of dream for as long as there's been light, but even we cannot change what has been. No, any changes to the past will always self-correct. That was never the lantern's purpose."

More tears welled up, but Caleb tried to hold them down. "What was its purpose then?"

"Possibility, dear Caleb. It is in the lantern's name, isn't it? The Lantern of Possibility. You went for its shadows, the things that might have been, but the flame was placed in your path to light the many possible branches of your destiny and help you choose the one most desired. You had so many to choose from."

The sadness in those last words hit Caleb hard. Had, as in, past tense. He could feel the cold numbing him and knew he had reached the last of his runs. He'd failed to save her.

"The music you heard could have been your composition, Caleb. There is so much creativity in your soul, and you had so much to offer the world, so much promise. As I said, we are breaking all the rules here, but no one deserves to go into the After without at least knowing what beauty they're leaving behind. It is a shame you never got to share it."

Behind Tres, countless other colored lights emerged and

began to grow, each holding another little figure, each with a sad but somehow grateful smile.

"You taught us so much. Thank you," Tres said. "I wish we could have given you more, but I am afraid your possibilities have dwindled to a single remaining light. You must have seen the dimming sun. Deep down, you must have known what powers the lamp. You must have felt the cold, the storm out there in reality – the storm you created to bring you here to this lost moment in time."

Caleb let go of his last tears and just nodded. Of course, he had known. He had felt it and had rebelled against it. "But how am I still here if she's gone?"

In answer, a few other lights behind Tres hovered over one of the beds across from Caleb, lighting the features of its occupant. Though badly bruised and bandaged, with what seemed a severe head injury, he immediately recognized her, and his heart froze – Tabatha.
"She's still here, at least in body, but not for long. We wanted to give you a last chance to say goodbye before you return to face your last sunset. I know it's not much, but we have tried, Caleb. We tried so hard. I am so sorry that, despite everything, we still failed you. It breaks my heart."

With those words, Tres and all the other Sparks shrank back into specks of golden light and said no more. All Caleb could do was stare at Tabby – his Tabby – and weep until the golden light blurred with his tears and the hospital faded away.

* * *

At the crack of dawn on October 29th, blind and deaf to most of the world, Caleb sat on his porch before a darkened lantern amidst a brown and yellow cloud of dead leaves dancing across his lap and the broken wooden floors. Around him lay a scene of destruction – the unexpected, unseasonable storm had hit hard, bringing the fall's first frost and taking with it many trees and most of his cabin, but strangely, it hadn't done much beyond the little cabin in the woods outside of Jackson. Caleb saw none of it, nor would he have cared – no sky above, no sky below. With the last few sluggish beats of his wounded heart, Caleb's frozen eyes turned, hopeful, to the golden light of the rising sun, lighting his last way back to the only possibility he ever desired, leaving the world to shadows.

I have been waiting for you.

As a rock journalist for Metal On Loud Magazine, Randy watches the world in search of both rhythms and answers. As an author, host of the Twitter poetry prompt tag #vsspoem, and a lyricist for four different bands, poetry is part of his every day – it even found its way into his novels.

His first self-publication: a collection of micro poetry forged into a single, two act epic poem called The Rhythm of Life, is now available on Amazon.

Randy's first published short stories Rain Must Fall and Days Gone By are now available in the anthologies Of Silver Bells and Chilling Tales and Of Mistletoe And Snow by Jazz House Publications.

The Grim Gallery

Jake Curran-Pipe

Amber had woken to the drizzle that signposted summer's imminent departure. Even the chatty wood pigeons of those gossamer mornings had been shocked into silence.

She and Sandy sat on a fly-tipped sofa in the ginnel between their streets.

"Did you see the shooting star last night?" she asked Sandy as he passed the before-school cigarette to her.

"What? When?" said Sandy.

"It was cool," Amber continued, only half-listening to her best friend. "Kind of purple." She didn't want to reveal she saw it because she was still up at two o'clock staring at the starry cloudless night after reading a folklore anthology for hours. "I only saw it because Jordan woke me up crying again. I swear he does it just to annoy me, the little gremlin."

"Fuming. I didn't see anything on the news, usually they—"

"You watch the news?" snickered Amber, returning the cigarette.

Sandy playfully slapped her on the shoulder. "We're adults

now, innit."

Amber gazed at the cigarette whilst Sandy gave it a final drag. "Surprised I saw anything at all. Everything's grey and now it's gonna get even worse and depressing until the middle of next year. I can't handle it anymore."

The two got up from the sodden sofa and continued the walk to school. It was their last year of high school and the threat of adult life loomed over them like the stormy clouds in the distance.

"Come on, man, there's loads to look forward to," said Sandy. "This is the best part of the year! Hallowe'en, Bonfire Night, Christmas, New Year, *my birthday...* and telly gets good an' all. It's not all that bad. Besides, this time next year, we might have jobs. Might be in college. We need to make the most of it."

Amber exhaled dramatically and looked up at the sky, the fine raindrops coating her eyelashes like morning dew on spiders' webs.

"I guess. But I still can't be arsed with going to school in the dark and then going home in the dark. It's not natural. We should be hibernating. Or living in Spain."

"What's with the Spain obsession you've been on lately?" asked Sandy.

"Just thinking about my cousins. Well jealous they moved out there. Pricks."

"You don't even like them!"

"That's not the point. Their mam and dad grafted so they could move out there—"

"They dealt drugs—"

"—And what do mine do? They just work because they have to. They don't have that entrepreneurial mentality Uncle Tony has. Like I do," she said, tapping an index finger on her temple.

"The universe owes me one, big time."

Sandy rolled his eyes at another one of Amber's monologues about how different she was from her family. She was always up to one plot or another to become loaded and leave the country. They always failed, of course, because being a scheming 16-year-old wasn't as prosperous as it was back in mediaeval times when all you needed was to leave town with a bindle and some magic beans.

"You don't have entrepreneurial spirit either, mate," said Sandy. "You barely lasted a week flogging them crisps in the playground. Did you even make a profit?"

"Yeah, well, the dinner ladies were catching on to me..."

"Aye, OK. Admit it, you're as much a layabout as your mam and dad." He smirked. "You're all bark and no bite."

Amber ground to a halt, her eyes glaring red and her mouth forming into an ugly, almost canine growl.

"D'you want another black eye?" she said, glancing at the one Russ accidentally gave him over the weekend. A shift in energy loitered between them as if the idea of a fight could actually happen. They both felt the sudden alien pang of despisal.

"Sorry, that was mean," sighed Sandy, catching the rising heat flushing in his cheeks. "So what's your next plan for the runaway fund then?"

"Ha, I'm glad you asked." She beamed, clearly entertained and impressed by her latest idea. "I'm gonna rob the harvest festival."

"What?"

"You heard. All them buckets with the tins of soup, toothpaste, corned beef... I'm gonna nick it all and then go round like Big Anita does selling it back to the neighbourhood. It's like shoplifting but without the jobsworth security blokes."

Sandy's eyes harboured a piercing intensity Amber had never

seen before. Her stomach jolted.

"Are you dumb? Big Anita was arrested."

"Well, yeah, so there's a gap in the market, isn't there? You're gonna have to help with the distraction though, it'll be well heavy. All them massive tubs."

Amber and Sandy turned the corner to the school gates toward the playground. What had been a frenetic circuit board of sunkissed delirium yesterday was now a mildewy wet flannel of teenagers realising their final summer as real kids had ended. Sandy lowered his voice.

"Amber, it's for the homeless and the needy. I'm not gonna help you steal that."

Her brow furrowed. "Don't be a big girl about it."

"*You* are a girl," Sandy laughed with a newfound contempt, his lip curled and eyes dead.

"Whatever. C'mon, man, don't be tight. This is how I'm gonna start all my business skills and that. Negotiating prices, meeting customers..." She could see the disinterest all across Sandy's face. "I'll give you a third of the profit, too!"

"Oh, thanks, I've been needing an extra two quid lately."

Sandy tried to pass through the school gates but Amber shot her arm across him, blocking his path.

"Alexander James Tulloch. I thought we were best friends," said Amber, feigning a cheeky smile.

"We are—"

"And best friends stick together no matter what. Best friends support each other's dreams. Best friends—"

"Best friends don't let best friends steal from *charity*," he interrupted, walking past her into the school building, shouldering her on purpose. "We're at a Catholic school! We could go up in flames! I'm not doing it."

"Don't wind me up, Sandy."

"I don't know if you've noticed, *Amber*, but I've been getting good grades this past year and Mrs Mullens said I've got a good chance of getting into the sixth form."

"Pfft... right," snorted Amber.

"I'm being serious. And maybe you should start being serious too," said Sandy as they made their way into the canteen for breakfast club. "Mullens has faith in me. I need to keep my head down this year."

"Have you been talking about me behind that old witch's back? School's a waste of time. You don't learn nothing here. You learn by being out there hustling." *And reading get-rich-quick books you sneak from the library*, she thought, but he didn't need to know that.

"And where has that gotten your family? Dropouts and drug dealers..." he said, his voice attracting the attention of passersby.

Amber's face shifted. Sandy realised that may have been one step too far.

"Look," he mumbled, lowering his voice and softening his frown. "All I'm saying is that for someone so obsessed with getting out of this dump, you need to realise school can help you with that. Not selling stolen crisps round the back of the bike shed."

A torrent of emotion washed over Amber's face as she looked over at the harvest stand tucked away in the corner of the canteen. Her face settled on a scowl.

"You know what, I don't need you. I'll do this myself. You watch."

Sandy sighed and walked over to one of the donation buckets. Plastic autumn leaves festooned the display in flourishes of bright orange. He smiled at the hedgehogs made out of multicoloured wool and cardboard. He unzipped his rucksack and felt the heat of Amber's glare as he placed a packet of ginger biscuits into one of the donation tubs. He turned around to look at her and she quickly shot her gaze to the other side of the room.

"That's your choice," said Sandy. "Maybe try and be a bit more giving. And maybe then you'll receive... or whatever the Bible says. Talk to me when you've grown up."

Sandy caught Russ and Sienna sitting in the corner waving over to him. Notorious shadow boxer Russ had a box of chocolate shoddily wrapped in a bow. Sandy felt the bruise on his left eye and laughed.

Amber seethed as she watched Sandy march past her to the friends he had slowly been hanging out with more over the summer. Not wanting to cause a fuss for once, she scanned the canteen for somewhere else to sit. Her eyes hooked on to a wallflower sat by himself, and thought *Maybe I will be more giving. It's harvest season after all.*

***

The first week back at school had been the longest week of Amber's life. Sandy avoided her gaze every time she tried to catch it. He was in all the top sets for classes and she was left alone in the middle sets with people she hardly knew. Amber was partly glad she wasn't in any of the top sets because it meant she could coast, but she secretly wished she could have at least gotten into top set English Literature. If the school offered Business, she knew she'd have been in that too.

The wallflower she had 'befriended' during the temporary rift she was waiting for Sandy to fix was called Clay Hornsby. He was in the bottom set for everything and could barely muster up an opinion of his own. Everything Amber said he yes-sir'd, no-sir'd, three-bags-full-sir'd right back.

Clay was a great lackey – he distracted the corner shopkeeper on Wednesday whilst Amber grabbed a fistload of chewing gums – but she was already bored of him. All she wanted was Sandy. He had been stolen by Russ and Sienna, and the three of them laughed loudly on purpose in the corner of the canteen whenever Amber and Clay sat in stilted silence.

The first weekend of the autumn term was unusually hot. *An Indian summer,* she had heard a teacher say once. The air clung to everyone like wet clothes and, despite the warmth, it was dismally overcast.

"How come you've not been out with Sandy this weekend?" said Amber's dad at Sunday teatime. She grunted a response and went back into her room once the beans on toast had been devoured.

Amber propped herself up against the headboard and stared out of the open bedroom window in front of her. The sky looked equal parts endlessly vast and suffocatingly tight. There was nothing it could offer her. The ceaseless grey was lifeless in the air. You couldn't even see the sunset. If Amber stared for long enough, the grey would ooze into black, and the wasted weekend would be over.

But she didn't want to gawk at the passing of time. Despite doing nothing all weekend, she was tired. More mentally than physically. She hadn't even thought of the next money-making scheme she was planning to stage after the harvest donation heist was kiboshed. Instead, she leant over to her bedside table and pulled out the folklore anthology from the drawer.

Maybe something in here will inspire me. Or send me to sleep.

Three stories down, and Amber flumped down onto her pillow with a snore.

***

A flash of purple jolted Amber awake. Even though she had her eyes closed she knew it was the middle of the night. There were no groans of cars, no ringing of bicycle bells, no dawn chorus.

Ugh, is it raining?

As Amber's senses came to from the slumber, she felt small droplets dot her face in haphazard rhythms. She opened her eyes and swirls of unnameable colour danced in front of her as they adjusted to the darkness. *I need to shut the window.* Another drop on her face, just below her left eye. She shot up from the bed.

"What the—"

It didn't come from the window. It came from above.

Phosphenes danced ahead as she tried to make out what was dripping. Was there a hole in the roof?

Then, something wet squelched and dragged in the darkness. Amber huddled into the corner of her bed and saw something small slither across the dresser below the window. At first she thought it was the cobra Beanie Baby she used to sleep with every night, but that thing definitely had a life of its own.

She looked down at the book on her lap and saw the pages wet with sluglike slime, the ink seeping from the pages. The paper was mottled with words sliding from their original place, the paper mulchy and glistening, as if the story itself was trying to escape the gruesome slime. She wiped her face, her hands flinching when they touched the snotty matter that coated her skin.

"Ugh!" The slithering mass disappeared out of the window. She got up from the bed and ran over to slam the pane shut. "Daaaaad!" she screamed until the light from the landing flushed through the crack at the bottom of her bedroom door.

***

Sultry September gave way to damp October. Amber had grown slightly fond of Clay Hornsby, despite his constant need for approval, but Sandy still hung out with Russ and Sienna. She hadn't told anyone about the weird thing that happened in her bedroom last month. Well, apart from Clay. He agreed with her parents that it must have been some kind of gastropod infestation. Whatever it was, Amber's stomach still occasionally churned at the memory of the slime on her face. Thank God that random purple flash from outside had woken her up.

The library wasn't best pleased with how she returned the folklore book either. She had only picked it up at random when looking for books on how to start a business. Finance and folklore were next to each other, and she fancied some rags-to-riches inspiration from the likes of Dick Whittington and Cinderella.

She had been feeling some entrepreneurial fatigue since the falling out with Sandy, but now that she owed the library fifty pounds stirling, she was considering bringing back her snack-selling business.

"Fancy helping me make a few quid?" she asked Clay in the playground.

"Yeah, OK," he said, more focused on his yoghurt but still as desperately loyal.

She zhuzhed his curly mop of hair.

"Thanks, cutie."

He smiled a dimpled smile. Despite being the year below, Amber didn't find him as annoying as the rest of them. He was the little brother she always wanted rather than the demon spawn she currently had.

"I don't suppose your parents have a suitcase we can borrow? I'm going to get a lot of stock. As soon as Hallowe'en is over, we're getting them discounted chocolates and flogging them here. Sound good?"

"I'll look in the attic tonight." He smiled. "That's really cool you setting up a business."

"Right? I'm all about giving back to the community," Amber giggled.

"Did you hear what's going on in the junkyard tonight?" Clay asked.

Amber was confused. Clay was never au fait with school gossip.

"Devil's Night, innit. People burn things," he said. "Like a 'fuck you' to the universe."

"Since when?"

Clay shrugged.

"So, what? People are gonna burn abandoned sofas?"

"Scrap heap cars I think. It's tradition."

"Pfft." *Whose tradition?* Amber thought. "Pretty lame they're setting fire to already broken cars. Shouldn't they be torching the Range Rovers on Ringley Road? Count me *out*."

Clay looked disappointed by Amber's lack of enthusiasm. He never wanted to do anything naughty but he always got a thrill from watching others do bad deeds. Like he was always in on the action but could easily play the fool if they got caught.

The school bell rang signalling the parting of Amber and Clay until the end of day. He felt there was one last chance to convince her.

"Well I'm going tonight," he said. "Sandy's going, too."

"I highly doubt that! He's gone all weird and studious now, he wouldn't be caught dead causing mischief," Amber said as she started making her way over to English.

"I heard him say to Sienna in science that he missed you," said Clay.

Amber stopped dead in her tracks, her back to Clay. She opened her mouth to reply but instead coughed and carried on her journey to the classroom.

***

Drizzle from above started to spritz the orange leaves as Amber made her way through the woods. The giggling and unintelligible commotion from her classmates were an easy crumb trail through these unknown trees, only she couldn't see the glow from the supposed arson they were committing.

She debated whether to call out Sandy's name. Clay had said he missed her, but would he really want to acknowledge her with his new-found friends?

The further Amber ventured, the less intertwined the trees became until eventually she came across a patch of dense fog.

"We should leave!"

Sandy's voice came from the abyssal murk.

Amber stepped forward into the clearing, pulling her hood up to shield herself from the drizzle. The ground was wet and dragging; she didn't have the shoes for this.

"Come on, guys, let's leave it. Everyone else is at the junkyard."

His voice was clearer now, amongst the giggles of at least two other voices.

"Sandy?" Amber called out.

The giggling stopped.

"Did you hear that?" said another voice.

Amber struggled her way through the mist to find the direction of the voice.

"It's me! Amber!"

Her heart started to race. She hated not being able to see more than three feet in front of her. Her memory flashed back to when she was trapped in a wardrobe during a game of sardines. The hot, bubbling fear of being closed in.

"Amber?! What are you doing?"

"I can't see anything!"

"Follow my voice!"

"I'm trying, you idiot! What is this place?"

There was a scream. Amber stopped in her tracks.

"Why aren't you at the junkyard?" shouted out Amber, her heart galloping.

Silence.

Something hard and heavy slammed into her shoulder. Amber let out a guttural, primal scream as she shut her eyes in submission. Whatever it was, she was too petrified to escape it. She was going to die a coward.

"We got lost," whispered Sandy in her ear.

Amber opened her eyes and screamed in his face, calling him all sorts of slurs, punching him in the chest for good measure.

"Sorry... 'tis the season of the witch after all! I had to," he smirked.

"Just get me out of this fog, it's creeping me out. I've had a weird month already with slugs invading my room..."

"What?"

"Never mind."

Sandy took Amber's hand and led her out of the other side of the fog where Russ Weir, Sienna Giuntoli and, to Amber's surprise, Clay Hornsby stood together hunched in their coats.

The Sandy gang's all here... thought Amber. But before she could utter a word out loud, her eyes were drawn to the hulking mass behind the trio.

It was a jet-black, gothic manor with a tower protruding from the centre. Straight out of a fairy tale. The drizzle had stopped and the sky had cleared to illuminate this humongous, jagged abode in the autumn moonlight.

"Wh–What is this place?" she said.

"Wise guy over there thought it would be fun to take a detour to the junkyard," moaned Sienna as she shot a glance at Sandy. Amber concealed a smirk; she had always enjoyed

Sienna's sassiness in school. "But instead we got lost. And then we found this..."

"I didn't even know there was anything *like* this round these parts. How come we never had a school trip here?" said history-buff Russ, genuinely upset that the school would obscure such a beautiful building from them.

The five of them turned to face the manor. No sign of life. No lights, no cars, not even an alarm system which was a necessity in this part of Manchester.

This is the kinda place I need to live in, thought Amber.

"What's inside it? Does anyone live there?" she asked.

"We don't know," said Sandy.

"They dared me to go up and knock but—" chirped Clay, who quickly stopped talking when Amber flashed him the evils. She couldn't understand why, but she felt betrayed by his presence here.

"I'll do it," Amber said. "I'll knock."

"N-no," said Russ, "No need, it's well late. They'll be cross if we wake them up."

"It's nearly Hallowe'en, we can just pretend we're trick-or-treaters," she said.

"With what costumes?" muttered Sienna.

"Well I don't see you going up there to knock," said Amber. "What? Thought you'd get Clay to do your dirty work you're too scared to do? You watch!"

Sandy went to say something but couldn't get it out in time before Amber stormed up the path to the oak front door.

Me and Sandy used to play knock-a-door-run all the time, I don't see what the difference is. Just because this place looks like something from Scooby Doo...

Amber stood before the door which was almost three times

the size of her and raised a first to knock.

A glimmer caught the corner of her eye from a nearby window.

She hopped down from the front steps and made her way across the eastern wing of the building to a large ornate window with undrawn velvet curtains. Inside the room was a crystal box containing a bejewelled crown. Amber's eyes lit up with the glint of the expensive gems before her. Her eyes darted across the room to other crystal boxes filled with an assortment of other expensive looking items. This must be some kind of a private collection. No wonder it was hidden away in the woods. Amber couldn't contain her grin and found her reflection in the window looking like a ginger Cheshire Cat. She giggled and sprinted back to the front door, giving it the loudest knock she could muster and waited.

Nothing.

Silence.

Nobody was home.

The universe had finally listened to her prayers.

***

It took at least twenty minutes to convince the other four to break into the manor with her. Amber allured them with the promise of riches. She told Russ that he might make enough money to get him and his family out of the council house they lived in; she told Clay that he could finally buy the games consoles his mum struggled to afford; that Sienna would be able to go on holiday for the first time. Sandy scowled as he watched her manipulate them into crossing the threshold. Scolded his friends for giving in so easily to Amber's temptress spell.

But secretly he too wanted in on those riches. He wanted money to support himself through university. His teacher had told him there was a chance he could succeed if he stopped hanging out with Amber and getting into trouble. But what could one more escapade do? Besides, did anyone even know this place existed?

And with that, Amber had rallied everyone into doing the second most traditional thing on Devil's Night... breaking and entering.

The five found themselves in the vast entrance hall of the manor. Amber had used one of Sienna's kirby grips to jimmy the lock on the front door. A building this old surely had no cameras or alarm system.

"Burglary is a piece of cake," laughed Clay. "This is so cool."

"Hey, don't jinx it," hissed Amber. "OK, I don't think we should turn on any lights. Just in case..."

"I guess I don't need to go to EuroDisney anymore. Got the Haunted Mansion right here," said Sienna.

The dark depths of the manor loomed before them. Amber tried to figure out which door would lead to the gallery she saw through the window. And maybe the place was full of other treasure troves.

"Maybe... maybe I should stand watch," said Sandy. "In case anyone comes, I'll knock on the door to signal."

Amber looked at Sandy picking at his cuticles, the way he always did when riddled with nerves. He never did like the dark. She wanted to take a moment to talk to him, away from everyone else. She wanted to confess how much she had missed him and that he was right: she *was* selfish and arrogant and that she was going to stop being so obsessed with being rich. She wondered what he was thinking about her.

"Sure," she said. "Knock three times if you see anyone."

Before he could reply, Amber ushered the other three further into the entrance hall. The creaks of old wood sent shivers down Russ's spine. They reminded him of hearing undesirable family members coming up the stairs at night.

"OK, so I think we should split up and steal as much as we can just in case," said Amber. "Russ, you go down that hall and Sienna go down the other. Clay, you're going upstairs. If you take your coats off and knot the arms, you can make a kind of basket like this."

She demonstrated, not noticing Clay's eyes dart anxiously up the staircase to the further dark.

"D-do *I* have to go upstairs? Why not you? You're the bravest," he said, his voice cracking in a mix of puberty and worry.

"I'm going to try and find that gallery I saw in the window and that wasn't upstairs," she replied.

"I could go with you," said Sienna.

"No, we need to cover as much ground as possible," said Amber.

"But what if there are larger things that might need two people?" said Russ. "Maybe being in pairs will be safer, too."

Amber shot them both a venomous glare.

"I'm shutting the front door," called Sandy from the other side of the hall. "I'll keep it open a crack to stand watch."

"Make sure to knock if there's any creeps about," said Sienna.

"Right, let's do it," said Amber.

Sienna nodded. Russ grinned but whether it was from nerves or excitement, who knew. Clay remained still and silent.

"Sure you'll be alright?" said Sienna to Clay as she walked past him to her designated corridor. He didn't respond.

"Something wrong?" Amber asked as Russ and Sienna parted from the group.

He gulped.

"Listen, Clay," she continued. "Everyone has to prove

themselves to be my friend. You're still on probation. Do this one thing for me, and I promise you've got a friend for life. Plus everyone at school's going to think you're dead brave if they ever find out about this."

***

Clay found himself at the top of the red-carpeted grand staircase with his knees knocking. If only he hadn't lied to Amber about Sandy saying he missed her, he wouldn't have gotten everyone into this mess. His stomach twisted in a dance of nerves and regret. His constant need for approval getting him in undesirable situations once again. One time in primary school he had taken the blame for one of the popular boy's defecating in a dinnerlady's shoes, purely for the hope of being invited to his laser tag party.

Clay made his way down the corridor in front of him. The almost pitch-darkness started to settle in his eyes and he could make out bureaus and vases and armour lining the seemingly endless hallway. *None of these are going to fit in my coat*, he thought, making his way past a very creepy painting of an earl. Clay stopped before passing it completely to ensure the eyes weren't following him.

A low groan tumbled across the ceiling. It sounded like creaking wood, or when a house would 'settle' in the night, but it also sounded wet. Squelchy.

Come on, hurry up. The quicker you find something, the quicker you get out.

There were two doors either side of him. He tried the handles. Locked. He made his way further down the corridor where the manor was starting to get a bit... smelly. Was Russ sneaking behind him? He had a tendency to fart more than the average human. But Clay didn't want to turn around. He had that same feeling creeping down his back like the one you get when running up the stairs to your bedroom at night. So he furthered down the corridor until it stopped, stubbing his toe on the door in front of him.

"Ow!" he whispered. Afraid of attracting too much attention.

That groan overheard again. What *was* that? He tried the doorknob. *Please work, please work.* He wanted nothing more than to run out of the manor and never look back, but he had to prove to Amber that he was brave.

It opened.

Thank God. Hopefully there's something Amber likes in here.

Clay stepped across the threshold and flinched at the sensation. He had stood on something soft. A large window at the back of the room washed the space in moonlight. The whole place was filled with sacks of wool with some of it spilling on to the floor.

And in the corner of the room the moonbeams sparkled on a large bronze structure Clay had only ever seen in fairy tales.

A spinning wheel.

Curious, he moved closer to it, careful not to lose his footing on the sleepy wool underfoot.

"Now, *you* look expensive," he whispered to himself as he gently touched the wheel. He glanced down at the sacks of wool and saw black printed words that made his eyes light up.

"Cashmere," he said.

His mum had always wanted a cashmere jumper. So surely that means it's expensive? Maybe he could save her some and she could make that jumper she had always wanted.

The room shuddered with that now all-too-familiar groan of the manor. This time it was louder and definitely wetter. Clay's heart began to rattle in his chest, the sound sending shivers right through him.

He turned to quickly grab a sack of cashmere but the grip on his shoes slid over the silken wool. He screeched as his balance gave way and knees buckled under him; he reached out to secure his balance but instead of the firm grip of the spinning wheel, he felt a sharp prick pierce his palm and tumbled to the ground. The pain raced through his body, his veins were aflame, the small black dot from where the spindle had jabbed him slowly oozing black. All Clay could do was lie amongst the cashmere in the moonlight as his body burnt and convulsed, twisting and choking him. He tried calling out for his mother, but he couldn't make a sound.

***

Amber hated old buildings. The smell of mothballs and mildew made her skin feel unclean. She wanted to be in and out as quickly as possible, and hopefully the other three were as efficient as she would be.

She followed her mental map along the eastern side of the house. The long corridor with windows on one side, exposing her to any watchers from the forest, and the oil paintings of historic faces she couldn't really make out on the other. They could probably give her clues as to who owned the manor but she didn't care in the slightest. She didn't want to know who she was stealing from.

A thud from upstairs.

She froze.

Was it one of the gang or something else in the house? She waited for a follow-up sound... nothing.

A golden door stood ahead, illuminated in the moonlight. *Bingo.*

Amber rushed to the door but found herself stopping dead in her tracks before turning the knob. It was another sound. But this time it wasn't a thud. It was a pounding.

Tap tap. Tap tap. Tap tap.

It felt like it was coming from above, from the sides and from below. It was everywhere and nowhere. The rhythm made her legs stiff and throbbing like she had just been electrocuted. She grabbed the doorknob and burst into the gallery, slamming the door behind her. The pulsing had stopped but now her heart was racing at the sight before her.

She looked up to the sky.

"Thank you, universe!" said Amber with glee as she faced the gallery with its crystal boxes of expensive looking items. She threw her coat into the centre of the room, just to check if there were any lasers, and then proceeded to take in a good look of all the artefacts. She had to choose wisely.

In one box there was a porcelain hand with an abundance of rings on every finger. Into the coat-bag they went. In another box there was – Amber presumed – to be one of those Fabergé eggs, or at least something like it. Whatever it was, it looked priceless and, thus, went straight into her coat-bag.

Amber then started to look at some of the larger items, their twinkling ornateness all competing for her attention. A glass casket with a golden frame was tucked away in the corner of the room like a sarcophagus with Germanic patterns engraved in the gilded base. Another crystal box this time with platinum statuettes of a mouse, a bird and, for some reason, a sausage. Something about them sparked an ember of familiarity that she couldn't quite place. It wasn't until she saw the large glass cabinet placed between the two windows that something started to feel peculiar.

KNOCK

KNOCK

KNOCK

"Shit," Amber muttered. She looked down at her coat of stolen treasure. She wasn't giving them up that easily. Sandy would have to wait.

She placed the loot gently on to the floor and ran over to the window, fingers groping the frame to find some kind of latch.

KNOCK

KNOCK

KNOCK

"We get it!" she hissed as she frantically tried to open the window. Still nothing – was the building so old that it had been built before sash windows were invented?

Her heart hammering her chest, she didn't even stop to think about her next action: she shoved her elbow through the glass. The pane shattered but before she could worry about health and safety, Amber grabbed her swag bag and launched it out of the window into the bushes below. She looked over the cabinet next to the drapes and touched the piece that was displayed inside. She debated for a millisecond... *No, a red coat wouldn't suit me.*

Amber put one foot on the window sill, ready to jump into the darkness and leave her friends to get in trouble but before she could, the most ear splitting scream vibrated through the manor.

***

"Sienna!" Amber could hear Russ shouting from somewhere in the manor. She barreled down the corridor and back into the entrance hall hoping to find Sandy but he was nowhere to be found. *Why had he knocked on the door?*

"Russ!" Amber shouted back. "Russ, where are you?!"

She heard him scream.

She hurtled down the western hallway, noticing a weird trail of mud leading toward the back of the manor.

"Russ, what's happening?"

"Get help!"

Amber ran so quickly her body was searing in pain. If something were to go wrong, she could get in serious trouble. She should have run when she had the chance, and escaped the town forever, but a part of her had thought it was Sandy in danger. She wouldn't be able to cope if anything happened to him.

She saw Russ's large frame silhouetted against the corridor, moonlight from an open door spilled out on to him. She could hear a contorted, high-pitched scream coming from within that sounded like a pig getting slaughtered. Russ dropped to his knees at the threshold. A gasp lodged in Amber's throat as she reached the door and saw what Russ was reaching out to below. And where the screams were coming from.

On the edge of the room Amber could see hinges along the skirting board; the first half of the room was a humongous trapdoor. Nestled between the two glowing windows was a plinth. Perched on top was a luxurious, deep-red cushion gilded with golden frays, and on it twinkled a single glass slipper. Amber could feel her eyes being hypnotised by the shoe's diamond allure that projected caustic shimmers in the vacuous room. Sienna's screams jolted her from her mesmeric stare.

"We need a rope or something," said Russ, stumbling over his words from fright.

Amber peered down into the trapdoor and saw something that made vomit rise to her throat. She gulped it down, she tried to step back from the frame, not wanting to see the grisly results of her own greed. But her body was frozen. She couldn't turn away.

Down in the depths of the trapdoor's floor, Sienna was laying on her back; her limbs awkward and angular. Jagged spikes of thick glass stained with blood jutted from her shoulder, her stomach, her thigh. The kaleidoscopic pit was slowly oozing into deeper and darker red. Blood poured from Sienna's mouth as her screams got more gargled.

"SIENNA! SOMEONE HELP!" begged Russ, his body dangling precariously from the ledge desperate to reach his friend. "She's going to die!"

Amber couldn't move, her eyes felt like they were bulging

from their sockets. She couldn't blink. Her eyes were hooked into Sienna's, her already pale face racing to sickly shades of grey.

A stench of bad breath.

A squelch, a grumble and a deep groan shook the corridor.

"I'll get some rope, if you're not going to help," said Russ; Amber could barely hear what he was saying over the din. "We need to pull her out."

Her vision stuttered, was fizzy like when she would stand up too quickly. The navy blue of the corridor drooped next to her, revealing sickly yellow, sponge-like walls that churned and groaned in the rhythm of the sound that rattled through Amber's ears. Still, she couldn't move, but her eyes remained on Sienna.

That breath smell. Eggy, foetid, invasive.

The walls around Sienna were cracking, the wooden panels bursting under a pressure in the building that hummed through Amber's body. Black, slimy flesh seemed to bulge from the cracks in the room. Like slugs. But Amber knew it *couldn't* be. And yet, they throbbed with lead-coloured veins in moist conviction. The wood and the walls were peeling away, disappearing under the mounds of flesh that had hidden beneath them.

A shot of colour. It was a mass of pink unfurled across Sienna's stomach. Her screaming had stopped. An astringent stench of rotten eggs attached Amber's nostrils as the pink mass wrapped itself around Sienna's body. Purple veins shimmered with slug-like slime on its underside as it consumed Sienna and dragged her into the bulging black mass.

KNOCK

KNOCK

KNOCK

"Are you all deaf?!" shouted a voice in the distance, breaking

Amber from her morbid hypnosis.

She vomited down her front and fell back from the door which slammed shut, throwing her back into darkness. She had no concept of what she had just witnessed. Her whole body felt like ice.

Something grabbed her shoulders.

"AMBER!"

It was Sandy.

She turned around, he jolted at the sight of her bloodshot eyes and sick-stained lips.

"We need to get out of here now," he said.

"Where's Russ?" she said.

"I haven't seem him. Where's Clay?"

Amber's mind was spinning. *He probably ran off, the scaredy cat*, she thought.

She looked at the navy wallpaper that just moments ago had borne yellow fat tissue. The gurling, groaning sounds had stopped. The deathly silence rang in Amber's ears. She giggled to herself. Was this some sort of psychosis? Had she been spiked? Was she even awake?

Sandy clicked in front of her wandering eyes.

"Where's Sienna? We. Need. To. Leave."

"She's... I don't know... Why were you knocking?" Amber asked, her brain a fug of confusion, fright and disgust. Amber looked down at Sandy's side. He was holding a large golden axe. "What's that?"

"I took it. It was in a cabinet under the staircase. I was getting nervous so I took it just in case... And then something started scratching at the door."

"Scratching?"

"And sniffing—"

"Like a dog?"

"Like a wolf."

***

Russ hurtled down the corridor to the kitchen where he had been exploring before hearing Sienna's screams. Surely there was a cupboard full of **DIY** materials? He didn't know how posh mansions worked.

His whole body felt like it was about to take off from the adrenaline that was surging through his blood. He wasn't about to let Sienna die in that room, no matter how unhelpful Amber was being. He and Sienna had been friends for much longer than her and Sandy, and they had never *ever* fallen out. He retraced the group's steps from the main road to the manor. Russ knew if he could pull Sienna up off those glass shards then he could easily carry her and run out to the main road for help. She was going to make it. He'd make sure of it. His fists and jaw clenched at the memory of Amber's gormless face whilst his best friend was in pain because of *her.* How could someone stand and do nothing when another was in desperate need? All the hearsay he'd heard about her was proven true in those few seconds.

Russ heard a clatter and clang of metal upon tile before him. He stopped in his tracks.

"Clay?" he called out.

Nothing.

Russ walked into the kitchen and saw pots scattered across the ground. There was a chill in the air: a breeze that had a dishcloth swaying from its hook.

Rope. Get some rope.

But before he could gain his bearings and figure out where such a thing could be stored, he heard a low growl coming from the dark of the kitchen where a crack of moonlight from the ajar back door split the room in two. Russ had heard a grumble coming from the walls before, but it felt too distant, too abstract to worry about. But right now, that low, guttural snarl felt very, very present.

Russ looked into the darkness at the back of the kitchen. And the darkness looked back.

Two pin prick, yellow-white dots.

The sound of saliva dripping on the ice-cold tiles.

He turned around and fled across the left side of the kitchen, his nape hot with terror. He made out a laundry chute door just before the entrance to the door back to the main hall. Within a split second he decided concealing himself in the chute would be much safer than being exposed in the shadowy chasm that was the manor's heart.

Russ slid the chute door open to see the pitch-black depths of wherever it led. The scrape of claw against tile pushed him into the opening, without logic, head first where he fell a stomach-churning height into the piles of linen below. He heard the character clawing at the chute door which had closed behind him; another growl and then silence.

Russ giggled hysterically as he realised he had fallen into the most perfect place. He could use the linen to help pull Sienna out from the pit.

"Come on, Russy," he muttered as he stood up and started pulling bits of chintz-patterned bedclothes together into his arms.

The air down in the laundry room was fuzzy, alive almost. Like there were a thousand dandelion clocks fluttering about. Everything felt close against Russ's body.

Satisfied with his linen collection, Russ tried to find the way out, but in the darkness it was hard to make out any doors without the brilliant moonlight from outside illuminating the way. The air felt warmer. *Was* it the air, or was it Russ? His cheeks were feeling flushed, his hands feeling shaky. His breath was shorter than before. He had never been a fan of small spaces but he definitely wasn't claustrophobic.

Hotter again, his forehead started to sweat.

And then the oddest thing: the distant smell of gingerbread.

A light, I need a light. Russ was starting to panic. He had lost all his bearings and couldn't tell which directions he hadn't checked yet.

"Sienna! I'm coming!" He choked, his throat drying out in the rising heat.

He ran forward, not knowing where he was going and reached out in hopes to feel a door handle.

"SHIT!" Russ screamed as he touched the wall in front of him.

The scalding heat seared the palm of his hand; his skin raged, crackled and blistered. The ice-hot pain surged through his arm as his body shut down in shock. He couldn't bring himself to move; his breaths were short and laboured. The stench of burning gingerbread scorched his nostrils and throat.

***

Sandy and Amber hurtled into the main hall. All was silent.

"Clay! Sienna! Russ!" shouted Amber.

"Shh..." said Sandy. "We can't bring attention to ourselves."

Amber felt like the whole room was spinning. What on Earth was that *thing* in the room with Sienna? Was she hallucinating? She had never seen, nor thought she would ever see, anything like that. Was it *alive?*

Whatever it was, she didn't want to stick around to find out.

"Come on, let's just go," she said.

"We can't just leave everyone here! Plus, there's a wolf outside!"

"We don't even *have* wolves in England," said Amber. "It'll be some rabid dog. It's not going to eat us. We're just going to have to run through the forest to find safety."

"Where did Clay go?" said Sandy, ignoring her rattling. "Upstairs might be the best bet."

Sandy grabbed Amber's hand. She pulled back in protestation but reluctantly joined him in running up the grand staircase to head to where Clay might be hiding.

"Did you hear that growling before?" said Amber as they reached the top.

"I'm telling you, it's a wolf—"

"Not the wolf. Before, it sounded like…" Amber stopped herself before saying. It sounded stupid.

"Like what?" Sandy said before signalling her to turn right.

"Like… a hungry stomach," she half-laughed. Clearly she was losing her mind. Was there some kind of curse on one of the artefacts she had launched out of the window?

"Here!" said Sandy, pointing to a slightly ajar door with moonlight spilling from it.

"Clay?" shouted Amber.

Empty. Just upturned sacks of wool twinkling in the hunter's moon. Their eyes drifted to Clay's coat on the floor.

Amber gripped the door until it hurt. Sandy sighed next to her.

"See, he ran off," said Amber, hoping it to be true.

"I hope you're right. This stupid little game of yours hasn't exactly gone to plan, has it?" said Sandy.

Something growled in the distance.

Amber and Sandy shot glances at each other. They both knew it came from the main hall. Sandy put a finger to his lips and then pointed to the corridor adjacent to them that had a spiral staircase right at the end.

They both stepped forward, overwhelmingly aware of every movement they were making, and started to slowly walk to the staircase. Amber's skin prickled with each step; the deathly silence in the manor seemed to turn every small motion into a cacophonous racket. Sandy and Amber furthered down the corridor, their pace picking up slightly before. The long, dark corridor felt like it was stretching out before them, teasing them with the notion of safety, and yet appearing ever so slightly far away. Amber just wanted to get to the stairs before—

Creak.

Sandy stopped dead in his tracks. His foot was on a depression in the floorboards. He moved slightly to alleviate the pressure on the wood but closed his eyes and cringed as another high-pitched *creak* bounced down the corridor.

Awoooo.

Amber's heart felt like it had shot from her chest as the chilling howl rippled through her insides.

"Fucking move," she hissed through gritted teeth.

Sandy moved his foot and the whole piece of floorboard creaked and groaned under the weight. Before they could start moving, they heard the pounding of paws upon the carpet.

"Run!"

Another howl tore through the air. At least she knew by Sandy's gaunt expression of fear that she wasn't imagining anything this time. She grabbed Sandy's hand and they bolted down the corridor, Sandy's golden axe clanging against the wall. Joy burst through Amber's body when her free hand finally touched the bannister of the spiral staircase. Both their legs were wobbly with suspense as they made the dreaded ascent upwards not knowing how quick on their heels the wolf was.

Almost at the top, Amber heard the wolf snarl as it made its way up the stairs.

"Quicker!" she shouted.

She turned the corner and saw the oak door in front that she launched herself into to make sure it would definitely open. She fell through the threshold, into the tower room, slamming her knee against the hard floor. Sandy tumbled in behind her not long after, wheezing desperately. He collapsed on to the ground, his lungs searing, but axe still in hand. The room was small, with one tiny window barely large enough to fit someone through it. The brilliant moon was still serenely shining on, unaware of the horrors inside the manor.

Before he could catch his breath, the wolf, with its yellow-white glowing eyes, emerged from the darkness of the staircase. It wasn't running; instead it stood with its tongue panting with saliva dribbling down on to the stone.

The beast bared its fangs and leapt for Amber. Frozen in fear, all she could do was close her eyes as the wolf tore through the air, its jaws aiming for her neck.

Thwack

A purple flash assaulted her eyelids. Something wet splattered across Amber's face.

Blood.

Amber raised a hesitant hand to her cheek.

No... not blood.

"What... the—" panted Sandy. Amber opened her eyes.

He stood over her, both hands gripped on the golden axe. Now blemished with black, seeping goo. Amber looked down to where she presumed the wolf was and saw something that felt distantly familiar.

Thick, oozing black tendrils squirming on the floor like beheaded worms. Amber stared at them, racking her brains for why they looked so familiar. She looked up at Sandy who was similarly aghast at the sight. *Yep, not hallucinating.*

"Do you think it's safe?" Amber said.

Sandy shot her a venomous look.

"We could have died just then. Good thing I had this," he gestured with the axe. "Your stupid little side hustle almost got me killed! This is why I had to stop being friends with you, Amber. You don't know when to stop to get what you want and you *definitely* have no respect for anyone else. If we'd have just all gone home we wouldn't be chased by wolves that turned into a pile of slugs. You're greedy and you're selfish, Amber. Haven't you learnt anything from those fairytales you read when you think people can't see you? "

Amber's eyes widened.

"Now get up. We need to find the others and get out of here before anything else happens."

Fairytales... Wolves... The glass slipper... The axe... Amber's mind swirled with the artefacts she had seen throughout the hours. *Slugs... That September night...*

"What the hell?" said Sandy, the axe clattered to the ground, breaking Amber from her trance.

She looked up and saw Sandy stood where the door used to be. He was banging on the stone that made up the walls of the tower. His balled fists pounded, pounded, pounded against cold slabs. *Thud, thud, thud, squelch.*

Sandy pounced back and put his hand on Amber's shoulder.

The stone had cracked away in chunks that cascaded to the floor. In the crevices, pink flesh pulsated with deep red veins. A deep, guttural groan rattled through the tower. The metallic stench of blood poured into the tiny room causing Sandy to retch. Amber grabbed his hand and they moved backwards toward the window. More stone fell away to expose throbbing mounds of flesh and sinew and veins and fat in the tower walls.

One stone slab in the centre of the room dropped, leaving a dark hole in the centre. The stomach growls grew louder. Amber wanted to peer over the edge to see what was down there but before she made a step, another slab dropped too.

A violent screech, like nails on chalkboards, clawed at Sandy and Amber's ears. They looked up and saw, almost opalescent in the moonlight, bright white teeth protruding from the ceiling.

Another slab dropped.

Sandy reached over and picked up the golden axe just as the slab it was resting on dropped into the groaning abyss. He ran to the window and smashed it with the hilt. He ran it along the sill, scraping stray shards of glass. Amber shuddered as her mind flashed to Sienna trapped in that pit.

"Quick," said Sandy, placing the axe down and cupping his hands together. "I'll be right behind you."

"You should go first, you've got the axe! What if something is out there?"

Another slab dropped, this time far too close to the duo. Amber felt hot breath on the back of her neck. A glint of a fang dazzled in the axe's golden head.

"Just *go*," Sandy urged. "You don't have to backchat about everything!"

Despite the terror, he managed a glimmer of a smirk.

Amber didn't need to be told twice. She hoisted herself up to the window, making a choice not to fuss as some rogue glass pierced her palms, and vaulted over the sill, as the tower made a deafening groan that sounded angry and moist.

She tumbled for a short moment onto the shingles of the roof. Amber threw out her hands, praying the friction would prevent her from plummeting off the side to her death.

"Run!" shouted Sandy, barely audible from the squelches and grunts of the tower.

There was a clang to the right and she grabbed the axe before it toppled over the edge of the roof. She looked back up to the tower and her stomach dropped at the sight. The window had vanished.

"SANDY!" Amber screamed so hard it felt like a vessel in her eye burst. "SANDY, WHERE ARE YOU?"

The roof lurched beneath her like a tidal wave. The bitter wind of the Hallowe'en midnight air chilled her to the bone.

He's dead, he's fucking dead. Just like Sienna.

But she had to believe he was OK or she wouldn't be able to survive the night. She picked herself up and grabbed the axe. She saw a dip in the roof on the other side with a drainpipe she could use to get to the bottom. It was too high to jump; she would definitely break a leg and would perhaps even die.

The whole manor rattled, almost sending her head first off the roof, but she steadied herself and began to run across the slippery slate. She looked behind her at the tower and saw it squirming and convulsing like the whole thing was alive.

"Clay! Russ!" she shouted into the darkness. She hoped they'd managed to make it out alive. She should never have forced Clay to go off by himself; she planned to apologise tomorrow when she, hopefully, saw him on the playground. She'd back him up on the tall tales of surviving the Devil's Night house of horror.

Her heart panged for Sandy but she knew he'd make it out somehow. He was wily like that. Always knew how to slip away from trouble without anyone knowing he was there. Tears pricked at her eyes as she recalled his scolding words.

Amber's foot trod on something soft and squishy. She stumbled over herself and landed face first on the slate feeling the bridge of her nose crack. Not wanting to waste one more second in, or on, the manor she pulled herself up and started to run forward.

But curiosity got the better of her. She wanted to know what she had stood on.

Amber's shock caught in her throat as she turned to see a colossal, bulging eye emerging from the roof of the manor. The violently orange sclera and jet black pupil glistened in the moonlight. She had never seen anything so...

Amber felt her whole body beginning to shut down. The pain from her bloody nose was numbed; her heartbeat non-existent; her trembling hands still. It was as if every notion of her own existence was being obliterated by the black hole of a pupil she was staring into. The orange sclera, as vibrant as autumn leaves but in no way as comforting. What she was looking at was grotesque beyond belief. An entity not of this world, it couldn't be. But it was too tangible, too visceral for it to be all in her mind. Amber could feel her face contorting into something that was neither a smile nor a frown; her mouth twisted, exposing her teeth. She felt her breath catching at the unison of her tongue and soft palate.

And it had seen *her.* The black chasm before her had looked into her eyes and acknowledged her existence, just like she had it. The axe fell from her hand and slipped off the side of the roof.

And then, a blinding purple light. The exact shade of the comet she had seen many weeks ago. Amber threw her arms up to shield her eyes and felt herself lose her footing. She fell through the air and into blackness.

***

The grass tickled her fingers.

Dull throbs pulsed in Amber's neck. She opened her eyes and found herself in a clearing surrounded by trees. Phosphenes sparkled in her line of vision as feeling returned to her body.

I must have fallen off the roof.

What roof? She looked ahead to see nothing. Just russet-leaved forest.

She recognised a tree stump she had passed from just before

she entered the foggy realm that Sandy, Russ, Sienna and Clay had gotten themselves lost in. Amber bent her back and let the vertebrae snap in crackling glee. The sharp twinge of a broken septum returned to her bloody face. The blood was still sticky, not dried.

I haven't been out for long.

"Sandy..." she pathetically whimpered. Her voice was tired.

Part of her still held the belief he'd got out of that tower of terror alive. He must have. She got herself up from the dewy ground.

A glint in a nearby bush.

She smiled as she recognised her golden puffer jacket. Her make-shift loot bag full of the valuable nick-nacks she'd thrown out of the window before...

Pushing all thoughts of the night's events out of her mind, Amber walked over to the count. She started to laugh. She was finally going to make those millions she'd always wanted. And much quicker than she had planned.

Amber reached for the golden jacket. It was laying on its side as if it knew the anticipation would already be killing her. She turned it over, ready to remind herself what jewels, crowns and precious artefacts she had managed to nick.

"NO!" Amber screeched. She leapt back from the coat, her hands trembling.

Inside wasn't gemstones or tiaras, but thick, black slugs that writhed in the hood of her golden jacket. Amber fell to her knees. She had nothing. The slugs oozed and slithered just like they had that one September night all over her copy of a fairytale anthology. Amber screamed so loud her throat felt like it was bleeding. She rocked her head up to the sky and stared up at the cloudless night where the stars and moon twinkled with pleasure.

In her search to have it all, she had lost everything. She felt her body shutting down just like it had when she looked into the eyes of that... thing.

Desperate for an answer, she stared up at the universe.

And the universe stared back.

Jake Curran-Pipe is a theatre producer by day and a speculative fiction writer by night. His work is inspired by Scottish & Northern English folklore and he is so committed to the macabre that he works in a theatre that used to be a Neo-Gothic church.

Acknowledgements

H. L. Macfarlane, editor

How have we made it here – the final season in this glorious anthology series? I know I certainly could not have done it alone.

To Adie, without whom I would have crumpled under the weight of editing and organising *Once Upon an Autumn:* to find such a dear friend and colleague through the creation of this tiny indie anthology has been a highlight of the last few years. Thank you for understanding the joys of semicolons and the woes of mixed US & UK formatting alike.

To every author in this volume: you did it. You made it. Whether you were with me from the very beginning or joined along the way, I am privileged to have worked with each and every one of you. The *Once Upon a Season* anthology is something to be deeply proud of. I know I am; I hope you are, too.

And to you, dear reader: thank you for picking up this volume, and the ones that preceded it, and for supporting us along the way. Know that, though this is the end, it is also only the beginning.

Here's to what comes next!